# HIDDEN MENAGERIE:

## A Cryptid Anthology

## Vol 2

*Hidden Menagerie: A Cryptid Anthology Vol 2* is published by Dragon's Roost Press.

This anthology is © 2018 Dragon's Roost Press and Michael Cieslak.

All stories within this anthology are © 2018 by their representative authors and are printed with the permission of the authors.

All stories in this anthology are original except "The *Anna Doria*" originally appeared in an anthology by Burning Willow Press

Artwork: Luke Spooner (http://caririonhouse.com)

All characters in this book are fictitious. Any resemblance to any persons living, dead, or otherwise animated is strictly coincidental.

All rights reserved. This book or any portion thereof may not be reproduced or used in any manner whatsoever without the express written permission of the publisher except for the use of brief quotations in a book review.

Printed in the United States of America

First Printing, 2018

ISBN-13: 978-0-9988878-2-1
ISBN-10: 099888782X

Dragon's Roost Press
207 Gardendale
Ferndale, MI 48220

http://thedragonsroost.net/styled-3/index.html

# HIDDEN MENAGERIE:

## A Cryptid Anthology

## Vol 2

Edited by Michael Cieslak

# Table of Contents

**Introduction**   11

**A Cruelty That Cut Both Ways**   13
Aimee Ogden

**Dendrophillia**   35
Kyle E Miller

**The Costs and Benefits of Lake Monsters**   51
Mark David Adam

**Night Quarry**   59
B.D. Keefe

**Wake**   73
Jennie Brass

**Hounded**   91
Lawrence Harding

**Moonlight Forest**   117
Soumya Sundar Mukherjee

**Nancy's Rumble**   135
Haley Holden

**Lifeboat**     151
Danielle Warnick

**Sky Demon**     179
Jeff Brigham

**Something in the Strawberry Fields**     211
Eric Guignard

**You Will Be Laid Low Even at the Sight of Him**     239
Kevin Wetmore

**O Christmas Tree**     265
Gregory L Norris

**The Basin**     279
Lauren Childs

**The *Anna Doria***     291
Ellen Denton

**The Ghost Tree**     307
Sharon King

**The Orphan and the Whale**     321
KA Masters

**Acknowledgements**     339

**About The Contributors**     343

**About The Last Day Dog Rescue Organization**     349

**About Dragon's Roost Press**     351

Introduction

### The Coelacanth

I have a vivid memory regarding my first knowledge of the coelacanth. I was already interested in oceanography, dinosaurs, and cryptozoology (as were many people my age). I was reading a book, possibly published by National Geographic for Kids, but I'm not sure. There was an entire section devoted to the discovery of this fish which was believed to be extinct *right up until the point where some fisherman caught one!*

Yes, there were dinosaurs still living among us.

This fueled my assumption that the Loch Ness Monster was actually a plesiosaur which had survived until present day. If a fish could do it, why not a larger dinosaur?

(Of course, there are many scientific answers to this question that my 8 year old brain was unaware of. I should also point out that I was certain that I was the first person to make this connection and would therefore be famous. Cut me some slack, this was during the pre-internet dark ages.)

The icy waters of Scotland were not the only places that

held monsters that were supposed to be extinct. There were the jungles of Africa and South America, lost islands unseen by people, and even the lakes and skies of our own back yards. Who knows what kind of monster one might encounter if one just strayed far enough from the beaten path...

*Hidden Menagerie Vol 2* contains all of the cryptids that did not fit neatly into the "beasts of the land" category. Inside you will find sentient vegetation, creatures of the deep, and terrors of the sky. While I did briefly consider grouping each set of cryptids by type -- all of the water creatures together, for example -- I discarded this notion. As result, you lovely readers will never know where the danger is coming from.

Just like in real life.

## A Cruelty That Cut Both Ways

Aimee Ogden

The thunderbird had left two carcasses by the barn overnight.

Ezra refused to call in the hands to help. It was Sunday, after all, and their God-given day off, whatever the devil's own bird might have done. It was only divine providence that the rest of the cattle hadn't escaped when the bird ransacked the Greens' barn--the blank-eyed creatures stood and stared from where they'd crowded at the back when Ezra cleared the wreckage of the door and let in the morning's light. He and Sarah cleaned the two dead cattle while Liza read the Bible to herself in the kitchen and prepared the Sunday meal. Sarah had assigned her daughter the story of Ruth and Boaz for today, and she could hear her daughter's voice drifting out through the open windows in between the rap of the knife on the wooden counter. She struggled over certain words--*Moabite* and *guardian* and *foreigner*--but her voice was clear and true as she sounded out the story of faith and patience rewarded. Sarah hoped she took the tale to heart.

Not much flesh to salvage from the dead cattle. The blood had run out to make dark mud of the dusty ground, and the hides had been shredded by the thunderbird's talons. But the livers and the tongues were still fresh and mostly intact, and Sarah used her best kitchen knife to cut them clean of the beasts. There would be gelatin from the bones too. Sarah said as much to Ezra, and he spat into the soil. Spittle clung to the dark whiskers on his chin, and his blue eyes glittered like ice chips in his face.

"So we'll eat for a day or two, and I'm meant to smile about that?" When he stood, his knees creaked. But she pressed her lips tightly closed against a retort, and he didn't come any closer. Finally he shuffled himself back down into the dirt, muttering curses as he sawed at the cartilage in the steer's hind leg.

Sarah peeled a slimy shred of muscle away from her steer's shoulder blade and added the bone to her pile. She hadn't changed out of her best Sunday dress--the only one of the three she owned made of store-bought cloth and not patched-up flour sacks--and she was brown to the elbows and knees. Well, it would wash, and so would she. She wiped the damp hair from her forehead with the back of one wrist and said, "You reckon it's brooding season?"

This time Ezra shot to his feet despite his crackling joints. He crossed the space between them in three steps and cuffed her across the cheek.

"I look like I've sprouted feathers to you, woman?" he shouted. "How the hell should I know when a creature like that sees fit to drop an egg? I raise cattle, not goddamn demon birds!"

She murmured her apologies, but he didn't return to stripping the other dead steer. He put his head down and stormed across the corral, muttering, hands clenched at his sides. She put her head down too. There was still work to be done, however many pairs of hands were set to it, and the blood that ran down Sarah's chin mixed in the dirt with the blood of the cattle.

The pain was a reminder, and one she'd earned. Not just that she had bought that sting and then some, with the secret sins she carried. But this too: that Ezra was more right than he knew. That bird was surely a demon, and the fate it bore on its leathery wings was Sarah's and no other's. For what wrong she'd done Ezra, whether he knew it or not, and what wrong she'd done Liza as well, of course. It would be a sin to deny that twist of the knife too. When it came for her and bore her downward, she would be ready. So long as her daughter was left safely behind, at least. Ezra had never, would never hurt the girl. And the thunderbird could bear her no ill will. If Liza had played a part in Sarah's misdoings it had been entirely a passive one.

Sarah's lip had stopped bleeding, though it felt puffy. Ezra was still pacing the perimeter of the corral, cursing his bad luck in women and land-claims alike. His cursing wasn't so bad. At least while he blasphemed, she could tell where he was without looking at him.

Back at the house, Liza's voice had fallen silent.

Monday morning the three ranch hands arrived by the time the sun was up. Matthew, Mark, and Charlie, who by rights ought to have been a Luke or at least a John, scratching their beards and shifting their weight from boot to boot as Ezra handed them each a weapon. For Matthew, Ezra's second rifle (the one with the bad trigger); for Mark the pistols from Ezra's desk; for Charlie, the wood-axe. They set out with Ezra on horseback, and melted into the red rising sun. "We'll be back by dinner," Ezra said before he mounted up. That meant Sarah would need to have dinner ready for four hungry men after doing their day's worth of ranch chores.

Liza helped her put the cattle out to pasture, then joined her in the corral to shovel manure. By then the morning was gone, and with it Sarah's opportunity to do the week's baking. Well, they could all eat flatbread for the next six days like the Israelites in Egypt and they'd be none the worse for it. Sarah and Liza went out to the east pasture to fix a bad fencepost, and to keep an eye out for the men riding homeward.

"Where do you think the thunderbird came from, Mama?" asked Liza. She leaned into the fencepost to hold it upright while Sarah dug the old rotted post out of its hole. They had both tucked their skirts up inside their apron strings to let off some of the oppressive heat that clung to their bodies. "Did they have thunderbirds back in Chicago?"

"No. Move that post closer, will you?" It hurt Sarah to have to ask that; her daughter was twelve years old and not built for ranch work. But Liza complied, and Sarah slipped the new post into the old hole. The barbed wire wrapped around it, front and back and front again, and helped to hold it upright. "There's not many of them, and no one's ever seen one but here on the prairies. From what your daddy and I have heard, at least." She stepped backed and fished the hem of her skirt free to wipe her brow. "As far where it came from, well … " She didn't dare say *Hell* lest Ezra decide she'd been stuffing the girl's head of fancy again. "Somewhere down south, maybe."

Liza didn't look satisfied with this answer, and small wonder that.

"Come on," said Sarah, and tucked the loose damp curls that had come loose back into her daughter's braid. "We've got work to do back in the corral and the kitchen before our day's done."

The men weren't back by dinner, and Sarah's tentative heart lifted as the shadows lengthened and the Dutch oven cooled. Maybe her prayers had finally been answered. Her lies she would carry around her neck until they dragged her downward to perdition, but she did have a daughter to see to, and in spite of herself she longed for the kind of reprieve only God in His infinite mercy could grant. A woman and a girl couldn't manage a ranch on their own, no, but they could sell the cattle and make their way back east on the money they earned from it. They could learn to walk with their heads high again, to raise their voices without flinching and to sing without looking around first to see who might hear. When the sun dusted the earth again, she nearly told Liza to start packing. But she bit her tongue and bided her time reading with the girl by lamplight. Half an hour past dark, and she heard the jingle of reins and raised voices outside.

"Daddy's back," said Liza, looking up from the Bible, and Sarah's belly twisted around her supper.

She lurched out of her seat as the door banged open. Ezra and Matthew crashed through the door with Mark's arms stretched between them. Charlie loomed in the doorway, a pale bloodstained ghost.

"Get us some clean water!" Ezra bellowed, and Sarah rushed to comply.

The men laid Mark out on the kitchen table, and Sarah gasped at the sight of his shredded leg. Had that been the work of the thunderbird's talons, or its beak? What a foolish question. She snatched up a pail and cried to Liza to start a fire.

Boiled water and bloodstains on the kitchen floor. When Mark finally slept, still stretched out to his full height on the table, Ezra sent Matthew and Charlie home. Sarah lingered in the kitchen doorframe, watched the light in the oil lamp dance in the beads of sweat on Mark's face. She told herself that it wasn't her fault, that Mark's fate wasn't her own misdirected punishment. Nor yet a cruel wish deflected off Ezra to an undeserving target. Well, now they'd both suffer for it. Mark trapped in the shredded prison of his body; her bent under the burden of a mouth to feed. A mouth without a back to bend to labor. The tiny twisting tongues of flame from the lamp licked at her like hellfire.

"Go to bed," Ezra grunted, when he pushed past her.

She folded her arms across her chest. Liza had already retired, exhausted by the day's events and the night's terrors. "I should stay. Do for him as can be done."

"There's nothing to be done for him." Ezra leaned toward her, and she put the doorframe between them. "I said go to bed. I ain't going to say it again."

Sarah fled, and dressed herself for bed with numb fingers. When she heard grunts from the kitchen, the feeble kick of stocking feet against old wood, she closed her eyes in prayer. The first plea on her lips was that Liza, at least, might sleep through this.

They buried Mark in the pasture, deep beneath the dry grass where the wind whistled. He had no family to stand beside his grave as it was filled, and none to ask any questions that might rile Ezra's temper either. Charlie didn't have his letters, and Matthew had a dreadful stutter, so Ezra read from the Bible when the wooden coffin disappeared beneath the pebbled dirt.

There wasn't proper food for a funeral spread, but Matthew and Charlie came back to the big house for a bit. Liza and Sarah put out bread and butter and cold sliced beef and the men ate and nodded their thanks. She wanted to reach out to them, touch them, reassure them of their guiltlessness. But she could hardly do any such thing with Ezra looking on.

When the men went out to get at least an afternoon's worth of work done--all the more important now there were only six hands to set to eight hands' worth of work--Sarah tugged at Ezra's sleeve before he could follow the others.

"This is the end of chasing that bird," she begged. "Isn't it?" Sarah could not abide the thought of another man bearing the punishment for trying to avert the fate that ought to be hers. A cruelty that cut both ways, that one.

Ezra slapped her so hard her ears rang. "I swear I'll never point a shotgun at that damn monster again, less it comes knocking at our front door." He jerked his shoulders up and down, and Sarah wondered what it was he meant to shrug off. "There's mucking in the barn that won't wait. Get Liza and get to work."

They had been married long enough that she spoke

Ezra's language, the pauses and the subtly emphasized words, the muscles in his face that tensed and slackened. Ezra would never again put himself between the ranch and the thunderbird, no. But he might see to it that someone else still would.

Liza had already bent her back to the soiled barn, and her hem was pinned up to keep it from dragging through the filth. She paused to straighten her back when Sarah arrived, and leaned on the handle of her muck rake.

"Mama," she said, and though her voice was dry as old bones, tears swelled up in her cinnamon-brown eyes. "Why is the thunderbird tormenting us?" Her voice dropped low. "Could it be something I did wrong? If I missed my prayers, or if--if I didn't mean them enough?"

Sarah reached out and pulled Liza into her shoulder. The smell of manure filled her nose and mouth: rich and grassy as God's green earth, and as tainted.

"No, my darling," she said, into Liza's hair. Too hard to explain to the child the particular taint of original sin that ran in her blood. "You didn't do anything wrong. It was never you."

Two weeks and three more dead cattle later, Sarah was in the yard when a stranger on horseback rode up. He had a hard-weathered face, brown as sun-baked prairie soil, but it relaxed in a smile when he greeted her. He wore a pistol on his hip and a pair of rifles slapped the flank of his sorrel mare. She offered him something cool to drink, and wished she could offer it as some sort of meager thanks. But he hadn't come here to save her, of course.

He told her he'd come to do the job advertised in town. "I've killed them birds before. Not always easy, but don't you mind--it can be done." He grinned at her over the rim of the cup of water she'd fetched. "You know, there's folk who like shooting them down because they think they're holy to the Indians, but that's not so. The Winnebago have a thunderbird, but to them it's a messenger to the gods. Not some ugly leathery sky-beast." He took another deep drink, then chucked the rest of the water into his own face. Droplets rained down from the gray-black stubble of his beard. "Besides: they die hard for birds, but pretty easy for angels."

Sarah dropped her eyes to her feet, not at the cowboy's words but at the sound of Ezra's voice. He was yelling, across the yard, at her or at the man, she couldn't tell. He didn't like it when she spoke to men without him present. She half hoped he would strike her in front of the stranger--earned or not, she would take freedom from this man's hands if he saw fit to offer it.

But no, Ezra had raised his voice in exultation at his hired gun's arrival, not in any fit of temper. He tagged up to the stranger, pouring out golden charm like a river of whiskey. Any reservations or doubts had to wash away under such a tide as that. Sarah's certainly had, when she married him. But then she'd had other reasons to let herself be carried along so easily. She'd been his mark as much as he'd been hers. In any case it was nothing strange for Ezra to present the Sunday-best version of himself in front of friends and neighbors and passers-by; it was only for Sarah and sometimes his hired men that he rolled up his shirt-sleeves.

They sent Sarah away while they talked money, until Ezra shouted for her to fetch the hired gun something stronger to drink than water. She fetched him a cup of Ezra's second best corn-juice, better than what he gave Matthew, Mark, and Charlie at Christmas but not as good as what he kept for his own personal use. Its smell peeled Sarah's lips back from her teeth, but the hired gun took a deep draft and barely pulled a face.

"Tastes like killing monsters feels," he said, and handed Sarah the cup. When he swung himself back into the saddle, riding so tall and straight and handsome, she could almost doubt the thunderbird's odds. Almost. But maybe if he failed in that quest, he might come back to the farmstead looking for another. A princess in a locked tower, a dragon at the gate ...

No--she banished that foolishness from her head, with a jerk of her wrist to fling the rest of the corn-juice into the tall grass. She was no innocent maiden, and never had been. Liza's daddy had been a handsome man, too, and look where that had gotten her.

Ezra's hand twitched, but he didn't slap her, not with the hired gun still in earshot. "I paid good money for that chain-lightning," he growled, and she knew he'd make her pay the wastage back later, in coin of his own choosing. She looked out to where the hired gun rode out through the ranch gate, which Charlie hurried to swing closed behind him. She shivered with fear and terrible desire when a shadow slid over her, but it was only the sun passing behind the clouds.

The tall handsome stranger with his rifles never came back, in seek of pay or otherwise. Other hired guns came and went in his wake, two or three a week at first, and then fewer as time went by and tales of the size of the monster that haunted the Green ranch spread. Some were as tall as the first, and some were as kind, though few were as handsome. But each and every one of them had eyes only for the prize, a reptile-bird hide to drag back to town and a pocketful of silver to spend on the resulting celebrations. Sarah didn't blame them, not when Ezra saved his vile outbursts of temper until after these men had come back empty-handed or not at all. Not until after they had disappeared into the sunset seeking easier quests to set themselves against.

And as charming as Ezra was, Sarah was his opposite. The years of marriage and the hot prairie sun had taken their toll in equal measure: her hair was so fair and her eyes such a pale blue, it was as if the color had been bleached out of them. If she'd had a clever way with words once, a sharp tongue that had turned heads, it had been a long time that her tongue had lain still and silent in the bed of her mouth. She was a piece of the landscape on the Green ranch and nothing more to these men. Maybe, she thought, as the summer days stretched out hot and dry, that was all she was to the Lord her God too. Her sins weren't great ones, but they were ugly little things. Ugly enough for her Maker to turn His head, maybe. And for Him to deny her the quick easy end of a visit from the thunderbird.

Or maybe He was waiting for her confession: not to Him, for she'd given her penance on bent knee a thousand times over. But to Ezra himself. And Liza. The sharp edge of Sarah's lie curved backwards on her, too. In the small quiet space they had together in the evenings, Sarah found herself studying her daughter's face. With Ezra out working late, his time pulled taut by helpless anger as well as necessity, she could enjoy her daughter's presence without the shadow of his nearness to darken it: her dark darting eyes and the delicate point of her chin. Sarah's hand-me-down nightdress hung too big on her body.

"Liza," she said, her voice dusty in her mouth. The girl hunched over the Bible by candlelight; she didn't straighten up at Sarah's voice, only slanted her eyes her mother's way. She looked like a startled coyote, trying to figure out which way to flee. The yellowed linen of the nightdress tented sharply over the peaks of her shoulder blades.

Sarah's tongue worked against her teeth, as if that might scrape the words free. The girl's frame barely held up under the thin layer of flesh it was clothed in; surely it would shatter under the cruel weight of unvarnished truth. She reached across the table and stroked Liza's brown hair. "Your papa and I are proud of how you've buckled down to work around here. Times have been hard, with Mark gone and with the extra work the bird makes for us. It's a blessing to have you." That last was true, though it hadn't always been so, had it? She let her daughter's curls fall from her fingertips and tried not to think of the girl's daddy. She swallowed the acid words that had pent up in her throat: that ghost could lie abed a bit longer. "Get to bed now. It's late."

When they got up the next morning, another rotting husk lay in the farmyard. This time, the body didn't belong to a steer.

Matthew's eyes stared heavenward; Sarah rushed to force them closed while Ezra stood over the body and Liza hovered just beside.

"I'm sorry," Sarah said, to Matthew's upturned face, and threw her coat over him to hide his cracked-open ribs from Liza's eyes. The sun bore down unblinking on her shoulders; there was nothing that could be hidden from heaven.

They had the body in the ground by noon. No one had the will to mutter more than a few words over the fresh grave, and Charlie only stayed long enough to see his friend buried. "Nothing tying me here now Matthew's gone," he told Ezra, and slung his half-slack bag up onto his shoulder.

If he had tears glittering in his eyes, Sarah took care not to look. She had big enough sins of her own without taking on someone else's. She put her hand on Liza's shoulder and watched the last of the hired hands walk away from the ranch for good. Out of the corner of her eye, she could see the tautly corded muscles in Ezra's neck and the vein standing out below his jaw. Time to keep her mouth shut and stay out of the way.

"I can help out more on the ranch, Daddy." Liza stepped away from Sarah, and Sarah's hand fell back to her side--too late to call back the girl's words, nor yet Ezra's sudden attention. No, he had never struck the girl. Not Sarah's sweet daughter. "I got a strong back, and I don't mind the work."

Ezra didn't move at first. Sarah reached for Liza, to pull her back and shoo her toward the house before she had to bear witness to one of Ezra's displays of temper. But Ezra's fist moved faster than her outstretched hand. He clipped Liza across the jaw and sent her sprawling. "Now you tell me," he bellowed, "how one scrawny girl's meant to replace three grown men!"

Blood dripped through Liza's cupped fingers, three red drops that stained her dusty apron. She yelped when Ezra stepped forward and swept back his leg for a kick.

Sarah moved. Not much, not far. A little sidestep that carried her across Liza's legs and the spill of her skirt. Her face pulled tight over the bones beneath, and whatever Ezra saw there made him pause. He stepped back.

"Just get in the house," he said, and turned away to dust his hands on his shirt. "It's past one and I already dug a grave this morning. Get some dinner on my table before it gets any later."

Sarah stood over her daughter until he'd walked out to the corral, and then hustled her to her feet and into the house.

Sarah and Liza worked silently, preparing the food and setting the table to Ezra's liking. Hot marrow soup with the last of the overwintered potatoes, liver fried in the pan, old bread softened with a smear of butter. Sarah sliced up a cold joint too, for Ezra's favorite sandwiches, and laid it in sight on the middle of the table, then turned to the pail of water to wash up her knife.

"I suppose you're not too hungry," she said to Liza, who hovered near the table. "Go sit in your bedroom for a spell. You can read, if you like." Liza vanished.

Sarah sat down at the table with her hands in her lap. Steam rolled off the marrow soup, and the over-rich stench filled her belly with sourness. It took another twenty minutes before Ezra banged through the door. He sat down, loosening the handkerchief around his neck, and looked about.

"Where is she?"

"Resting. You ready?"

"Damn right," he said, and shoved his plate toward her. She served him his supper.

Early the next morning she led the sheriff's deputy from town out, far out past the ranch's fences. Out, on horseback, to the great nest that lay hidden in the scrubby trees, out by the cliffs that fell down toward the drought-shriveled river. She showed him Ezra's body, torn nearly beyond recognition, where he lay amid the shattered remains of three enormous eggs. The pinkish things that lurked beneath the fragments of shell were too terrible to look at, and the deputy kicked them out of sight into the corner.

"Damn fool," he said, and covered his mouth as he frowned down at Ezra's mortal remains. "Not the first idiot this bird's claimed, and sure as shooting won't be the last."

Sarah shook her head. "Don't think ill on him. He was protecting me and Liza to the last. Got it in his head the thunderbird must be brooding, to linger around here so long." She dragged her sleeve across her face. "Well, he was right, rest him."

The deputy tipped his hat, guilty and solicitous all at once. "What'll you do now, ma'am, if you don't mind me asking? That's a big ranch for you and the girl to manage all on your own, even if new hands do hire on. And it's not altogether safe, a widow woman and her girl all by themselves."

"No, I'll sell the ranch." Sarah studied the ruins of Ezra's face. Not enough left of him to tell what sort of expression had colored his final moments, whether he had left this world behind on wings of regret or surprise or terror. "Go back east if we can. My sister still lives in Chicago. Liza ought to grow up around family if she can."

The deputy replaced his hat on his head. "Ezra's got kin in Independence, too, hasn't he?"

"Yes." Sarah nodded slowly and so stiffly she was surprised her neck didn't creak. "But I can get more outwork back in a big town like Chicago, I hope."

"I suppose that's so." He sighed, and settled to one knee beside Ezra. Sarah didn't envy him the task of dealing with that human wreckage. "Well, you'll be missed around these parts, Miz Green."

"Thank you," she said, and walked out of the shelter of the trees, where she could stand up straight, where the sun's white heat poured down on her face. She took two deep shuddering breaths, and swallowed her rising gorge.

A shadow blotted the sun's warmth off her face. She

looked upward, and found the thunderbird wheeling overhead, wings spread.

Her throat tightened. Not now--she wasn't prepared to go now, of all times. Better to leave Liza behind with no protection at all than with a man as likely to harm as to help, yes. But not by much.

Sarah fell to her knees. There was no forgiveness to be had, not from a dead man twice wronged and not from the Creator God whose punishment she'd so terribly flouted. And Sarah wasn't sure she would have wanted forgiveness anyway, even had it been there for the asking.

The thunderbird gained height, then tucked its leathery wings. It dropped toward Sarah in a free-falling dive.

"I'm sorry," Sarah said, but it was Liza who she sent those futile words to. She closed her eyes.

A gust of wind beaten on leather wings, lashed Sarah's face, and she screamed. But not alone. Another cry raked the air, so close that it drove the breath from her body. Pain drew her belly back toward her spine, but not her own pain: secondhand pain, borrowed pain. She opened her eyes.

The thunderbird huddled not ten paces from her. Its claws tightened in the spilled innards of a yowling mountain lion. The lion kicked twice, gave one last feeble cry, and relaxed into death's waiting embrace.

The thunderbird's red-gold eyes found Sarah's. The beast was too big to be believed, the size of a pair of circus elephants put together and then flensed down to bones and dry leather. The bony crest on the back of her head was nearly as long as Sarah standing to her full height. She held Sarah's stare as she raked into the mountain lion's exposed belly. Gore stained her fleshy beak and spattered the wrinkled leather of her belly. New gore and old.

"I'm sorry," said Sarah again, not to Liza this time. To the bird, demon or angel or creature of the earth. The bird stared her down as she staggered out of the copse of trees and out onto the open prairie. Eastward, toward the ranch. Time to go home to Liza, help her pack up. They'd have to travel lightly, two women alone. A few changes of clothes in Liza's hope chest, the brass candlesticks, the Bible. A pot and a pan, and, of course, Sarah's best kitchen knife.

## Dendrophilia

Kyle E. Miller

His heart had always been in wood. And so, when late July lightning struck the old sycamore and tumbled its limbs into the garden with a crack and scrambling rush of branches, the storm struck him too. There was one fewer tree to climb. One fewer pile of leaves in the autumn, one fewer pool of shade in the summer.

Ashley came out from beneath the covers of his bed, his two pit bull terriers trailing him, pressing their noses into his palms and the backs of his knees as he went up to the window and looked. Twigs had impaled green tomatoes and a whole bough had been driven into the potato patch like a shovel, unearthing them too early. The rain would wash them all away. Thunder clapped, and Ashley jumped. He was afraid of storms and stars and flying, anything unfathomable, lonely, and far away. And so when he saw someone standing in the garden rain drenched and sodden under the thunderclouds, he was torn.

"Dad. There's someone out there." He looked over his

shoulder. "Mom?"

No one was coming to help, and he was shaking in his socks.

Maybe it was the way he had been born (in the air, from one belly into another, flesh to steel), or maybe it was the way his father shut down the house before a storm and looked out the front window, watching, he said, and waiting for the siren. Maybe it was the stories he read about falling stars and falling ships and the things that lived light years away, or maybe there was nothing up there, and all those bright white shuttles he saw on TV and the internet returned with only men inside. Maybe they were alone after all, and maybe that was even worse.

"Mom? There's someone. Someone out there."

Had it been night, Ashley would not have left the house. But there were no stars to watch him, only the eye of the storm, and he was tired of being afraid, weary of missing moonlit walks and hiding under covers. He was seventeen, not seven. And so he went out, running toward the garden and the broken tree, the splintered fulcrum on which teetered all his fear and wonder. The pit bulls watched and whined from the open door.

The wind made lashes and whips of the rain, pushing water into Ashley's eyes and mouth. He stumbled into the garden and grabbed hold of the boy's wet wrist and pulled, but the boy wouldn't move. It was as if he were rooted to the spot, and it took all the strength Ashley had to move him, and down he went, into the mud.

Ashley had to drag him. It was like dragging a waterlogged length of wood, and when Ashley got him through the door and into the porch, he wondered if that's not exactly what it was. All that leaf and bark, pith and soil muddying the porch linoleum--had he made a mistake? But there really was a boy in there somewhere, a boy about Ashley's age. He could make out the little nubs of his toes, the shiny knobs of his knees, and two sharp knotty elbows. His skin was mottled gray and brown and white, paler near the neck and face, beautifully bone white. His hair was long and soft green. He had hair down there too, and it matched. Ashley blushed and quickly covered him with a towel. He dried him with another, gently pressing it into his temples and then his cheeks. The pit bulls nosed about, pawing at the boy's limbs and sniffing. Ashley pushed them away, but he was too late: one of them took a toe in his mouth.

The boy opened his eyes, and they were green too. He was looking at Ashley.

"I know you," he said.

The dogs howled and howled.

They sat on the sycamore's fallen trunk the morning after, their butts growing damp from the still soaked wood. The pit bulls wrestled on the grass.

The boy had stayed in Ashley's room last night. Ashley had given him the bed, and he slept beside it on the floor. The dogs stayed with him, waking once or twice to sniff and growl. Ashley's parents seemed not to care or notice, assuming the boy was a neighbor and not looking too closely, content, perhaps, that Ashley had a friend at last.

"What's your name?" Ashley asked.

He mumbled something Ashley didn't catch.

"What?"

"Would wose." In the sunlight, Ashley could see inside his mouth, the tongue like a polished stone, his teeth little chips of wood. Ashley had gotten him to wear pants, but not a shirt or socks or even underwear. His chest was broad and smooth, full of something like muscle. "Would wose."

"Would what?"

"Wouldwose."

"Wood woes?" Ashley laughed. He blushed often and for many reasons, and he blushed now and turned away. "Something else. What about a nickname?"

"Wuduwasa. Faun. Silvanus. Orke. Satyr. Bigfoot. Green man. Pan. Jack o' the Green. Leshy."

"Leshy?"

"All the same. Not always hairy though. A myth."

"I like leshy."

Their eyes met, the boy grinned, and Ashley felt a prickle up his spine. His penis hardened all at once and in an instant. He crossed his legs and looked away, blushing once again. "Um. So. Where did you come from?"

Leshy tapped the sycamore. A shard of bark fell away, the trunk defoliating even in death.

"I thought so," Ashley said. "You said you know me."

Leshy had seen everything Ashley had ever done beneath the tree. Sitting among the roots and reading day till dusk, waiting for a ladybird to fly off the page before turning it. Playing in the sandbox when he was a child, marching toy animals across a desert. Leaping in fallen leaves on bright October days. And Leshy had heard him talking to himself long after it was considered normal, on rinsed spring mornings when there was nothing better to do but talk to the earth and the ants and the roots.

But Ashley wasn't embarrassed, not this time, not with Leshy.

"Will it be okay if my dad cuts the tree down?" Ashley asked. "He's going to chop it up soon."

"Leave the roots."

"Okay. I'll tell him." Ashley paused and rubbed the sun from his eyes. He would tell his father to set aside some wood for him too, enough for a cabinet. With drawers, he thought, full of acorns and peeled twigs, thorns and seeds. Whittled figurines of wooden men, fairies and gnomes and forest folk. A chest to hold his treasures. He would be a joiner when he grew up, maybe a boat builder or wheelwright, even though he didn't think they were needed anymore, with everything being made of steel and plastic. He felt as if he had been born too late. "How old are you?" he asked.

Leshy stretched his arms to the sky. He had hair under his arms, little green curls, close cropped and stubbly. Ashley found himself staring.

"What are you doing?" Leshy still hadn't put his arms down.

Leshy looked surprised and then lowered his arms. "Oh. I forgot."

"Forgot what?"

"You'll have to count my rings."

"Rings?"

"To know how old I am."

"Oh. Okay." Ashley hopped off the tree and moved toward the break in the sycamore, where he might see its rings.

"Not those. My rings."

"Oh. Okay. Where are they?"

Leshy hopped off the trunk and pulled Ashley into the shade underneath. "I'll show you."

In autumn, Leshy's hair turned pale yellow and fell off. In winter, he had none, and Ashley could see and touch the little knobs on his scalp, two of them just inside the hairline like a fawn's ungrown antlers. In spring, his hair began to grow again, lighter green than before.

"I thought you only existed in like, England, or something," Ashley said. To him, America seemed so young, as if had sprung up after all the other continents had already formed. Too young for myth, a history too shallow yet for power to take root. America had no dark age like England, no castles and knights, no time for the glory of a grail to spread its magic and seep into the forests. But Ashley had forgotten that all land is old. He had forgotten that magic is quick and that science is the slow one.

Season by season, Leshy showed Ashley the forest as he had never seen it before. The forest behind his house had never seemed so large, not even when Ashley was a child and the world had a way of getting bigger the farther in he went. Leshy taught him the secret language of wood. Leshy taught him to follow the currents of the forest. He learned wortcunning and woodcraft. He learned to name every plant, every animal, every insect and their signs. Every scrape, scat, den, and spoor. Leshy showed him the plants that did not belong, the ones that might do harm, the invaders. He called them by name: wild parsnip, garlic mustard, purple loosestrife, honeysuckle. And Ashley learned about wood. The best wood for walking sticks, for arrows that flew the truest, and--to Ashley's surprise--for the hottest and longest fires.

"You're not afraid of fire?"

Leshy laughed his birdsong laugh. "A myth, Ash."

"When you were, uh. Before. Did you ever get scared? Being so high off the ground, so close to the stars? And lightning?"

Leshy grinned and shook his head. "No. It's easy. Let me show you."

And that night Leshy led Ashley out under the stars, their hands clasped. At first, Ashley cried out, took a step back, and fumbled for the door knob. The stars pressed down on him like needles, pins that held him in place. He was paralyzed. But Leshy raked the tips of his twiggy fingers across his back, and Ashley let all his muscles go. Leshy pulled out the pins, and it didn't even hurt.

"Like this?" Ashley said. He was tiptoeing: quiet, or the stars will hear you. "Like this?"

"Like this," and Leshy darted into the forest, dragging Ashley along until they were laughing.

Leshy led him to a meadow. It was a different place at night: sweetly damp and singing. For the first time in his life, Ashley saw the flowers all shut up, the spider webs that just might last long enough to hold the morning's dew, and the katydids that filled the night with their loud guiro song. And he was almost free, but he could still feel the sting of the night, the moon's glare, the dreadful watching of all that was dark and far away. It burned at the stem of his brain like a little black star pulsing.

"I can still feel it," Ashley said. "It's not gone."

"Not yet," Leshy said, and he pulled him to the ground.

They tangled, a welter of wood and flesh limbs. Ashley felt Leshy's roots questing up and inside, farther than he thought they could go, stretching upward like a second spine, and his head spun and his eyes fluttered as something burst behind his eyes, and then the roots were retracting, pulling something with them.

"Leshy."

They ended up on their backs staring star-ward. Ashley turned to whisper something in Leshy's knot of an ear and found him sleeping. He sighed and wondered what purpose Leshy might have for entering the world of humans. Did leshies always cross that line, or was he unique among them? Maybe he did it for the reasons humans go to Elfland and outer space in the stories. Or maybe he had been given no choice: lightning simply struck. Or maybe he was there to make more of his kind. Ashley imagined a little baby leshy growing somewhere inside his stomach. How long would it take to sprout and where would it come out and would it hurt?

There was so much he didn't know, and he was afraid to ask, afraid that the wrong question or the wrong word would break the spell. That if he put a name on what they had, it would be broken.

Leshy tugged on his hand, and Ashley forgot about it. He would figure it out later. For now, there were the stars.

But once they got back inside, Ashley wouldn't watch the shuttle landing on TV. He had had enough of stars. He wanted soil, dark and rich and nourishing. Earth, and the things that grew in it.

"You didn't miss much," his father said afterward. "Seen one, you've seen them all."

You never saw what they brought back, if they brought back anything, only the dwarfed figures of the men walking proudly, safely on the ground again. There was never even the chance of seeing an accident, a botched landing, a little excitement, your heart in your throat. It had taken a long time, but they had finally made it safe to send men and women to the stars.

Ashley watched summer ending in the apple trees. The fruit ripened and fell, sweetening the ground and the air all around. Yellow jackets feasted on the fallen harvest and flew drunkenly away. Days were warm, evenings were golden, and nights were cool.

"Leshy, what's that?" They were walking toward the pond where they swam in peace and silence with the swans when

Ashley noticed a black mark on the back of Leshy's knee.

"Canker."

Ashley stopped, his heart dropping. "What? Cancer? What?"

"No. Canker."

"Oh. Okay." Ashley wasn't sure if that should make him feel better. "What is it?"

Leshy looked over his shoulder. "Nothing. Let's go."

That night, Ashley looked it up on the computer when Leshy wasn't around. He found images of trees covered in dark, weepy wounds. Blotches of illness. A pestilence.

Someone tapped him on the shoulder, and he spun around.

"Oh. Leshy. I just looked it up. I'm sorry if you didn't want me to know, but. Are you okay? Is it? Will it? Does it hurt?"

Leshy shook his head, but said nothing and stood there until Ashley pulled him into his lap. They sat a long time like that, one in the other's lap, Leshy kneading Ashley's scalp and Ashley drawing circles around the whorled knot on the back of Leshy's neck. What Ashley called his birthmark.

"It'll go away," Leshy said.

Ashley believed him through September. They watched

summer burn itself out together. They plucked tomatoes from the vine and watched poplar leaves turn gold, the first to go. They shined like coins in the evening and fell into the pond, where they had their last swim of the year together. Ashley came out shivering, his teeth chattering, and Leshy wrapped him in a towel and rubbed him dry.

Another black mark appeared in the crook of Leshy's elbow on the last day of September.

That night, they took a walk down the road, the asphalt cold on Ashley's bare feet. Ashley meant to ask him everything that night, drag the answers out of him as he had once dragged his body out of the storm, but Leshy fell before he said a word. In a fit of tears, Ashley carried him back to the house and put him in bed. Should he draw a bath? Would hot water and Epsom salts draw out the darkness? Pesticides? Fungicides? For all Leshy had taught him about trees, Ashley knew nothing about how to care for a leshy, a woodwhatever it was he once called himself.

Leshy partially recovered by morning. He could talk, stand, and even walk, but his hair began to fall out. His skin fell black and ashy. His teeth decayed. His eyes grew dim and bleary, a dark smoky emerald color. Ashley spent whole days in the sun with him, telling him stories of his childhood, things Ashley had done beyond the eyes of the sycamore tree, hoping to give him another life to live in for a while. Leshy smiled, his eyes closed to keep the sap inside and his feet in a bucket of cool water. Sometimes he murmured, but his body wasn't responsive. His xylem, his phloem were drying up and dying.

"Tell me what to do," Ashley said. He was in tears. "What is this, Leshy?"

Leshy shrugged, as if he didn't know.

One evening in October, Ashley returned to the sycamore cabinet he had begun the summer before. It stood in the dark and sawdust of his father's garage, still a skeleton of what it would become. He had neglected it because of Leshy, and now he returned to it because of him: to get away, to put his hands to work and keep the canker from his mind. The pit bulls curled up nearby, and he set to work sanding its edges to softness.

The garage door slid open behind him, and the dogs lifted their heads, their brown eyes soft and full of light.

"Ash," Leshy said. "Let's go to the pond."

Ashley put down the sandpaper. The cabinet would have to wait. He would need it, later.

Ashley had to help him walk all the way there. The

water was too cold for swimming, but they sat on the bank and watched the sun set behind the pines. Leshy lay down and put his head on Ashley's lap, and they stayed until the stars came out. Some fell and others scooted across the sky, not stars at all, but satellites. Shuttles, maybe.

"I wish I could take it from you," Ashley said. He bent down and kissed the knot of Leshy's ear.

"I took it from you."

Ashley sat up. "What?" Tears welled in his eyes. "What? Why?"

Leshy pulled his head from Ashley's lap and sat up. Their hands still touched on the ground. "Maybe for the same reasons you would take it from me."

"But what do you mean you took it from me? I made you sick?"

"And I made you well. A bad thing came, and now it will go."

"But there's a cure, right? Leshies don't die."

"They do."

"But there's a cure."

"No. There's not. Not here."

"Not here? Then where? Why not here?"

"Because the sickness isn't from here." He touched the earth. "It doesn't belong here."

"What? Then where's it from?" Ashley was shivering now. "Where?"

And Leshy pointed to the stars.

## The Costs and Benefits of Lake Monsters

Mark David Adam

"Let me get this straight," Jake said. "You want to sell us a lake monster?"

"Not sell," the older man said stroking his trimmed beard, "arrange for you to have."

Jake squinted and the others in the room looked on. The man was sure the distinction was not the main thing they were wondering about.

He ran a match along the table top, held it to his pipe, puffed til smoke surrounded his face like clouds around a mountain, then exhaled into the air above him.

"I can arrange for the waters of your lake to be inhabited by a noble water serpent," he said.

The people in the small pub stared; surprisingly, no one laughed or ridiculed him.

"Think of the tourism it could bring in," he went on as casually as if he was offering to build a ski lodge. "And then, of course, there are other benefits as well."

He looked at each in turn, pausing at the woman who had brought him his scotch, whose hair hung down over the left side of her face, but did not quite hide the bruise around her eye.

"Protection," he said, letting the word hang for a moment then waving his hand, "of these beautiful waters and forests." He looked around at those who had edged their chairs closer to his table. "A purifying presence," he said softly.

Jake, acting as spokesperson for the town, not because of any standing, but because his size and strength and dislike for outsiders made him bold, said again, "You want to sell us a lake monster?"

"Arrange," the man said. "Of course there would be certain reparations due. A contract to be fulfilled and maintained. And there is my own," he paused, "small fee as intercessor, which is, after all, not without its difficulties."

"And you would have it that our lake would be home to a Loch Ness Monster?" Jake asked scowling.

"A giant water snake," the man corrected. "Elusive, showing itself enough to arouse interest and respect, but not enough to become commonplace." He looked around him like a teacher handing out exams to children. "It will not be caught, nor appreciate attempts to do so, nor will it appear in photographs."

The door of the pub opened and everyone looked up as more people entered. The man noted the surprise on some of those sitting when they saw who had arrived, but his deal was with the town, not just the regulars of the pub, and the people of the town were responding to his unspoken call.

"You want to sell us a lake monster," Jake repeated, not because he had not heard the man's use of the word arrange, but because he distrusted everyone, especially those he did not know.

"Like I said," the man replied, "arrange. But let's not quibble. I take your meaning. You are wondering what it will cost you."

The man lifted his scotch, took a slow drink, then looked around the room at each and every person in turn.

"A life," he said, when he had finished acknowledging all with his eyes. "A life. Every three years. That is the arrangement."

No one moved or spoke. There was not a whispered protest or exclamation of disbelief. The man sat back, turning a large ring of dark tourmaline on his finger. He knew his audience could not only feel the truth of his words, they were stirred in an unconscious way back to a time of pacts and tributes paid to powers that the blood, if not the mind, remembered. A harsher time, to be sure, but one more honest than rents and taxes. A time of compacts that did not drain one's life in small parasitic measures, but was stern and true.

"I heard about the Barlow boy," he said softly.

"What parent? What community, would not remove such a threat? A sickness like he had...what he did to Holly."

The room stilled even more.

To hear this man speak so plainly, so knowingly, of a private, secret matter that many had only known as rumour was more unsettling than his offer.

"Thankfully," the man went on, "situations such as the Barlow boy are rare. But," he lifted his hand in a cautionary gesture. "We mustn't fool ourselves. There is a price. At times it will be easy to pay. At others...it will be a sacrifice."

"Strict rules must be maintained," he said. "Outsiders, while they will be accepted by the serpent, and may be taken by it of its own accord, are not substitutes. The contract is with the people of this town...If you choose."

He got up then, going outside to look at the moon and leaving them to speak among themselves. He waited, quite awhile, until a man called him inside. They informed him that

## The Costs and Benefits of Lake Monsters

Mark David Adam

"Let me get this straight," Jake said. "You want to sell us a lake monster?"

"Not sell," the older man said stroking his trimmed beard, "arrange for you to have."

Jake squinted and the others in the room looked on. The man was sure the distinction was not the main thing they were wondering about.

He ran a match along the table top, held it to his pipe, puffed til smoke surrounded his face like clouds around a mountain, then exhaled into the air above him.

"I can arrange for the waters of your lake to be inhabited by a noble water serpent," he said.

The people in the small pub stared; surprisingly, no one laughed or ridiculed him.

"Think of the tourism it could bring in," he went on as casually as if he was offering to build a ski lodge. "And then, of course, there are other benefits as well."

He looked at each in turn, pausing at the woman who had brought him his scotch, whose hair hung down over the left side of her face, but did not quite hide the bruise around her eye.

"Protection," he said, letting the word hang for a moment then waving his hand, "of these beautiful waters and forests." He looked around at those who had edged their chairs closer to his table. "A purifying presence," he said softly.

Jake, acting as spokesperson for the town, not because of any standing, but because his size and strength and dislike for outsiders made him bold, said again, "You want to sell us a lake monster?"

"Arrange," the man said. "Of course there would be certain reparations due. A contract to be fulfilled and maintained. And there is my own," he paused, "small fee as intercessor, which is, after all, not without its difficulties."

"And you would have it that our lake would be home to a Loch Ness Monster?" Jake asked scowling.

"A giant water snake," the man corrected. "Elusive, showing itself enough to arouse interest and respect, but not enough to become commonplace." He looked around him like a teacher handing out exams to children. "It will not be caught, nor appreciate attempts to do so, nor will it appear in they were not interested. No one questioned the validity of his offer, or inquired about different terms.

He nodded.

"Thank you for your time," he said. "I will be on my way in the morning."

He walked to where he was camped on the lake's edge. He sat for a long time watching the reflection of stars on the surface of the water. After the waxing moon had drifted behind the trees of a distant ridge he heard footsteps, as he knew he would.

The woman, Jake's wife, who had served him scotch looking out from behind loose hair, approached while other women stood behind.

The man rose and pulled out a silver chain from around his neck. Attached to it was a small oval, no larger than his thumb. It pulled in the light of stars and glowed softly in his hand.

He held it out to her.

"Place it in your womb," he said, "and when the time comes, enter the lake and set it free."

She held it for a time, not to question her decision, but

to honour the moment. Then she put her hand beneath her dress and up between her legs.

It wasn't always the women that accepted his offers. The children of a mining town had taken on the duty of being host and friend to a goblin. In exchange for their first teeth it protected them from the darkness their father's acquired working beneath the surface; a darkness that would have otherwise manifested in violence and neglect. In another town, the men who worked the land always left one field fallow in which they constructed a maze. At the heart of it they left the first and best of their harvest for the deva who protected their crops from disease and blight.

A woman, behind the one who he had given the egg, had her arm around her daughter whose belly was extended, five months pregnant, the father being her own. He knew this would be the first sacrifice.

The man motioned with his hand, gathering the women in. He sang the song of the serpent until they had learned it and its rhythm was woven into their breathing and pulsing of blood. By the rippling of the lake's water he taught them how to mark someone so that if that person ever went on the water, or to the lake's edge at night, they would not come back.

And in the dawn light he received his fee, a kiss from each of them, that made him smile and erased the wrinkled lines of his face.

## Night Quarry

B.D. Keefe

Seneca legend had it that the thing could be seen at night during certain cycles of the moon, or in earliest morning when mist clung to the water. Jari gwado, they called it, great horned serpent, and the elders said that it sometimes took fowl or otter thrashing from the surface. A brave even claimed to have witnessed it swallow a yearling as the deer swam in the black water off Long Point.

Most of the townspeople dismissed these stories as the queer superstition of the Indians. A professor traveling through town by stagecoach, on his way to New York's western frontier to study the Allegheny, wrote a treatise for the local paper comparing serpent legends from around the world. He was briefly a guest at the Golding House Hotel, the large if somewhat shabby hostelry that sat on a bluff overlooking Onondaga Lake. The professor held court in the hotel parlor for a number of evenings, explicating to anyone who'd listen how primitive myth universally featured the serpent as a symbol of wickedness. It was as true of the Seneca as it had been for the Hindu of India and even the European peasants of the not-too-distant past. After all, was St. George's famous adversary so different from this creature of which the Seneca whispered?

The professor, as it happened, never made it back from the western country. Some ravaged clothing and a bloody folio of papers was recovered at a desolate crossroads; a notice about the tragedy appeared in the same paper as had the lesson on serpents.

The first white man claiming to have seen the creature was Hiram Smith, though he was near-sighted as a mole and simple as a post, so little attention was paid to his account. Nevertheless, one night not long after, a gang of apprentices from the brickworks - their bravery no doubt improved by the corn liquor endemic among that class – found their way onto the water in a skiff.

For reasons merely hypothesized about, some convergence of weather and geography created large swells that arose seemingly at random and moved in a southwesterly direction from the lake's middle. On the night in question, one violently rocked the skiff. A boy fell overboard and, unable to swim, was saved by a line tossed from the side. In this way the others pulled him aboard. All five would later swear oaths attesting to what they saw next: a vast creature, its head alone the size of a calf and with teeth like arrowheads, exploding from below the surface and snapping at the place where the boy had flailed just seconds before. Almost as quickly as it had broken the surface, it dove back down into the nocturnal water. Its tail was more than twenty feet long, they all agreed.

The story would have been dismissed as a prank had all five not come back to town shivering and white as the Lord's robes.

Thomas Golding got up from the remains of his solitary dinner, swallowed the last of his brandy and, wiping his mouth on a linen napkin, went to appraise the body of his wife.

The hall at the top of the staircase was steeped in opaque silence. Normally the grandfather clock would have ticked softly in the parlor below, but when the last of the hotel's seasonal guests had departed a week ago Golding disabled it. Now the place was still and quiet as a tomb.

In the bedroom, Clarissa was just as he had left her. Flickering candlelight gave a muted view of her corpse; the nightgown billowed around her like the wings of an angel. Some angel, Golding thought, recognizing the perverse humor in it. There was a dark blossom on the sheets from his work with the hatchet. Something held him back from using it on her pretty face, so instead he'd brought it down again and again on the back of her head, hacking through the heaps of lovely black hair, through the scalp treated with every exotic tonic money could buy, through the skull which shattered like porcelain, and, finally, into the brain beneath. Not that the last was any great loss. Clarissa had a reputation for many things, but wit wasn't among them.

She had outwitted Golding for a while, though, he had to concede. She might have continued doing so had the blacksmith not been a braggart. Golding had nursed his suspicions for months, but it was only after overhearing the innuendos of some regulars in the Black Horse Tavern that he resolved to undertake a proper investigation. What he found neither pleased nor surprised him.

Two weeks had passed. In the intervening days, Golding seethed with the knowledge of the infidelity. He indulged in dark thoughts, not least of which was how easily the thing could be resolved. It came to him like an epiphany late one evening: her loveliness was that of a prized pet, nothing more. Even a pet needed putting down once it had gone feral.

The blacksmith was a coarse sort known to strut shirtless outside his shop. His mustaches, full and black, gave him the appearance of a circus strongman more than a craftsman of upstanding moral character, and he cursed in fouler terms than even the firemen who shoveled coal in the lake's steamships.

Golding had reservations about working with the man from the very beginning, but he saw no alternative. The job called for someone as skilled in technical matters as he was lacking in scruples. The blacksmith fit the bill on both accounts.

Golding's face was met with a chill draught as he opened the door to the attic. He ascended the staircase and gazed to where the machination lay. It was more than sixty feet when drawn to its full length, though now that the steel hoops of its frame were coiled and obscured in large measure by canvas tarps, it was like any other piece of disused machinery. Except the eyes. A patch of moonlight illuminated them, and the red and yellow lacquer with which he'd meticulously painted them seemed to glint with menace. He wondered if perhaps he should have partaken of less brandy tonight.

The blacksmith wasn't due for another hour, when Golding was reasonably sure he would meet no one on the high road. He had some work to do in the meantime. He turned to the contraption beneath the tarp. All summer and into the beginning of October it had been submerged in the lake, sunken with a series of weights and counterweights devised by the blacksmith, then elevated to the surface by means of the enormous smith's bellows secured below the southern boathouse. The great rush of air from the bellows was fed through an ingenious system of rubber piping. If the whole enterprise hadn't been a fraudulent ruse, Golding could have taken it on the road as an exemplar of modern engineering. He might have fetched a nickel per head in hayseed towns throughout the New York countryside.

Instead he had operated it in secret and the Golding House reaped the rewards. The "serpent" appeared a dozen or more times after the original reports, and people began flocking in droves to Onondaga in the hopes of spotting it. The hotel received nearly two hundred guests from as far away as Illinois in the first month alone.

Golding lifted the tarpaulin and found what he had come to the attic for: the weights used to hold the "serpent" underwater, forged of black iron and at least fifty pounds apiece.

He remembered watching from the doorway of the smith's shop as the rogue - shirtless torso gleaming with sweat and face demonic in the glow of the embers - pounded the irons with his anvil until they were cannonball-shaped spheres. Golding seized one with both hands now in the dark of the attic and lifted it unsteadily. It would serve other purposes tonight.

There was the snorting of a horse in the lane. From the lantern's glow Golding could see the distorted silhouette of the animal through the etched glass panels in the door. He took another swallow of brandy for his nerves and then went to the door, weaving a little as he did.

Through the window he could see another silhouetted form, this one a man's.

"Abraham," Golding said as he opened the door.

The blacksmith grunted and brushed past him into the shadowy parlor. As always, his movements put Golding in mind of a great circus cat pacing its cage.

"I've had enough of these late night spy games," the blacksmith said. He swiveled to look at Golding, great hairy arms crossed over his massive chest.

"We can't very well meet at the noon hour on Main Street," Golding said, easing the door shut behind him. "The only way a secret is kept is for the those in confidence to never utter a word to anyone else. Loose talk has undone many a man." His words slurred some.

"I've about had my fill of your prattle," the blacksmith said. " I been thinkin', and our arrangement ain't to my liking."

"Oh?" Golding said. He tried to contain it, but a new swell of anger moved in him.

"I'll be getting half the profits now."

"Half the profits?" Golding said, his voice a tangle of confusion and rising indignation. "Now wait just a--"

The blacksmith held up a hand to silence him. "Like I been sayin', I don't want no more of your fuckin' prattle. It's like talking to a woman."

"You can't speak to me that way," Golding said, and edged further into the dark of the parlor.

"I'll talk to you how I like," the blacksmith said, taking a step forward. "Speaking of women, where's that pretty wife of yours? In bed?" When he said the last part a hint of a smirk appeared on his face.

"It's none of your concern where my wife is," Golding

said, taking another unsteady step into the depths of the room.

"She ain't much of a housekeeper or a cook," the blacksmith said. "If she were my wife I'd keep her in bed all the time. She's got to be useful for something."

Golding was now completely hidden in the shadows of the room's corner. He bent over and lifted one of the weights from where he had secreted them beneath a sheet.

"What're ya doin' back there?" the blacksmith called out. Before he could say more, Golding was rushing toward him, a great iron orb held tremblingly above his head. He brought it down with all the force he could manage and it met the blacksmith directly in the face, freeing a spray of teeth and nearly removing the man's jaw in one brutal motion. The blacksmith stumbled backward and sprawled in a bloody heap on the floor. Golding, despite gasping for breath and nearly losing his balance, retrieved the weight from where it had fallen. He lifted and then dropped it once again, this time on the blacksmith's heaving chest where it collapsed the sternum and rib cage in a crater of viscera. The blacksmith tried to speak but all that came out was a wet gurgle.

"That will be enough of your prattle," Golding said, leering at the ruined jaw that hung by a skein of flesh like that of a ventriloquist's dummy. Abraham the blacksmith wouldn't be swearing, or insulting anyone's wife, or making any more demands. Tonight or any other night.

The lake was still and obsidian, and the waxing crescent moon above gave off no more light than the cracked door to an illuminated room. Golding felt fatigue in his arms as he rowed; the weight of the trash in the stern meant he had to work twice as hard as usual, and he'd undertaken considerable labor already. Moving the bodies, as well as the weights, and launching the rowboat, had proven just what poor physical condition he was in. If it weren't for the brandy he was unsure he would be able to see this last part through.

He was out past Long Point now, and from his memory of the depth chart he knew the water was forty or so feet deep here. This wasn't far from where they had first submerged the "serpent," and Golding knew that if he kept rowing five hundred strokes beyond the point he would be in the deepest part of the lake, where it dropped off sharply into a deep submarine valley.

He was nearly to his destination when the first swell hit the boat. Despite the absence of wind, a wave rolled directly toward him. The bow bobbed over the wave's crest and Golding felt the spray on his bare arms where he had rolled up the shirtsleeves. A second swell appeared, larger than the first by half, and its spray soaked his trousers. He rowed harder.

Once he was done convincing the constable that Clarissa and the blacksmith had run off together, he would sell the hotel and perhaps head west to Nebraska or Kansas. He'd heard that the cowhands there had a thirst for whiskey and snake oil. They needed someone to sell it to them.

A third swell struck the boat. Water was pooled at his feet now. Four hundred and fifty strokes? Four hundred and sixty? He'd lost track. This was deep enough.

Golding crawled aft toward the mound of refuse. Clarissa's body was at the top of the heap, weights already cinched around her tiny waist. With considerable effort, he hoisted half of the corpse atop the starboard gunwale. He thought of saying a few last words, but no inspiration was forthcoming. With a final push the whole macabre parcel splashed loudly in the water. It sunk instantly, and within a minute the last ripples had dissipated and the lake's surface was still again.

Golding knelt beside the heaped oaf, who had to weigh two hundred pounds even before the weights were added.

Wrapping both arms around the abdomen, he lifted with as much vigor as he could manage and felt a stabbing pain in his back. He also felt the port side of the boat dip dangerously into the lake, and water came rushing over the gunwale. He quickly corrected this by leaning to the starboard and lowered himself again, ignoring the pain. This time he managed to get the blacksmith's shoulders over the edge of the boat. Another push or two and the deed would be done.

He gave a heave, now against the blacksmith's legs, which were like the trunks of young oaks, and the weight he had secured around the corpse's chest helped pull most of its considerable mass into the water. In the final moment as the body tipped forever into the lake, there was the sound of fabric ripping, and the weight he had secured around the ankles came loose and tumbled into the boat. The deck was instantly splintered by the impact, and a frenzy of black water came lapping through the hole.

The last thing Golding saw as the boat submerged, as frigid water engulfed him, was the creature rearing with terrible ferocity to engulf the blacksmith's body. It seemed to swallow the entire cadaver at once, not bothering to chew. It looked nothing like his serpent had, nothing like a Chinese dragon, or the monster slain by St. George, or any cheerfully colored grotesquerie rotating on a carousel. This creature was blacker than the water or the night sky, and so much bigger than anything he could've dreamed up. He could hear himself screaming, but it was like someone else's scream, a sound heard far away, or in a dream. His focus was entirely on the serpent and how impossibly dark it was. Its eyes were the blackest part of all, and as it swam toward Golding, he knew that even under a full moon they would reflect nothing.

## Wake

### by Jennie Brass

"Come out, come out wherever you are!" Willow's dirty hand cupped her mouth and amplified the taunt. Her naked toes wriggled in the muddy stream bank. She didn't mind the chill creeping up her bones. The familiar sensation welcomed her.

The distant toll of the village bell called her from over the hill. She didn't so much as turn her head. The memories of the other children's clumsy rhymes plagued her.

*Weeping Willow,*

*Weeping Willow!*

*Cries in her pillow.*

*Can't even say 'hello'!*

Of course she'd uttered no words to her fellow orphans. Not one of them ever showed any interest in understanding her. Let them believe she was mute. Let them play their childish games. She was certain now what she had glimpsed in her vague dreams, knew now what she had searched for these past four years.

The breeze threatened to steal the tattered page clutched in her hand. She tightened her fist and cast her teary eyes on the foaming stream at the end of the forest's path.

She had to have her answer before the headmistress dragged her back to the orphanage.

"You have to be here. You just have to! I can't go back." Her legs trembled and she fought to stay upright in the ankle-deep mire. The search for the truth had taken so long. Her heart thrummed at how close she had come to never glimpsing the revelation. How close she had come to overlooking that humble book, *The Terrible Journeys of Tasgall the Bard.*

The stream carelessly churned by her. Its banks were lined with rocks draped in the moss of undisturbed years. Not even a marsh bird flitted about the pylons of the collapsed wooden bridge. All that remained were the moldering frame boards in bits and pieces.

And a memory.

She closed her eyes and ignored the hair lashing against her face. There it was in her mind. The majestic wooden bridge stretched over babbling waters. Birds dove into that deep channel and surged up with a fresh catch of fish clutched in their bills.

Rays of sunlight dappled the shingled roof. A soft ka-thunk ka-thunk ka-thunk, ever present. The steady turn of the water wheel. The cadence of life.

Yes. This was the place.

Finally the place.

"Where are you?"

The hungry woods swallowed her shout.

"Please! I know you are here." Her voice faltered. A moment later, so did her knees. Willow crumpled into the mud and sobbed into her ragged dress. The precious page clutched to her heart.

In the squelching mud, the clomp of steps approached her. She froze and held her breath. Had she heard it?

The drip drop of water slapped the ground. She suppressed a tremble. Had she *truly* heard it?

Warm breath caressed her bowed head. The scent of salt marshes stung her nostrils. Willow lifted her gaze. Wide brown eyes, turbulent as the stream, stared down at her. A horse with a coat as black as the sky on a moonless night stood before her, swishing his tail lazily. He pressed his nose toward her.

She quivered and reached out to brush his soft muzzle.

Once.

Twice.

At the second stroke the stallion bucked back. His ears flicked. He nickered and stomped a hoof in the mud.

Willow stood to reach toward him again.

The horse reared up and turned his side to her. His head bowed, curious eyes watching her every move.

She embraced his neck.

At this, the horse wheeled. He pulled his ears back and narrowed his eyes.

Willow lowered her hands. "Easy. I know what you are, Kelpie. I know *who* you are."

He neighed and shook out his mane, stomping his foot impatiently.

"I am not like the other children you have taken. You'll never stick me with your trap." Willow knelt before him and presented one hand to him. With the other, she clasped the page to her heart.

The wind drifted from the far bank and brought with it the scent of stale ashes.

*Fire.*

Flames reflected on water danced in her memory. The cries that haunted her dreams since that night lingered in her ears.

"You see." She choked back fresh tears. "I *want* to go with you."

The kelpie shook his head. Wet strands of mane thrashed his neck.

"If you know what I am, child, why have you risked coming here?"

Willow did not retreat, her outstretched hand still waited for him. "You cannot trap one who is willing. Your hide won't turn to tar and trap me."

The breeze rustled the leaves. Her eyes snapped shut.

*The crackle of the flames.* Hands grasping her. Yanked from her bed. Thrown out her window into the bitter night. She'd landed on the slope, rolled, and in a tumble came to a tangled rest in her blanket against the bridge pylon. A thunderous crack rent the air as the supports of the building gave way. The ka-thunk of the mill wheel had ceased. Familiarity … gone, washed away in the current of the water behind her. Carried away into the dark shattered night, as she had been so long ago by the arms of a stranger. Whispered words dulled the memories to nothing but a shade.

Gone. Everyone. Everything. So long ago.

She opened her eyes and wiped the tears away. "No one ever came to the orphanage to bring me home. No one ever will." Gently, she unfolded the page from the book pilfered from the orphanage library. "Only you have come now."

She held out the page to him. An illustration of the bridge over the stream, the kelpie's shadowed silhouette rising out from the mire of the swamp. A dire warning of the peril.

For a long moment he stood, motionless.

The night before, Willow stole through the silent halls of the orphanage. Like so many nights before, the flicker of a lantern provided her sole companionship. In the library she passed by all the shelves that had failed to explain the visions that plagued her day after day. She searched each book title in hope of a glimpse beyond the illusive vale.

She didn't belong here among the other children. Whispers called to her, unceasing, night and day.

She pulled out one book of fairy tales and thumbed through it. All were familiar, none helpful. About to put it back, she paused. Pushed back on the shelf, a leather bound book had been hidden. The name on the spine rung like the village bell.

*The Terrible Journeys of Tasgall the Bard.*

Tasgall.

That name lingered in the fog of her mind.

Willow opened the book where a loose page had been tucked. She froze.

The illustration on the page was familiar. The mill, the bridge, the stream. She set the image aside and devoured the story.

*Many a fellow bard will look upon this passage with sorrow. Or perhaps will offer me a scathing rebuke for my naivete. As a bard I am required not to omit a passage simply to avoid the admission of oversight. And so hearken to me now as I record the tale, even though my scars have yet to shed their scabs, of a terrible night by the enchanted stream.*

*The* Song for Safe Passage *died in my throat the moment I came around the bend in the path. Everything had changed. How had a cart bridge come to stretch across the unspoiled stream? On the other shore the rhythmic ka-thunk of a waterwheel drew my gaze to the mill nestled on the bank. Banished were the stretches of wildflowers that edged untouched forest. In their place, fields of cultivated grain pressed into the groves.*

*Cautiously I approached the stream. The water rippled past, undisturbed. Beneath the peaceful surface I searched for the concealed threat. Instead, fish of all sizes dragged their tails in the tangled weeds.*

*None of this was as it had been when last I stood here. My throat tightened with dread.*

*Hooves struck the timbered stretch over the river. I spun at the sound. An auburn horse attached to a cart neighed as a man leisurely crossed the bridge to my bank of the stream.*

*No song asking permission to cross a guarded territory hung in the air.*

*What had happened here?*

*I leaned forward, watching the surface of the water. The cart reached my bank and the man offered me a nod as he passed.*

*I caught my breath and forced my feet to venture onto the structure that should not be. The wood had settled nicely, unmolested. Ruts worn into the center betrayed years of use. Below me in the water nothing stirred.*

*There was only one way to get an answer.*

*I dusted off my tunic and pressed on toward the mill. A man swung the wide door to the mill room shut. At the scuffle of my feet he glanced up and smiled.*

*"And a good evening to you, sir. Name's Leathan. You look like a wise fellow, I'm sure you can guess what I do here."*

*I placed a hand on my chest and gave half a bow. "Tasgall, the bard. At your service."*

*A wild moan carried across the field. The sky above twisted clouds into ominous knots.*

*I trembled and once more searched the placid waters. There was no sign of any presence in their ripples. Then why did the wind carry the faint presence?*

*He held out a hand to me. "Come, not a man alive ignores that sound if he is wise. A storm is brewing. Would be a scoundrel of me if I left you to the weather's foul mercy. I have a warm hearth and fresh bread."*

*I followed him inside, comforted by the invitation. "And I bear tales to pass the time."*

*I dropped my travel sack by the hearth and let my*

fingers warm in the glow of the fire. Leathan coaxed a few oil lamps to life. "Ailsa, my love, we have a guest for dinner."

Even in here the rhythm of the mill wheel continued the cadence. Ka-thunk, ka-thunk, ka-thunk.

His wife came in with a steaming loaf of bread on a tray. Tangled in her skirts, a bright eyed girl grinned at me and waved. "Ma! Ma! Look at his pretty red cap."

I plucked the garment from my head and held it out to her. The child darted forward and snatched it.

"Willow." Her mother clicked her tongue. "We mustn't take things that don't belong to us."

"It's just a hat, Ma."

I shook my head. "Oh no, sweet child. That is more than a mere hat." Willow tenderly placed the hat beside me. Obediently she took her seat at the table before a serving of hearty stew and a slab of fresh bread. I followed her there and between mouthfuls of my own meal I explained, "It's a bright garment that tells the world I am a bard. A teller of tales, a singer of songs and legacies. That hat is a magic all its own."

Her eyes widened. The candlelight rippled in her deep blue irises.

My heartbeat quickened. Was it a trick of the light?

Or, something else.

A mug of ale pressed into my hands stole my attention. Ailsa met my gaze, tension lingered in her eyes. "A bard? Well, with the storm tonight perhaps the distraction of a song or a story would be a pleasant distraction."

"The honor is mine." I sought refuge in a study of my idle fingers. "It is with regret that I confess it is my only form of payment."

Leathan lifted his mug. "A payment gladly received. Nothing is more rewarding than the gold of a well *spun tale."*

A gulp of ale burned my throat before I replied, "Then may I give my gracious hosts my best performance this evening."

Willow hastened to slurp up her stew. Her gaze never left me.

When the meal was finished, Leathan stoked the fire while Ailsa and Willow settled down beside the hearth-light to the accompaniment of the raging storm.

Willow watched over my shoulder as I sketched the stream with its new neighbors, the mill house and the bridge. "Leathan, my travels take me all over the land. So I confess, it has been many years, perhaps close to a decade since I have been here and the banks of the enchanted stream were left to the wild. Tell me, when did you build your home here?"

"This place? Oh, about five or so years ago. Good luck for us too. Ailsa and I came looking for a new place to live. By some luck we wandered onto this stream and suddenly everything in our lives fell into place. You call it enchanted, *truly you have a gift for words. You cannot know how right you are.*" He rested his hands on Ailsa's shoulders.

She blushed, her gaze cast into her lap.

"Within the first season here she was with child. This fertile land blessed us with our little Willow."

At her name the girl grinned and waved a hand. "That's me. I's a blessing."

In the candlelight I could no longer deny the waves rippling in the blue of her eyes. Enchanted. The word lingered in my thoughts, troubling them. Even without looking, my hand sketched a figure in the stream.

"What's that?" Willow pointed. "Looks like a horsie."

I lifted my hand, my eyes searched her parents as

*I spoke to their daughter. "It is a type of magical horse. A creature called a kelpie that claims stretches of water. They lurk there waiting to ensnare unwitting humans, especially young children who might fancy a ride. Crafty beasts, they can even appear human for a time should they wish. Did you know, sweet one, that if you ever see one there is a way to capture it?"*

*"There is?" She leaned in closer to me.*

*"Don't touch their skin, for it is tarry and you'll stick to it and be dragged down into the waters. But, if you take their bridle they are slave to your will until it is returned to them."*

*A mug crashed to the floor from Ailsa's slack hand. Her skin paled under the flash of lightning outside. "Oh, how I hate the howling wind. Willow, it's getting late. Time for bed. Come Leathan."*

*"But my love, there has been no time for a story."*

*"Aww Ma, I want to hear more about the watery horsies."*

*She stood and whisked the child into her arms. "We need hear no more howling of monsters on this stormy eve. Good night, humble bard."*

*I rose to my feet and offered my hosts a full bow. "I should enjoy the warmth of your hearth over a bed, if that is alright with you."*

*Leathan nodded as he led his family from the room. It had not escaped me that Ailsa's gaze drifted to a trunk on the floor.*

*Once the house stilled, I crept over to the trunk. Rusted hinges squealed and shattered the silent night. I froze, and held my breath long enough I should have turned blue. When my transgression remained undisturbed I dug through the contents. Deep under a pile of odds and ends I discovered the braided pond-weed cord bridle. Swiftly I tucked it into my sack and swung it over my shoulders. No wonder this land was so well tilled. No normal horse could have possibly changed the reed choked banks of this stream into viable farmland. Only one creature could will it so. No one deserved this fate, if I was right.*

*I crept out into the night and slipped through the door into the mill room. Bathed in the lamplight, a black horse stood in the rear of a stall. His half lidded eyes dull as a parched stream bed. I reached into my sack and pulled out the bridle. Careful not to touch his hide, even though nothing of the sheen suggested a tarry nature, I slipped it over his head and tied it in place.*

*He reared up with a malevolent scream.*

*Turbulent waves formed a maelstrom in the once dull eyes.*

*In a single blink I watched the horse change into the form of a dark-haired man. His hand reached for me. "How dare that woman! How dare she trick the mighty Caochan into surrendering his waters!"*

*I stumbled back from the miasma that lingered around him. The mill suddenly reeked of a putrid swamp. "Please, you are free now. Make haste and you may find an unoccupied stretch of a stream to call your own."*

*"Call my own? This stretch of the stream is my own. Where is that accursed wench? She and her family will know my vengeance!" Caochan threw his hands in the air. At once his form shifted back into the powerful horse. His hoof drove down and broke through the boards. Flour dust drifted into the air in a fine cloud.*

*"Leave them be. They didn't know!"*

*"Oh, she knew. Get out of my way, foolish bard!" He bucked the lamp from my hand. Flames licked up into the air following the path of the flour. By the gods, what had I done?*

*"You'll kill us all!" I tried to beat the flames out. My efforts only managed to spread them.*

*"As sure as a stream floods its banks."* He kicked the door open and galloped through.

*I abandoned the efforts to douse the flames and darted to help the family. He headed to the house where I lost sight of him.*

*"Wake up!" I screamed.*

*Inside the house lay in shambles from the sharp hooves of the kelpie. Smoke oozed in from the attached mill. The steady ka-thunk of the mill wheel droned on over the growing roar.*

*Ailsa screamed from the other room. I tried to penetrate the choking smoke, but it stole the air from my lungs. I was forced to flee the engulfed house. Caochan's raging fit echoed within the confines of the burning timbers.*

*The wind howled, but it bore no rain. The house blazed like an inferno. A window shutter opened and a blanket wrapped bundle tumbled down the bank to rest on the bridge pylon. I shuffled over to it.*

*Willow. Her wide eyes stared at nothing. The ripples in her irises whipped up to frothing waves. I clutched her to me.*

*A section of the roof groaned and fell. The fire within roared with the fresh fuel. There was nothing I could do for her parents. For those foolish enough to steal a kelpie's bridle and ban him from his own stream, their fate was sealed.*

*But I could help Willow.*

*Halfway across the bridge I gazed back when Caochan burst out of the side of the building dragging the screaming Ailsa tacked to his side. A sickening crack rent the air as the axle on the mill wheel snapped and groaned to a halt. The ka-thunk had ceased, replaced by the crackle of hungry flames. No one else had left the building.*

*I looked over my shoulder. Caochan reared up, his tarry hide engulfed in flames licking his imprisoned victim while she pleaded wordlessly. He dove toward the bridge at breakneck speed. The moment his hoof struck the bridge it trembled from the impact. I stumbled to keep my footing.*

*With Willow in my grasp I put everything into reaching the other end of the bridge. Timbers creaked and groaned beneath us. The blazing heat of Caochan's pelt cast sparks out to strike me. I was on fire, but I could not stop now.*

*I leapt for the bank.*

*His hoof came down on my leg with a crack.*

*The night sky turned orange. Every timber of the bridge burned and screamed under the weight of the beast. He reared back onto his hind legs. Ailsa wailed out, flailing her legs in vain.*

*The middle of the bridge snapped. His eyes widened as the splintered timbers cast him into the waters. The waves swallowed both kelpie and the woman who dared to bind him whole. Steam rose up in a spiral.*

*I rolled into the mossy reeds on the bank rewarded by the hiss of the extinguished fire. Still in my arms I clasped the entranced Willow. My fear banished most of the pain, but I was no longer able to stand enough to carry her.*

*"Fire!" Voices from the nearby shire carried over the night wind.*

*Relief washed over me, I would not have to carry her. As I gazed into the betraying ripple of her irises I knew the danger was far from over. There was only one way to protect her. I laid back and tried to weave the spell in my words.*

*In fitful gasps I whispered into her ear, "Speak not a word of this nightmare, little Willow. Take care where you build your bridges."*

*I can only hope it was enough to keep her safe.*

*Water is such an insidious element.*

On the far bank of the stream, nestled beneath the fallen timbers of the mill house, a field mouse rummaged through the debris. Through a hole no larger than his head, the mouse slipped into a trunk. He had been here before and pulled threads from the fabric found within until the cloth was little more than shreds.

Today his target was crisper. Deeper inside, nearly at the bottom, he had discovered a stack of books. Some were shut in their covers. But one remained open, the edges perfect for his sickle teeth.

Of course, he being nothing more than a humble field mouse, was not privy to the secrets on the page. The words were nothing but streaks of black against the light paper.

Had the gods gifted him with the ability to read, he may have lingered for more than a quick nibble. For this is what they said.

> *I write this now as I can scarcely believe it myself. I have hesitated in committing this to paper, lest I be deemed mad. Or worse. I shall begin when Leathan first believed we had stumbled upon a font of luck.*
>
> *It was late spring when we came to the banks of the most enchanted stream. Fields of colorful wildflowers danced in the breezes at the foot of towering trees. Even the mire of the shore could not spoil the beauty of this glade.*
>
> *"Can you see it now, Ailsa?" Leathan's eyes glazed over as he pointed at the rock ledge on the far shore.*

*"We can build the mill and our house right there. The fields are fertile here, much better than the over-trod plot we were forced to abandon." He held me tight and stroked my flat belly. "Perhaps here we might find the future so long denied us."*

*Shame burned on my cheeks. "I am sorry."*

*"Hush now. There is still time for children. I will fetch wood from the forest for a cooking fire and see what else I can find to eat."*

*I removed the pack from my shoulder and gazed at the meager contents. "There is little left to cook."*

*He kissed me before I could say more. "You will make a feast of it, my love, as you always do. I'll be back before dark."*

*I watched the woods swallow Leathan before I turned to the gently babbling stream. Perched on a rock to keep my feet from the grasp of the squelching mud, I washed my hands in the cold water.*

*Drops of water rained down on me from a cloudless sky. This was not the right sky for rain. I looked over my shoulder to find a strange man leaning over me. Water cascaded down him in rivulets. His deep eyes pulled me up to my feet. The color in them churned and swirled. I could not look away from him.*

*He reached out a hand and filled the air with the sweet tang of salt. I grasped the hand as he pulled me from the bank into the reeds. My mind drifted deeper into a haze with each step. We slipped into the reeds.*

*There I lingered on the edges of memories. I hardly recall how the sun had sunk so low on the horizon, or how I had come to be lying in the shelter of the willow in the arms of the strange man. His warm breath stirred my damp hair.*

*I should be somewhere, doing something. The thought plagued me, and yet I could not fully recall my purpose. All I desired was to rest my hands on him.*

*He wore a simple necklace, the pendant nestled in the hollow of his collar bone. I turned the river stone pendant with my finger and whispered the word written there. "Caochan."*

*The cord glowed. As I withdrew my hand the necklace came with it and changed into a bridle woven of pond-weed. The fog that crippled my mind lifted as I scrambled back.*

*The man beside me opened his eyes. A maelstrom of fury flashed in them. He arched his chin down and his form shifted into an immense tarry stallion.*

*Gods help me, a kelpie!*

*As swiftly as the storm exploded in his eyes, it vanished. The pools within grew placid, dull as a mud puddle. He stood before me with his head bowed. I took a step, he followed.*

*"Is it true?" I stared at the bridle in my hand. "Now you cannot harm me? As long as I possess this, your will belongs to me?"*

*He only blinked in reply.*

*"We are saved!" I gazed at the far shore. "With your strong back my husband will surely be able to break this land. Leathan was right. Oh, what a blessed day."*

*So it had seemed. The mill foundation is well laid. I have not told Leathan of how the stallion came to me. I had intended to, along with the news that I am with our first child. But he is so elated with that news that swells my belly, I can hardly dare to think how we would receive the rest of it.*

*I now dread what happened in the time I cannot remember. This I know. The kelpie must never regain his bridle and thus his freedom. For I fear what would happen if his fury were unleashed.*

For a long moment the kelpie stood motionless on the stream bank, pondering little Willow.

Then, ever so slowly, he sank down onto the ground.

Willow crawled onto his back and hugged his strong neck tight. Her tears trailed down his mane and mingled with the river.

Step by step he carried her into the currents, the water lapped up his sides higher and higher. Willow smiled for the first time in years.

"Take me, Caochan." The dark waters swirled around him as he sank to his broad shoulders. Chill water kissed at her neck as he kicked into the deep channel.

The page floated in the eddying wake of his strokes. Captured in vivid detail in the old illustration at the other end of the bridge, barely visible in the parting trees, a quaint mill house peered out.

"Take me ... back home."

## Hounded

Lawrence Harding

Carl rang the till and nodded at his customer. "That'll be twenty dollars."

Seamus nodded and began counting from a sheaf of notes. He tossed four fives on the counter. "There y'are, Carl."

Carl tucked the notes into the till drawer. "Everything going all right up at the farm? You're looking tired."

Seamus grinned and ran a hand through his sweat-slicked hair. "Oh, the farm's grand, just grand. I've just had trouble sleeping. It's this heat…"

Carl laughed. "Well, paddy, you'll have to get used to it eventually. It's only taken you what, ten years now?"

Seamus joined in the laughter, which soon gasped to an awkward halt, stifled by the heat. "Aye, and it'll take ten more, no doubt. We Irish weren't built for this weather!"

Carl shrugged. "You're the one who chose to live here."

Seamus hesitated, on the edge of speech, then snatched up his supplies and made for the door of the general store that served their humble patch of Outback. Carl blinked, then shrugged again. He was a funny one, that paddy.

The door banged shut and a dog barked. There was a crash as Seamus dropped his stack of groceries, half-hurling himself back into the store. He caught Carl's eye, then turned away and began gathering up the spilled tins and packages. The dog barked again, and Seamus cringed as the last packages disappeared in to his bag. The barking was replaced by laughter from across the street.

"It's just a dog, mate!" yelled some wit as Seamus hurried away, eyes downcast and fixed on his groceries. Carl shook his head. Yep. Definitely a funny one. What kind of an idiot moved to sheep country when they were afraid of dogs?

Seamus couldn't sleep again. He tossed and turned, always just on the edge of slumber. But whenever he drifted over the edge, he found it waiting for him in the deep.

Sea-slick fur. A flash of scales. Then darkness; but he knew that it was there, in the dark, toying with him. Silence. The stillness of knowing that you are in your final moments. The sensation of eyes prickling at your neck. Even the wind caught its breath.

Then – a keening cry, a gust of movement, a gleam of white, the glint of needle teeth; it was about him. He was flailing, battering at it, but it sank its fangs into his calf. He fell to his knees, and it had him.

Pain. Screaming. Blood. Darkness.

It took Seamus a moment to realize that he was awake. It was night. That was why it was dark. He was in his room. He was safe.

But he knew that it was out there, somewhere. It always would be.

But it could never follow him here.

Seamus poured a second cup of coffee down his throat, letting caffeine do what sleep could not. He tried not to smell it. The smell always reminded him.

Aidan had been drinking coffee that night; the night that ended both their lives. Maybe Aidan had been the lucky one, in the end. He didn't have to suffer any more.

"It's got to be round here somewhere," muttered Aidan as he took another swig from his flask. "Keep your gun handy."

Seamus nodded, peering ahead at the shadowy landscape that their head-torches picked out.

"Aye, Aidan. We'll get the bastard."

His foot slipped, and he only just avoided pulling the trigger. He swore and looked down. "Shit, Ade. More of them."

The ground was peppered with scraps of half-eaten fish. Scaled heads peered up at them with vacant, confused eyes. Tails and fins were scattered among the grasses.

His fish. Their fish.

Something, or someone, had been going at their stocks for weeks. Sometimes that happened to a fish-farm – you couldn't stop every heron, try as you might. That was the game you played with nature.

But whatever was poaching from them didn't even finish

its meals. That rankled. It was bad enough that fish were being taken, but it was worse that they weren't even needed…

Well, they had to do something, and they were doing it.

The fish-ponds seemed quiet, at first. There wasn't even a breeze to stir the surface of the water. The two men walked to the edge and tracked their shotguns to and fro, waiting for something to show itself.

There was nothing but silence. Too much silence. Seamus began to wonder if they'd wasted another night chasing shadows.

But then he heard the soft sound of something breaking the surface. It was immediately drowned out by the roar of their guns. Both shots hit the water. Both men cursed their poor aim.

Then a high, keening cry arose from the far bank. Seamus and Aidan dropped their guns as they instinctively clapped their hands over their ears as the screeching rattle tore at their hearing. It was like nothing they had ever heard before. It was like something out of the bedtime tales that glitter-eyed grandparents told you at night, tales of the banshee or the Morrigan.

The cry faded into a silence deeper than the one they had broken. Seamus and Aidan lowered their hands.

"Jesus, Seamus. What the hell was that?"

"I don't know," replied Seamus grimly, taking up his gun. "But we'd better get a closer look."

They crept closer along the circular bank of the pond. Something was half-slumped on the bank ahead, surrounded by water that was dark with blood.

"What is it? An otter?"

"Too big. It's the size of an Alsatian at least."

Aidan whistled, impressed. Suddenly he clammed up and raised his gun. "Shit, Seamus – another one!"

He was right. Another huge shape had surfaced next to their kill. It seemed to be nuzzling the corpse, trying to wake it. Aidan took aim. "Stay still now, there's a good bugger…"

The creature raised its head to the sky. Another shrill shriek split the night, but this one had a different cadence. The first had been woven of fear and agony; this was threaded with pain and mourning, and rage. Seamus gritted his teeth against its assault.

Aidan was not so lucky. His gun went off wildly, sending

its slug off into the void. He swore and tried to reload.

He never had time. As the shotgun roared, the creature's head snapped around. Seamus' headlamp illuminated it for a brief moment that would live with him for ever; an enormous otter with terrifyingly intelligent eyes, with fin-like ears protruding from water-smoothed fur sprouting from scaled skin.

Seamus saw no more than that, because it dived into the water and then, suddenly, it was upon them, and all that he could remember after that moment was Aidan's screams.

He could never quite remember how he got away. It was unfortunate, as it made the police even less inclined to believe his unlikely story.

Seamus blinked away the memories and downed his third, cold coffee. It tasted like the stuff the police had given him. Some memories were inescapable.

"So. You were hunting a beastie, were you? And it just happened to eat your mate and let you off scot-free?"

"Yes."

The detective inspector sighed and shook his head. "Your

story's straight, I'll give you that. Can't prove you wrong until we find the body. Which we will," he added with a pointed glance.

Seamus looked back impassively. "I didn't kill him."

"You're the last man to see him alive. You were alone. You both had guns. You were found covered in another man's blood. Fish-ponds are reasonably deep." The detective inspector shrugged. "It's a cliché that the obvious answer is usually the right one, but it's a cliché for a reason. It'd be a lot easier for all of us, yourself included, if you stopped telling me fairy stories and tried the truth instead."

The implied question hung in the air, but Seamus just stared through it.

"I'm telling the truth."

The detective inspector sighed and reached for a cigarette. "Have it your own way, then. Sergeant, take him back to the cells."

It was only when the dredgers found what was left of Aidan that Seamus was released. He'd never seen the body, but he'd once forced himself to read the autopsy report.

Flesh torn. Teeth-marks on bones; angles in-keeping with those expected from predatory bites. Too little material for conclusive identification of assailant. Cause of death an attack by an unknown animal.

Material. That was all that his friend had become. The thought sickened him even now, but at the time he had felt like he was walking on air. He was vindicated. He was free.

The authorities combed the surrounding countryside in search of the creature. The official story was that a big cat had escaped from a private menagerie. It didn't occur to anyone that it could be anything else.

Seamus knew otherwise. He had seen it. But his story was dismissed as a deluded false memory concocted to cover up the trauma. He could live with that. He was free.

But so was the beast, and they never found it.

When coffee didn't help, whisky always did. With a little spiritual help, Seamus was able to get a decent morning's work done with his modest flock.

After a few hours of drudgery, he headed back to the house to avoid the midday heat. His fair Celtic complexion wasn't made for a place like this.

There was a flicker of movement in the corner of his eye. He froze. Despite the heat, a chill shuddered through him. His body might be in Australia, but his mind's eye transported him far, far away…

There it was again. He hadn't imagined it – had he?

He knew all the windows were shut. He knew the doors were bolted. He knew he was alone in the house.

He should have been happy to be vindicated. He should be relaxing now. But all he could hear was the sound of snuffling around in the darkness behind his house.

Something big.

And occasionally a distant screeching that he couldn't quite believe was the nearby train-line.

It took a few days for some friends to come over to celebrate his release; and to find out why he wouldn't leave the house. They were understanding, of course. It was terrible that he'd been left with no mental health help. Seeing someone eaten alive had to be traumatic. It was no wonder he kept seeing things.

A few pints and a bit of bantering helped a great deal. They even managed to persuade him to go out onto the patio. But as soon as he heard the distant screeching, he fled back inside.

His friends managed to convince him that it was cats fighting in the street out back. But he still didn't leave the house for six weeks after that.

Seamus shook away the past and stomped inside. Several clicks tinkled in the heat as he turned the locks.

He warmed some beans and grabbed a can of lager from the fridge. Once sat at the kitchen table with his simple meal, he flipped open his laptop and began scrolling. He chewed mechanically, barely tasting his food as his eyes devoured the words on the websites he had bookmarked. His mind sank into the drudgery; so familiar, so comforting, so nerve-wracking.

He'd first turned to the internet during his self-imposed house arrest. It was the natural thing to do. Though his friends tried to stop him, telling him that trawling through report after report of beast attacks was far from healthy, they couldn't be around him all the time.

He told himself that he was facing his demons. He told himself that if he found out what kind of animal it had been, it would banish those deep, nagging dreams that tugged at his rationality, screaming at him in the night; the thoughts that what had happened to Aidan just wasn't natural. If he could prove it was, then he would be free.

He couldn't quite banish them yet, but image after image of rent limbs and torn flesh drowned his horror in dull familiarity. In time, his nightmares settled into mere bad dreams. Weeks passed, and his friends finally managed to coax him out of his fortress.

Nothing happened. He felt no presence. The screams in the distance were just the trains. It seemed that he had banished his demons at last.

His brief sojourn in the light would last maybe three weeks.

Seamus realised that he'd been staring out of the window for some time, watching the scrub dancing in the heat-shimmer. It rippled, like water being disturbed by something slowly, purposefully pressing through it.

He tried not to remember. He always tried not to. But, as always, despite his struggles, he was pulled down, down into the depths of recollection.

He had decided it was time to go for a walk on his own. He had been on a few rambles with friends recently, as they gently pulled him out of his isolation. They claimed the fresh air would help, and so far they had been right. He was sleeping better. The nightmares had all but faded.

They never discussed what he had seen, or thought he had, by mutual and silent agreement. They wouldn't believe the stories, and they wouldn't encourage what he knew was an unhealthy obsession.

Now, he felt ready to face the world alone. So he wandered down a familiar country lane, enjoying the breeze as it wafted fresh spring scents through the air. His thoughts were pleasantly empty. For the first time in weeks, Seamus was content simply to be.

He came to the fork in the road. To the right, the path wound out across the meadows and back round the way he had come. To the left, it led towards his car – and the river.

Seamus hesitated. He had intended to follow his usual path. But something was tugging him down to the water. Hair prickled beneath his collar. He clenched his hands uncertainly. He hadn't seen natural water since…

…since that night. The night that… it happened.

He had to go down to the water. It was the last fear he had to face. Once he had done that, then he could be free. He took a deep breath, set his shoulders, and marched down the winding path.

The river was deep and wide, with a surface that was smooth and still. Sunlight danced on the ripples left by fish nipping at flies. Seamus drank in the view. He was surprised to find he quite enjoyed it. The sight of the flowing water soothed him. He felt calm, calmer than he had felt in months.

He felt, in fact, almost too calm. So calm that some deep part of him, some long-buried primal instinct, sat tense and on edge. This time, it was what saved him.

When it broke the water, it did so in utter silence. Only the vaguest of movements at the edge of his vision alerted

Seamus; or rather, his inner watchman. It was on the far bank, maybe four hundred metres away. It hadn't noticed him.

He was struck by how strange it looked, yet so familiar. How could he have ever thought it was a normal animal? From the fins that fanned from where its ears should be, to the fur sprouting in tufts between its scales, to its wide, webbed paws, he knew it was the creature that had killed Aidan. The very same one.

For a moment, he was too surprised to be afraid. After so long, he had almost convinced himself that he had imagined that night.

The beast turned its head. Its eyes seemed to bore into him. Even from so far away, he could feel their intensity pierce his breast. As it unleashed that weird rattling cry, his living nightmare came flooding back. His mind was frozen. Only instinct moved his limbs as the creature pounced into the water, making straight for him. Seamus fled, scarcely aware he was doing so as he pounded up the hill to where his car stood waiting.

The path was a blur. All his thoughts were focused on

the next step forwards. He never looked back. He could feel it coming closer. The keening whistle began to pierce his ears again, and he knew that it had left the water. He had no idea how fast it could move on land. He could only keep running, and pray that he was faster.

He was lucky. The carpark wasn't far from the river. Even that short distance seemed insurmountable as the keening grew closer and closer, louder and louder. He could almost feel the creature snapping at his heels. He could almost feel its breath.

As the carpark came into view, he fumbled for his key fob. He was never more grateful for technology than when he saw the lights on his vehicle flicker as the doors unlocked. He wrenched the door open and dove into the car.

He didn't close the door fast enough. The creature managed to get its head and a clawed forepaw through the gap. Saliva sprayed as it fought to close its jaws around him. Seamus threw himself back and kicked it in the snout once, twice, thrice. It fell back, whimpering. Seamus took his chance, lunged forward and slammed the door shut.

He could hear the creature howling as he revved the

engine. It leapt at the car, scraping its claws across the windows in a frenzy. He watched it chase after him for a time as he sped off, until it disappeared behind him.

He drove aimlessly for hours. Eventually, he pulled into a service station, and began to cry as shock, relief, and fear released themselves. He hadn't been imagining it. It had all been true. He was right, though he wished he wasn't. He was lucky to be alive.

But now he had had a proper look at the monster. Now he knew what he was looking for.

Large otter/dog. Fins for ears. Webbed paws. Needle-like teeth. High-pitched cry. Scales and fur.

He typed in everything he could remember about the beast, and pressed enter.

It was one of the first results that came up. The picture was only an artist's impression, and it was slightly off on one or two details – the skull was too canine, the skin not scaly enough – but there was little doubt that it was the same creature.

The dobhar-chú. The water hound.

He read the entries. Not much seemed to be known

about it. They were almost exclusively seen in western Ireland, they lived mostly on fish but would eat land-based animals, including humans. Apart from that, there were only physical descriptions, most of which contradicted one another. Except for one detail that he hadn't known, which made everything make terrible sense.

The dobhar-chú mated for life. If one of them was killed, then the other would hunt the killer down, mercilessly and without forgiveness. That was the one thing that every story was in complete agreement on.

It had already got Aidan. Clearly that wasn't enough. Seamus wracked his brain, trying to drag the details of that night from memories he had taken great pains to bury. Which one of them had fired the fatal shot? Did that even matter to the dobhar-chú? He paced around the house for hours, convinced that he was a dead man walking, trying to convince himself that he was not. He failed.

He did manage to reassure himself a little. Even if the beast was after him, it had taken weeks, months even, to find him. Even then, it was he that had stumbled across it. There was no way it could have followed his scent in the car. He just had to be careful, that was all. It might want to kill him, but how could it find him without a trail to follow?

There was a high-pitched wail, almost a scream, from the garden. Seamus leapt out of his skin, the shook himself together again. It wasn't the same sound. It was a cat. He'd heard them fighting enough times before.

Still… it was best to be sure…

As he entered the kitchen, the yowling suddenly stopped. The world seemed to take a deep breath as he looked out of the window.

It had been a cat. And the mangled mess that had been the cat lay at the feet of his nightmares made flesh.

The dobhar-chú did nothing. Blood dripped from its maw as it stood over its victim. It stared at Seamus. Their eyes locked. He half expected it to throw its head back into the howl he had learned to fear, but it did not. Instead, it lowered its head and began to feed. After a few bites, it looked up as if to see if it were still being watched. If it had been a human, Seamus was sure that it would have smirked.

At last, Seamus realized that it wasn't just some dumb,

ravenous beast. It wanted revenge as much as it wanted his death. He was being toyed with. He drew the curtains and fled to his bedroom.

It didn't take long to throw a few necessary items into a suitcase. Clothes, phone, passport, cash. Anything else could be replaced. He had to get away now, before the hound decided to test the strength of his door. He hurried down to his car. Blind fortune had helped him again here. A covered garage hadn't been high on his priorities when he bought this place, but it was saving his life now as he bundled himself into the car free of savage jaws and slashing claws. He started the engine, punched the open button on the garage door remote, and sped out onto the road, heading anywhere but there. He hoped it might have come out onto the road, that he might drive over it and end the nightmare there and then. But it was nowhere to be seen.

Even so, he could feel it somewhere in the distance behind him. Somewhere, it would always be hunting him.

Seamus closed the laptop. He'd been looking at it for what seemed like an age, but he'd scarcely read anything. His memories kept getting in the way, as they always did. He'd read enough to be reassured. There was no news, no reports of odd animal attacks, no brutal unsolved murders. There'd been nothing to give him pause since a couple of shark attacks off the north coast a couple of weeks ago, but this was Australia. That sort of thing just happened sometimes; frequently enough that he could convince himself that it wasn't… anything else. It was one of the reasons he'd chosen to come here.

He'd known immediately that if the thing was going to follow him, he needed to outrun it. There was no way it could outpace a plane, or follow him to the other side of the world, especially not somewhere so hot and dry. He had to be safe here. He had to be. The dobhar-chú wasn't entirely natural, but surely it had limits?

His own had been tested enough. Seventy-two hours after the incident with the neighbour's cat, he had landed in Australia, with only his suitcase.

He'd done pretty well to get this place in the time he had been here, all things considered. He felt a little pride in that. He was, it turned out, not a bad farmer. If only he could relax enough to enjoy it.

Seamus dreamed of the keening cry again that night. He

tossed and turned, unable to shake it off. No matter what he did, the accursed sound was always just on the edge of hearing.

It was only when he got up to use the can that he realised that he could still hear it.

Cold dread filled him. Surely it couldn't be…?

No. No, it couldn't. It couldn't have found him here. His overtired mind just couldn't let go of the dream. That was all. That was all.

He was sure of it.

When Seamus went out to his fields that morning, he was too shocked to be terrified.

The sandy soil was stained a dark ochre, peppered with viscera and tufts of wool. At least half his flock had been killed. No, not killed. Savaged. Ripped apart. Eviscerated. Vacant eyes stared up at him from sockets already crawling with flies. The blood of the dead sheep seemed to cry out to him from the earth, asking why this had happened to them.

It was because of him. Seamus fell to his knees and wept. These sheep had become more than his livelihood. He had loved them, after a fashion. And now they were dead because of him. That moment from all those years ago overwhelmed him. The knowing look of the dobhar-chú as it gorged on the cat. It was out there somewhere now, watching with that same look. It was toying with him. It was eking out the pleasure of its revenge. That realization gripped his heart in an icy fist.

It was here. Somehow, it had found him. Would he ever be free? He turned and ran back towards the house, his heart pounding desperately in his ears. The world felt oddly silent around him, as if he wasn't really there. It was as if in all the world there was only him and the dobhar-chú; he could feel it waiting in the wings for the perfect moment to make its entrance.

He just had to reach the house. Then he could plan and prepare. Maybe he could fly back to Ireland. He'd have a good decade's head-start at least. He just had to reach the house. He ran on and on, expecting that eerie cry at any moment, or the raking of a claw, the needle-piercing of its fangs. Any of them would have been a sweet release. But he was consumed by the thought of escape and the horror of imminent death.

Gus from the next farm over nearly ran him over with his

pickup.

"Christ, mate, you ok?" Gus leapt out of his truck and pulled Seamus to his feet from the ditch he had stumbled into. "You ran out in front of me, you bloody idiot! You're lucky you're not dead!"

Seamus didn't respond. He tried to pull away from Gus, who saw his expression and frowned.

"What happened, mate? It get your sheep too?"

Seamus blinked. "It? The dobhar-chú?"

Gus' brow knotted. "I don't know anything about a dovvy cow, but something had a bloody good go at my flocks this morning. Big old bastard. Made a weird noise, like a whistle."

Seamus yelped and started to run. Gus laughed. "Don't worry, mate. I got it. Stone cold dead."

Seamus nearly collapsed. He turned to look at Gus, and began to laugh. He laughed high and loud, with wild, burning eyes, until he began gasping for air. Gus thumped him on the back until he stopped laughing. Seamus wiped a tear from his eyes and took a deep breath.

"Can I see?"

Gus grinned. "Thought you'd never ask. I wanted to know what you thought of it. Bet it's worth a few bucks," he added archly as he swept the tarpaulin back to reveal the body in the back of his truck.

Seamus' eyes widened. There it was. The very same beast. The fur had greyed, the scales were perhaps less lustrous than they had once been. But it was unmistakably the beast that had ruined his life. It glared up at him through bitter, death-glazed eyes. Between them, congealing blood seeped from a bullet-hole, mingling with the gore around its maw.

"Queer-looking thing, ain't it paddy? What do you make of it?"

Seamus started laughing again. It began as a chuckle, then a stronger laugh, until it erupted from him. He drew long, ragged breaths as he collapsed in the dirt and rocked himself as wide-eyed relief consumed him.

The Beast was the talk of the area for months afterwards. It even made the little town famous, a magnet for monster-hunters and cryptid fanatics.

The locals never mentioned Seamus. It seemed cruel to involve him any further. Besides, the ward they kept him on these days didn't allow him too many visitors. Not that Seamus would have noticed.

He was still there, still howling with high, keening laughter that rattled in his throat.

He'd been a funny one, that paddy. Poor, mad old paddy.

## Moonlight Forest

Soumya Sundar Mukherjee

The three old men were sipping their evening coffee and idly gossiping when the door of the restaurant opened and a stout-bodied man in his thirties entered. The yellow light from the counter fell upon his face and it appeared to be pale and exhausted. He had a suitcase in hand and a faint smile on his thin lips. He looked at the fourth empty chair at their table and asked politely, "Mind if I join you?"

Ross, his beard as white as the silver moonlight outside the window, shook his head and said, "Please have a seat."

The man sat and ordered coffee. Dave, a good-looking old man with powerful glasses on his nose, tried to observe this newcomer who sat just opposite to him. "Right from the station, eh? How did you get here from there? I mean, by which road? The Windmill Alley or the Wheatfield Road?"

"No, Sir," The man casually said, "I came through the forest. Nice shortcut from the Railway Station."

There was a long, uncomfortable silence between them.

The three old men looked at each other.

Ross, combing his silver beard with fingers, said, "So, you came through the forest, did you, lad?"

"Yes," The man looked at him and found the uneasy expression on his face. "So what?"

Jim, the third old man, observed, looking at the crisscross of shadows coming through the closed glass window, "A full moon night. Quite interesting."

The young man stared at him, "Interesting, why?"

The waiter came with the coffee. The young man thanked him almost inaudibly and took up the cup to his lips when he found that all three of them were looking at him as if they were seeing a ghost. When his eyes met theirs, they quickly started observing their own cups.

"What's it?" He demanded, looking at Jim. "What is quite interesting?"

Jim looked at his two ancient companions as if to ask for permission. Dave nodded, "Tell him, Jim. He's new here and he's somehow done the impossible, but it is unlikely that he'll be able to do it again. He deserves to know, for his own safety."

The young man looked at them curiously. Jim said, "We're glad that you're alive and good, but, believe me, you shouldn't have taken the forest road, lad. Not in a full-moon night like this. Not ever."

The young man only raised a brow. The old folk were still thinking.

Then Dave said, "We were four friends, once. Now whenever we old friends get together, there's always a chair empty."

Ross added, "Yep, lad. You occupied Tom's chair."

"He left you?" The young man asked.

"Yes," Dave looked at the window through which the dense body of the forest was visible in the pale moonlight. "He died. In the forest. In a moonlit night like this."

Now the young man seemed to have gained more interest. He leaned forward and said, "How?"

Ross said, "It's quite painful for us to remember our friend's memory. But you need to know it so that you never go back to that forest path."

"You tell him, Jimmy," Dave said. "You're quite good when it comes to telling stories."

Jim coughed a little and started.

**Jim's Story:**

How old are you, young man? Thirty? Thirty-two? Good. It's hard to believe, as you see me now, old and decrepit, that thirty two years ago I was thirty-two myself. These two old rascals, Dave and Ross, were my friends. And Tom too. Ah, Tom! Such a fine hunter. He could shoot down even a tiny sparrow from just above the horizon.

Excuse me, gentlemen. It's the old age; it makes you exaggerate things. What was I speaking of? Tom! Yes, Tom. Thomas Conway. He died. In the Moonlight Forest. Yes, that's the name of the forest you came alive through tonight, only God knows how! It's a cursed forest, young man. No mother's son in the world should go in there, especially in moonlit nights like this, if he wants to see the light of the day again.

But Tom went there that night. Why? You ask me 'why'? It's always a girl, young man; it's always a girl. Thomas Conway went there to meet this girl, Ella, to meet his death.

Ella was beautiful, wasn't she, Dave? Yea, you remember, I know. She was a woman of heavenly beauty, and Tom fell in love with her. Our dear old Dave, too, had a crush on her, but you see, he was too shy to admit it, and Tom won the girl from him. But no malice, we were all friends. Dave believes in self-

## Moonlight Forest

sacrifices, don't you, Dave?

But the forest… Yes, the Moonlight Forest! You're perhaps thinking why the forest has such a strange name. The forest has its own history.

When we were all little boys, when we were forbidden to touch the ale, a meteorite crashed in that forest. You know meteorites, young man? The shooting stars! They whoosh from one end of the sky to another like a quick, bright scratch upon the darkness. When these things crash onto the earth, they are called 'meteorites'. Perhaps you know all about those cosmological stuff. You seem quite an educated fellow to me. How much have you studied? University, eh?

Pardon me for this side-tracking. Old age makes you talkative, you know. Well, yes, the meteorites. I remember that night even today. The thing that fell from the sky set the forest on fire. Our houses shook violently. The water in Mrs Forster's well came jumping out of the hole and the pond behind the southern playground flooded the fields. Ah, I still remember my school-books from the rack falling thud thud thud and my mother shouting, "Come out here, Jimmy! It's an earthquake!" All the men, women, and children of the village came out of their houses. Many temporary huts fell to the ground by the sheer power of the quake. Then we saw the forest burning.

It burnt for two days and turned the whole forest into ash. The vast area was a hot, gray colored wasteland. The heat died gradually, but the ashes remained. We collected the powder-like ash in little packets to play smoke-bombs with it. All of us did that silly thing, you remember, Dave? The four of us took lots of ash for which our parents scolded us. Ella's parents did not let her take that dirty thing with her. So Tom secretly gave one of the packets we collected to her. Ah, I remember, it was the first time she kissed him upon his cheek.

The next monsoon brought rains. Rains brought twigs to the ashen land. The burnt land became a forest again in the next five or six years.

But this time the forest was not the same. There were some changes. The trees have changed. They've now developed a taste for animal flesh.

All of us have sometimes seen some ignorant cattle moving into the forest. The trees now can sense it when meat reaches within their reach. They grow sharp teeth and tight tendrils which are strong enough to fasten even a healthy horse. They tightly bind the prey and bite it to the last like hungry piranhas.

Ross said that the meteorite might have brought some changes to the DNA of the trees; the simple photosynthesis is now not enough for their nourishments. I can't tell you much about scientific theories; for that, you'll have to talk to Ross here, the wise school teacher, who knows about things: mutation, spirals of the gene, evolution, and other weird stuff. I'm not very educated myself, you see.

We learned to avoid the forest, especially on moonlit nights. For some unknown reasons, the trees become more ferocious in these nights. I've heard of werewolves, but I'm not sure whether these can be called 'were-trees'. Moonlight makes them crave for flesh; and it was a moonlit night like this when Tom went there.

Ella's father wasn't ready to give her hand to Tom. Tom was a poor man; he didn't inherit much from his parents. Ella's father was a wealthy businessman and he disliked Tom. So the lovers decided to elope. We helped them to prepare for their journey, didn't we, Dave?

We friends planned to assist them in their adventure. Dave is the brightest among us. He said that they should escape through the forest road, because no one will be there at night to chance to see them.

I know, I know! The carnivorous trees in the forest – you're thinking about them, aren't you, young man? That was the beauty of the plan. Nobody could have thought about this but Dave the Genius.

I told you about the packets of the ash we took from the burnt forest, didn't I? That's the thing! We noticed that when one carries the burnt ash of the forest, the trees seem to get away from that person. Perhaps they loath the smell; perhaps the terrifying burning sensation of their forefathers is etched in their unconscious mind, if they have a thing called 'mind' at all. But we've discovered this and we've decided to keep it a secret among the four of us. And Ella knew, of course. But the bottom line is, if you have a little bit of ash of the meteorite-burnt forest with you, you're the perfect exorcist to drive away those hungry tendrils from your dear body.

So, that night when the moon was up, Tom came out of his house. He was a brave boy. He came to the Fig Tree Lane where we three were waiting for him. All of us were happy and sad; happy in our friend's happiness, sad because this was going to be a hard goodbye, for we were such good friends for a long time. He hugged us one by one. This old sentimental fool Ross wept like a girl. I checked my tears with a great effort. And Dave, he hugged him like this was the last hug in his life. We didn't know that this was indeed going to be Tom's last.

Tom had the packet of ash in his pocket. So he was sure that nothing can harm him in the forest. We waited in the shadows of the Fig Tree Lane, waiting for Ella to appear. The moon was full and cold; its dark patches looked like burn-wounds.

She came almost gliding in the moonlight, with a suitcase in her hand. We all minutely observed her graceful walk, the moonlight pouring upon her perfect body. She knew where we would wait, and she came like a goddess in the silver glow of the moon. I still remember the hiccup you got, Dave.

As we were still inside the village, it was not wise for the lovers to be seen together. We accompanied Tom to the verge of the forest. Ella was supposed to follow us, maintaining a reasonable distance. And she did so. She, too, had a packet of ash with her; so she was safe, too.

When we came near the forest, it was the real good-bye time. Tom smiled and said, "Miss me, friends, when I'm gone," without knowing how true his words were.

He entered the forest and passed by two or three trees. We could still see him as he waved to us. Ella was coming closer to us. Soon, she too was going to get into the forest. Tom's tall figure was half covered in the thin, leafy shadows. Then suddenly all hell broke loose.

The trees somehow sensed his presence and but they did not attack him at once. They waited for some time so that he might go deeper into the forest. Then suddenly their branches shot down like whips and they bound him just like a spider binding the hapless insect caught in its net. Tom began to shout: "Help! Help!" In that moonlit forest, the trees were dancing like enormous shadowy serpents with a taste for human flesh.

We were helpless. As none of us was going to enter the forest, we didn't bring with us the packets of ash. Dave told us that we won't need it. Ella saw the scene and screamed, "Tom!" and ran towards him. Dave shouted, "Stop her, Jimmy!"

Ross and I ran towards her. I got to her first and grabbed her by the shoulders and dragged her back from the forest. The trees were then biting out chunks of Tom's flesh from his body. He had stopped screaming. He had stopped struggling. Black blood came trickling from his wounds. I realized for the first time that blood looked so dark in moonlight; it oozed out of the curls of the tree that had wrapped him.

Ella fell senseless in my arms. The scent of her hair

reminded me of summer fruits and exotic flowers. But in front of us, my friend's body was quickly turning into a fleshless skeleton enclosed inside a vicious plant's coils. We stood there motionless, unable to look away from that horrifying sight.

Later Dave discovered the cause of this unfortunate incident. When we were waiting for Ella in the Fig Tree Lane and hugging each other, the packet of ash somehow fell from Tom's pocket. Dave discovered it there next morning.

So, young man, a word of advice from an old man: never go into the Moonlight Forest unless you have the 'magic' ash with you. I don't know how you survived tonight, but miracles don't happen regularly.

**The Man Goes out of the Restaurant:**

The young man was looking at his own empty cup of coffee when Jim finished his story. He sighed and said, "I've just one question for you, Dave."

Dave, who was silently looking at the moonlit window for such a long time, stirred a little in his chair. He adjusted the glass on his nose and said, "Yes?"

"Your friend, Ella's future husband, died that night. How could you propose to her the next morning?"

Ross and Jim both looked at Dave with an unspoken "What," and then at the young man. Dave hoarsely said, "How do you know that? I've told nobody about it!"

The young man placed his suitcase on the table. "Does this thing look familiar to any of you?"

Ross stroked his white beard rapidly. "Oh my God! Jim! Dave! Don't you recognize it?"

They looked at the old suitcase in a way as if it were a time bomb.

"Ella was my mother," The young man answered. "When they were departing from here, she was already with Tom's child. Thomas Conway was my father."

All the three old men looked uncomfortable. Then Ross said, "Yes, you have his nose. And the upper lip…"

"Answer my question, Dave," The young man said.

"I'm not answerable to you, lad," Dave said bitterly. "But yes, I admit that I did it. So what? I did it for her. After Tom's death, she needed a supporting shoulder."

"No, Dave," The young man's voice was bitter, too. "You did it for yourself. My father was your friend. How could you give a marriage proposal to the fiancé of your friend who just died the last night?"

"Look, I'm sorry for that. But these are the things of the past. Why're you digging them up now?" Dave said.

"I know the answer, Dave," The young man ignored his question and continued. "You were afraid that Jim might propose to her in the absence of Tom. So you had to hurry."

"What nonsense!" Jim protested.

"Don't tell me that you didn't love her, Uncle Jim. Anybody who has listened to your story knows that you did have a soft corner for her. But I don't blame you for that. Love's no crime; but murder is."

"Murder!" The three old men looked at him sharply.

"I know I can't prove it, but one of you took that packet of ash from Tom's pocket in the Fig Tree Alley when the hugs were going on. I can't prove this, but, you know, suspicion falls upon the man who discovered it there the next morning. He found it because he knew that it would be there. Or, he simply said that he found it there and showed the others just what he took that night from his friend's pocket."

"That's enough!" Dave growled. "I've had enough of this nonsense! You're my friend's son, and I'm glad to see you here, but I'm not going to sit here and hear you talking rubbish! Excuse me, friends, I've to go home now. It's getting late for dinner."

"Please be seated, Uncle Dave. It's getting late for me, too. Please bear with me for ten more minutes. I want to tell you why I came here after so many days, and I promise that I'll make it interesting for you," The young man said. "I, of course, didn't know that I would meet my father's old friends here. I'm here for my own personal business."

"What business?" Jim asked. "Why have you come to this place after so many years?"

"Just what you said earlier, Uncle Jim. It's always a girl. I fell in love."

"You fell in love with some girl from this village?" Ross asked. "Who?"

"No, no, not from this village," The young man corrected him. "She is from the city. Lily is one of the most beautiful girls I've ever met. It was love at first sight."

"Another love story?" Dave sneered. "I should have expected nothing better from a Conway."

"It'll get better, Uncle Dave, I promise," The young man said. "Listen carefully now. She was beautiful, she was heavenly. I loved her so much that it seemed impossible to live without her. I'm sorry if I sound hopelessly romantic, but I can't help it.

Now comes the turning point of my story. One day I decided to please her with a surprise visit. I went to her place and saw her lying naked under a trusted friend of mine; her eyes half-shut, her mouth open to give away beautiful moans of pleasure. Can you believe that? False friends are not very rare in any generation, what do you think?"

None of the listeners uttered a single word. The young man continued, "And this friend of mine? I've known him for almost six years. Met him in a party. His name might seem familiar to you. Roger Alden."

All of them stared at Dave, who whispered, "Where's he now, Conway?"

"He is well and good still, Uncle Dave. Don't worry; let me finish my story. I saw them together in bed. I knew that both of them had betrayed me. Yet I said nothing. I, then, remembered the story I heard from my long-dead mother, and I remembered you. I should have expected nothing better from an Alden. Like father, like son, don't you agree?

"I came to the Moonlight Forest a month ago, because I needed to do my homework. It was another moonlit night like this. I had the packet of ash that my mother once carried with her. I took a guinea pig with me. I released it in the forest and saw how the trees took their time to let it in deep inside the forest and how ferociously they killed and devoured it. But they did nothing to me. So I went back to my town, happy with the results of my experiment.

"Then tonight we came here. All three of us. I asked them to visit my ancestral village with me. Lily knew nothing of my history. Roger knew nothing too, because you got divorced after two years of your marriage, Dave; and your wife had wisely told him almost nothing about you and your background. She wanted to keep your influence out of her son's life. So I accompanied them through the forest road from the Railway Station. Quite a fine moonlit night this is, you must agree with me. I had the packet of ash in my coat pocket, so they were safe as long as they were with me, until, half an hour ago, I suddenly disappeared behind some bush and left them there and came here for a cup of coffee. Seeing you three here is a bonus, dear Uncles."

Dave's lips trembled. "Don't do this, please, Tom!"

The young man laughed. "Tom's dead, David Alden. They are now just taking their time. Be alert, and you'll hear it any moment now."

Ross and Jim were contemptuously looking at Dave

who was staring silently at the moonlit forest. His hands were shaking. The young man stood up and said, "The coffee's on me."

He placed the money on the table, picked up the suitcase of his mother and with a little nod to the three old men, went out of the restaurant.

After one more minute of unbearable silence, two violent screams of a man and a woman from the dark forest shattered the silence of the cold, moonlit night.

**Nancy's Rumble**

Haley Holden

"The Honey Island Swamp Monster is actually named Nancy," Hannah Spotts told her cousins as she popped gum. The sound cracked in the mid July heat, interrupting the waves of heat rising off the blacktop under them. She scrambled on top of the monkey bar, sitting with her legs spread even though she had a skirt on. At eleven she had more important things to worry about than her underwear showing. "And anyone who calls her The Honey Island Swamp Monster and runs into her gets drowned in the swamp."

"You mean in the lake," Tanner said, because he wasn't stupid. "You can't get drowned in a swamp."

"Have you ever been in a swamp?" Hannah shot right back, because Tanner was kind of stupid.

"It only takes like two inches of water to drown," Taylor said.

Tanner turned to glare at his sister from his spot at the top of the slide. She was never on his side, an almost know-it-all with big teeth and glasses that she didn't really need. Tanner hoped the Honey Island monster drowned her in a whole three inches of water.

"I don't believe in monsters anyhow," Tanner said. The vocabulary word made him feel surer in his stance. Anyhow, he remember reciting to his mother, spelling it and giving her the definition. He was even pretty sure that he had used it correctly.

"You don't have to believe in monsters for them to be real," Hannah said, her long black hair touching the ground as she hung by her knees on the monkey bars.

"Only little kids believe in monsters," Tanner said. Hannah was two months younger than him, she never knew what she was talking about. And Taylor, the know-it-all in training, was only ten.

"I know how to find Nancy; my dad used to go see her all the time," Hannah said. "If you don't tell your parents we can go tonight when it's dark."

"Who?" Tanner asked.

Hannah rolled her eyes and loosened her knees to fall from the monkey bars, landing on her hands and quickly snapping to her feet. "You can just call her the Honey Island Swamp Monster and get drowned," she told her cousin. "Come on, Taylor, we can go look up facts about Nancy on my mom's computer."

Taylor hopped off of her swing as if it were her duty to collect the facts the way that other kids collected Matchbox cars or Barbies. Tanner thought that girls were stupid to want to learn. It was easier not to be afraid if you didn't know better. At least that's what he told himself, swinging his feet off the edge of the platform as he watched his sister and cousin cross the street back to their aunt's house.

Nancy was created when a train wreck left circus animals running around Louisiana. A monkey and an alligator conceived her. Taylor asked Hannah if there were really crocodiles around. Hannah didn't correct her, because she knew there were alligators in Louisiana. So, without lying she could send a big smile to her smaller counterpart and claim to have never seen such a thing as crocodiles in Louisiana, they couldn't take the cold in the winters, or something like that.

One of Hannah's teachers had told her the year before, she thought.

At dinner Taylor and Tanner's father sat at the head of the table, even though they were guests. The kids' Aunt Susan pretended not to care.

"I wish y'all could have made it out here when Nathan was still around," Susan said as she set the salmon in the center of the table.

"We're sorry about that," Taylor and Tanner's mother said. Their father was already reaching for the food.

"We pray first," Hannah said as she rocked up on her chair. She didn't like her uncle, she hadn't before her father had passed away and she didn't see why she should pretend to now.

"I'm just setting up my plate," he said back to her. Kids didn't question adults, where he had been raised. And his sister's kid had always loved to speak out of turn. Neither of them glared right at each other, instead they both tightened their grips on the silverware in their hands.

Susan didn't bother to correct either one of them, going back to the kitchen to get the peas.

Nancy was tall. Taller than any of the kids' fathers. And she was covered in what looked like seaweed. She had either yellow or red eyes and Tanner scoffed when his sister told him that as they got ready for bed. That was cheesy, he had told her, and all made up monsters had yellow eyes. Taylor thought that must have meant Nancy had red eyes.

The Honey Island Swamp Monster wasn't real. Tanner

was sure. But not sure enough that he doesn't steal his father's Swiss army knife. The wildlife everywhere was receding, the forests doubling as the hairline of the civilized world, but Louisiana swamps had no need for toupees as far as Tanner could see with his flashlight.

Taylor was traveling a step behind him, because almost knowing everything didn't keep you safer than a knife, and Hannah was leading because ignorance and confidence were a combination that projected a false shield.

"Nancy likes to stay near a big tree this way," Hannah said, pointing away from the direction they had come.

"I didn't read that in any articles," Taylor spoke up, her hand curled in the back of her brother's shirt.

"Well we can't just post that on the internet." Hannah soldiered ahead, snapping branches and crushing bugs in her path. "If it was out there then everyone would come bother Nancy and she'd have to change her favorite spots."

"How do you know about it?" Taylor asked.

"My dad showed me," Hannah answered. "He knew Nancy. That's why I know her real name and know that she'll drown Tanner if he calls her anything else."

"If I call her anything else or if I call her The Honey

Island Swamp Monster?" Tanner said as he ducked under a low hanging branch.

Hannah didn't answer, arriving to a familiar spot and tugging her camouflage off the little boat her father had hidden in the backwoods property. The creek in their woods led into the Honey Island Swamp and Hannah knew she could get there on her own. She and her father had taken the trip a million times.

"You can't take us in that boat," Tanner said, looking at the rotting vessel. "Are you trying to get us all killed?"

"If you're scared of Nancy then don't come." Hannah didn't even look up from her work, tugging the boat towards the water.

Taylor came out from behind her brother to help push the small boat.

"I'm not going out there," Tanner said, shaking his head. "It's not safe, come on Taylor."

"I want to meet Nancy," Taylor said. She held her hand out, furrowing her eyebrows at him. "Give me the knife."

"You don't even know how to use the knife," Tanner objected.

"Can't be that hard," Taylor said, closing and opening her hand quickly to beckon him to pass it over to her. "I'm not scared of Nancy, but just in case she has friends we didn't read about."

"You should be scared of Nancy," he told her as he slammed the Swiss army knife into her palm. "You should both be scared of the stupid monster."

"I thought monsters weren't real?" Hannah asked. The boat rocking up and down in the water as it waited for them.

"Screw you!" Tanner shouted before he turned on his heel to head back.

"You're going the wrong way," Hannah sighed. She handed Taylor her flashlight. "Wait with the boat for me, I need to get your dumb brother home. I'll be right back."

The boat bobbed up and down behind Taylor and she turned to look at it. The vessel looked reminded her of a puppy, jittery with excitement at the idea of being played with. Taylor didn't want to disappoint the little boat so she climbed in, deciding she could wait for Hannah in her seat.

Nancy had three webbed toes on each foot and she smelled bad. In Taylor's imagination she didn't smell that bad, just a little bit like wet dog. If she lived in the swamp she probably played in the water a lot, Taylor reasoned. Her grey hair, or green seaweed, or whatever covered her to keep her warmer than the crocodiles who lived in Florida instead of Louisiana probably just needed washed with shampoo. After a bath Nancy would smell just like Taylor's mom, strawberry hair and vanilla body wash.

Taylor hadn't meant to fall asleep in the boat, but when she woke and turned her flashlight on the first thing she caught in its beam was a big turtle sitting in the opposite end from her. A red eared slider, she noticed, just like the one her classroom had kept as a pet the year before, except bigger. The second thing Taylor noticed was that she was moving.

She checked in front of her again, but Hannah wasn't paddling the boat. In fact, upon inspection, Taylor realized that Hannah wasn't even in the boat with her. She looked in the direction she was traveling and saw grey shimmering in the moonlight.

Chest tightening and heart racing, Taylor laid back down. She meant for the movement to be sneaky, but her speed rocked the boat. Her eyes were snapped closed, breath held as her boat slowed to a stop. She didn't open her eyes. Nancy was bigger than she had expected, much bigger than her dad.

What if Nancy was taking her to the big tree? What if

Nancy wanted to eat her? Taylor wracked her brain for anything she had read on the monster's eating habits and couldn't think of any. What would she do if Nancy was trying to eat her? She couldn't swim faster than the monster and probably couldn't run faster either.

"Nancy," she said, cracking her eyes open to look at the monster.

Nancy was already leaning to look into the boat and her red eyes blinked when Taylor spoke. Her head craned, more seaweed than grey hair and Taylor could feel the cool metal in her palm moving as she shook.

"Nancy." Taylor cleared her throat, as if a scratch in the back of it was her real problem with speaking. "I want you to take me back to my Aunt Susan's house,"

The monster made a noise and headed back to the front of the boat to pull. Her arm was disproportionate to the length of her body, too short in human standards. She continued in the same direction they had been going.

Tanner would have told her to take the knife out and then pretend to sleep until Nancy stopped and got close again, then she could attack and make her escape.

Instead, Taylor sat up.

"Nancy, I don't need you to drown my brother," she told him. "He might not call you what you want, but that's just because—"

She paused, looking at the monster's back as they moved. It probably got lonely living in the swamp, at her favorite tree with only Hannah and her dad to visit her. And now, Nancy would only be getting visits from Hannah. Maybe Nancy wanted to talk instead of listening.

"Nancy, do you get lonely?" Taylor asked.

The monster might have understood simple English, after listening to the people who searched for her constantly. Or maybe instead she understood how the tone at the end of a phrase could make it something to be answered.

Nancy began making noises and although Taylor couldn't understand them, she appreciated being answered. The noises started off quiet and baritone, increasing slightly in pitch and volume as they traveled. The boat rocked to a stop as Nancy quit moving and Taylor watched as an alligator crossed their path. The alligator's growling sounded a lot like Taylor's father snoring. Nancy gave a similar growl back and Taylor fumbled with the Swiss army knife, accidentally slicing her pinky in the process.

The gator rolled along, although Nancy moved to the

back of the boat, pushing backwards so she could keep watching it. Her noises began again, returning to low and baritone.

Taylor listened, Nancy grumbled. They traveled together like old friends.

The bank of the river bumped the boat and Taylor couldn't tell if it was sooner or later than she expected, since she hadn't been expecting much at all. She looked at the land, then glanced back at Nancy, who was already moving towards the front of the boat. The monster reached in, taking a hold of the rope and walking out of the water with it to tie the boat to a tree.

Taylor still had the knife out in her hand, the cork screw on the other end of the knife pulled out as well in her panic. She closed it and rolled it into her pocket as she stood, keeping the flashlight on in her left hand.

"I appreciate the ride back, Nancy, I'm not sure how I got unhooked in the first place. I know Hannah tied it," Taylor said to the monster as she walked towards the front of the boat.

Nancy rumbled at her.

"I hope our talk helped. I'm sorry that my uncle can't come visit you anymore," she said, trying to step from the boat to land. The boat rocked and she hit more mud than solid land, sending her sliding back towards the water. Nancy reached out to stop her with a hand on her back, pushing her up onto solid ground.

"Nancy," Taylor said again, because the last thing she wanted to do was upset the monster by calling her something she didn't like. "Thank you for getting me back safely. I'm sure my cousin was very worried about me."

A light noise came out of the swamp monster, making Taylor feel fond.

"Tell me more about yourself?" Taylor asked, because learning wasn't always understanding, sometimes it started with just being. The staccato hums vibrating between them didn't make sense to Taylor, but she knew that they made sense to Nancy as she rumbled.

When noise started coming through the woods Nancy shrunk back into the water. Taylor stood from where she had been sitting on the bank.

"I think it's just my cousin, Hannah," Taylor said, not wanting Nancy to go. "You know her. Her dad is the one who always came to see you."

Nancy either didn't understand or didn't care, continuing to back up into the water.

Tanner's voice rang though the woods, reverberating off

the water. Taylor wondered if Nancy had heard him first. Maybe she had remembered what Taylor had almost said about her brother.

"I can't believe you lost her," Tanner said. He sounded angry enough that Taylor almost wanted to climb back into the boat.

"She climbed in the boat, she must have untied it," Hannah shot right back. "I only had to leave her to make sure you didn't get lost on the way home." Flipping the blame was almost a family tradition at this point, handed down generation to generation.

"I'm right here guys!" Taylor called out, her hands cupped around her mouth.

"Did you even really lose her?" Tanner asked as they marched through the woods towards his sister's voice.

"At least I found her too," Hannah snapped. "Instead of an alligator."

"I saw an alligator," Taylor called, "And I met Nancy, she was super cool!"

Through the rustling emerged Tanner and Hannah, both brandishing flashlights. Taylor had to hold up a hand to block their light from her face, scowling.

"The swamp monster doesn't exist," Tanner said, grabbing Taylor's arm when he got close enough. "Get away from the water, you just said you saw a crocodile."

"Alligator," Taylor corrected. But she let her brother pull her away anyway.

"There's no way you saw the swamp monster," Hannah said as she caught up to them. "It's not real. Monsters aren't real Taylor, and you could have gotten killed out there by a real animal. Do you know how dangerous the swamp is at night?"

"But you said she was real, your dad used to see her," Taylor objected. "She's real, I saw her."

"My dad used to tell me that as a stupid fairytale when he didn't come home at night. Fairytales aren't real! You could have gotten eaten, are you not hearing that?" Hannah asked, tugging the small boat in off the water. "That was stupid and reckless. Stupider than anything your brother has ever done."

"You're the one who told me what to call her!" Taylor objected. "And I read about her."

"Not everything you read is true!" Hannah shouted. The boat emerged out of the water, setting ripples across the surface. If Taylor had gotten eaten both of the eleven year olds would have been in so much trouble.

# Nancy's Rumble

"You could have killed her," Tanner said, keeping his arms wrapped around his sister as he backed her away from the water. "Filling her head with that junk."

"I just meant to scare you guys a little bit," Hannah snapped right back. "It was a joke."

Taylor could see Nancy's back, shining against the dark of the water. It was Nancy, she was sure. She could see the movement and if she listened hard enough she swore she could hear a low rumbling, like she wasn't comfortable using her staccato tones with the other kids around.

"She's right there," Taylor said, pointing at Nancy's back so the older kids could see.

"That's the moon's reflection," Hannah said as she covered the boat back up. "And this," she motioned to the tarp over the boat. "Is a boat cover, it's not a magic chameleon."

"Chameleon's are real," Taylor said, clearing her throat. It seemed harder to speak to her cousin and brother than it was to talk to the swamp monster. She watched Nancy's retreat and let a soft vibration raise in her chest instead of fighting.

The Honey Island Swamp Monster didn't come to Hannah's father's funeral. Some woman named Nancy did, with hair that smelled like lilacs instead of the swamp, she sat in the back and left early. But Taylor's Nancy stayed home, under the big tree, trying to rumble her child given name.

## Lifeboat

### Danielle Warnick

He wondered if her cheekbones and jaw stuck out like this before. Had her wrists always been so knobby and brittle? He should know, he'd touched them a hundred times.

For an instant he thought that the hunger killed her: that Mia had curled up against the edge of the raft like a bundled skeleton and died in the middle of the night without a sound.

When he couldn't decide if her chest was moving or not, Shawn felt the beginnings of panic prickling at the base of his neck.

He reached toward her parted lips, certain he'd feel hot breath on his fingertips.

His wife's face, more skull than skin, opened its eyes and said, "Hello, love."

Startled, he jerked his hand away as if she had taken a

snap at him.

Shawn was so astounded that he didn't say anything, only ogled Mia as she sleepily pushed herself up from the boat-floor.

She frowned. "My stomach really hurts."

"That'll be the hunger." He said.

"What'd you say, honey?"

"You're probably really hungry."

"Oh." She said, "Yeah…"

She trailed off, blinking prettily as her train of thought ran away from her.

"Have we gotten anywhere new yet?" she asked.

Shawn looked around, the ocean stretched far into the pink light of the fading sun. Silence. Waves lapped the raft. Gulls cawed.

"No, love, I don't believe we have."

"Crabs," she said, smiling, "I was dreaming about eating crabs," the smile faltered, the bottom lip pouted, quivered, "I'm starving. Don't we have anything else to eat?"

All their marriage he'd drop everything and give her whatever she wanted, that smart phone that cost more than a house payment, a steak sub he'd fry up at six in the morning if the mood struck her, to not be able to do so now perplexed and frightened him. He searched about him as if he'd find something edible knotted up in the raft's safety-ropes or hidden under the middle seat. Nothing was there, of course.

"I'm sorry." He offered.

Mia smiled and patted his arm. "It's alright, love. It's not your fault."

Mia originally suggested they visit Daytona Beach. They could shop along the strip at night, swim in the ocean hand in hand during the day, but Shawn had already been to Daytona Beach in college, and explained that they wouldn't enjoy shopping the strip because of drunk kids staggering out of bars, and not to mention Florida's nasty history with sharks, he added, so much as putting a toe in would be nerve-wrecking.

Mia seemed a little hurt at first that he'd shot down her idea, but there was nothing wrong with her ideas, he assured her-- he adored her ideas, and went on to say he didn't care what they did, where they went, so long as they were together.

They had a knack for smothering any dicey situations such as this.

In the two years they've been married they hardly ever argued.

Sure, they had a few tiffs every now and then, usually him griping whenever she fed and baby talked any sort of animal that happened to wander into their yard, be it a raccoon or filth-faced possum (her saying "Isn't the wittle' baby so cuuute!" while she tossed out bread or any leftovers, and him, tightlipped and going red in the face to keep from bitching).

He found these annoyances endearing more often than not, though.

So...not Daytona Beach, they decided, where would they go then?

Shawn's older brother once mentioned letting him borrow his thirty-five-thousand dollar yacht.

Sailing the blue waters of the Hawaiian-coast had always been a dream of Shawn's and he challenged anyone to come up with a more romantic proposition than that.

He phoned Charles about the yacht a week later, hoping to God it hadn't been one of those things a man says to his brother at a barbecue and doesn't mean.

Their getaway had a marvelous start, Mia bought him a navy blue captain's hat at gift-shop in Honolulu, the kind with the little gold anchor stitched down the middle. She pulled it down on his head as he stood at the helm of the boat. She'd kissed him and called him "Skipper" and then they were off, sailing the blue waves.

The first few nights they had quiet, calm sex during which he insisted she leave on her orange and green palm-tree bikini top. He loved it when she called him Captain or Skipper or matey. Even more than that, Shawn enjoyed pretending to know things about boats when in reality he knew absolutely nothing about them.

That was a distressing fact with which he was about to become grimly acquainted with.

He was sleeping when he heard the first crack, a terrible wooden rending that split his dreams right down the middle.

Then he felt the water.

A cold gout of it doused the bed and soaked his clothes.

He shot bolt upright and saw Mia gawking at a massive fracture in the wall that gushed black seawater. The captain's hat slumped on his head, he'd fallen asleep with it on.

"What's happening?" she screamed over the noise.

Shawn had no idea.

But it was obvious that his brother's thirty-five-thousand dollar yacht was sinking once he saw that the water had reached Mia's knees.

Luckily, his brain kicked into gear and he remembered the lifeboat, that bright orange lifeboat that hung on the side of the yacht by thick ropes.

He and Mia floated on that small raft and watched his brother's ship get swallowed by the waves. So shocked he couldn't think of anything else to say, Shawn muttered, "Sorry."

She grinned at him. Mia could always hold herself together so well in a crisis. "No worries, love. I'm sure we haven't drifted too far from shore anyway."

"Surely." Shawn agreed.

The next morning they dug into the snacks Shawn had remembered to grab before the yacht went down. Mia peeled a chocolate-bar open and ate it still inside the wrapper.

"You were so clever grabbing these, so, so clever." She said, lips smeared brown.

They burned through the food in almost a week, and that was the first time Mia had turned her sunburned face toward him and asked, "Do you suppose we're going to die out here?"

She'd been smiling when she said it.

A light scraping woke him up. A sound like a razor against leather. Shawn opened his eyes and saw thin, curled feet hooked into the side of the raft. Dull, bluish black eyes stared at him, and an elongated bill opened with a squawk.

Feathers and wings fidgeted.

A pelican.

His stomach murmuring, Shawn tried to make like he wasn't trying to grab for it, a fake yawn and stretch. His hand nearly reached the bird's fluffed breast when a small, oily body knocked hard against the lifeboat, rocking it in the sea, scaring the pelican into flight.

That was alright, he hadn't really wanted to eat the bird anyway.

The small, unidentified body smacked into the raft again, from underneath this time, and Shawn thought he heard some sort of noise.

A cry.

A dolphin, he guessed.

Mia stirred, yawning.

"Did I hear something?"

"There was a bird." He told her, "A pelican, I think."

"Pelican," she said, smiling at the word as she twirled a lock of hair around her finger, "Pelican. That's a funny word. Say pelican once."

"Pelican." Shawn said, "Yeah, that is a weird word."

Mia knotted hair through the four fingers of her clenched fist.

"Pelican." She muttered, and Shawn flinched when she jerked those long blonde strands out of her scalp. "Pelican, pelican, pelican."

Shawn was certain that she surely couldn't be doing what it looked like she was doing.

"I wonder why it's called a pelican?" she asked, and he saw that, yes, she really was putting the dry tufts of hair she'd ripped from her head into her mouth and chewing on them.

He thought about saying something but didn't want her to feel self-conscious. He ignored the wiry strands dangling from between her teeth instead.

"I'm beginning to think we should have gone to Daytona Beach like you said." He admitted.

"Don't start in on yourself, love." She crawled closer and patted his thigh with a hand that was all bone. Shawn almost screamed.

"You couldn't have known this would happen." She whispered.

He wished to God she'd stop eating her hair.

Her eyes fluttered closed, "I think I'm going to have a little nap."

"A nap." He was glad, "That sounds like a brilliant idea."

As Shawn watched her eyelids twitch with dreams, he wondered about the dolphin that knocked against the lifeboat, and if whether or not dolphins were known to cry so piercingly like that.

It gave him a bad jolt seeing her when he first woke up. He should have prepared himself for what she'd look like lit by the bright tropical sun: spidery limbs and very little hair left on her red, irritated scalp.

"I'd like one of those bagels we get from the gas-station," she said, "I've been thinking about them all morning."

"Mmmm, yes. The ones with the raisins."

Shawn tried not to imagine the bagels, or the greasy paper bags they came in, it'd be too painful.

"Do you think you could go get me some, love, there's some change in my purse."

He realized then how much her pleasant grin unsettled

him, that calm, complacent grin that's been on her face ever since they watched his brother's yacht go down, it wasn't pleasant at all, he saw. It was delirious and lunatic, swallowed-fear and screams hidden just behind her prominent teeth.

"You do know that we're stranded on a raft, right?" he asked.

"Of course I know," she said, getting testy, "It's just I'm so hungry, can't we find anything else to eat?"

He frowned.

"I wish I could give you something. I really do."

"Then what fucking good are you then?" she yelled.

Shawn actually winced.

She'd never cursed once before, let alone snapped at him. He just didn't know what to say.

She turned her head and looked the other way, and that stung a little, like she'd completely dismissed him. Shawn decided that if she was going to be that way then he wouldn't look at her either. He stared up and watched some gulls pinwheel back and forth in the hazy white sky.

He wondered if all birds circle dying things or if that was just buzzards.

When he looked back, Shawn found Mia leaning over the edge of the raft, watching something that splashed around in the water.

She made strange noises it took him a moment to recognize as giggles.

"What've you got there," he asked, and came beside her for a look-see.

It was some type of fish, that much was obvious, but he'd never seen a fish like it anywhere before.

He nearly cried out in revulsion when Mia reached in to grab it.

"Isn't he the most beautiful little thing you ever saw," she asked, delighted, hugging the fidgeting creature to her breasts, "oooh, what'd you think he is?!"

Shawn didn't know, and for reasons he'll never be able to understand, he hated the thing on sight. It had a glistening scaly tail like other fish, but it had arms. The fish had arms. Fish aren't supposed to have arms. Tiny spiked and webbed fingers flexed and opened on the end of each one. It had a face.

A small, humanoid face, almost Creature from the Black Lagoonish' with a fin-Mohawk running through the middle.

He thought it looked immature, half-formed, a thing you see on a gratuitous flyer handed to you by an outraged activist outside a Planned-Parenthood-Clinic.

"Aww, lookit' the wittle' baby's gills opening up when he breaths." She'd meant to show him this, bringing it closer, but Shawn violently tore the fish from her grasp, and bit deep into its midsection.

Cold coils of guts slid easily down his throat and Shawn sank his teeth in for more.

Mia battered him with skeletal hands, trying to wrestle the dying fish from his grasp and begging him to stop, to just please God Stop!

"You're hurting him!" She shrieked, "You're hurting him!"

Only a needle-work of bones and pinkish white stringy meat hung in each fist by the time he finished.

Some shreds of scales too.

His upper lip curled at the way she glared at him, and he snapped, "What, you said get you something to eat!"

"You're horrible," She whispered and picked up the tattered remains he'd tossed on the boat-floor, her bottom lip trembling, "the poor little baby." Her gaze settled back on him and disgust cast a sheen across her eyes.

"How could you do that to a little baby?"

There it was, that soft part of her that grated him. He remembered once that she told him she believed any baby lost in the womb, be it miscarried or aborted, went straight to heaven, and Shawn had been slightly creeped out at the time hearing her say that. It'd put an image in his head of a heaven strewn with curled, dead fetuses. Of course a woman who believed a thing that ridiculous would overreact like this.

"We can't just starve." He grunted.

"Just leave me alone." She crawled to the farthest corner of the lifeboat away from him and curled up, hugging her knees to her chest, "I don't want to talk to you anymore."

They didn't see any more of the strange fish for quite a while.

Mia kept so silent that Shawn nearly forgot she was there at all. Occasionally he'd catch her glaring at him and he would try to make things right again, but Mia wasn't having any of it; she'd snort and whip her head in the opposite direction when he gently whispered her name and, once, she quickly scooted backwards and actually hissed at him when he tried crawling toward her.

Her actions made him feel cheap and small. Couldn't she see he was trying to apologize here? It was absurd.

She was absurd.

Night fell and more of the odd fish came in around the boat, droves of them. He could hear their slick bodies knocking around. He wasn't going to eat any at first, honest. Mia was fast asleep by then, and Shawn thought that he'd better not, she'd wake up and catch him in the act and be absolutely sickened with him. He didn't want her to hate him more than she already did.

Best to leave them be, he decided.

He tried to see the fish from her perspective---cute, cuddly things, puppies of a sort---he even made himself picture one: its spiky head, gilled throat. He tried to smile at the image, but the more he listened to their splish' and splash in the sea the hungrier he became.

He had turned and peered at them before he realized what he was doing. At night they had a glow. An eerie green glow shone through the translucent skin, making their needle-thin network of bones and squishy arrangement of organs shine in X-ray. He saw a gleaming wad inside one pulsing, beating. Its heart, he thought, and slid his tongue across his lips to moisten them.

Did she expect him to starve to death?!

In any case, she was asleep. What of it if he ate just one more, especially if she never found out. He'd go about it quietly, that's all.

Wasn't any of her business what he put into his mouth anyway.

He jammed a hand into the moonlit water and fished around, bringing one into the life-boat jerking and bucking in his grasp. The creature made no sounds, only breathed through its perforated gills, its chest rising and falling. Its eyes, lens colored and small, stared at him complacently as his mouth yawned wide open.

He closed his jaws around its neck and wrenched its head off with his teeth. He felt the fish's skull cave in between his incisors, its eyes pop from their sockets and squirt sweet tasting juice down his throat.

Mia screamed.

"You're horrible. You're awful!" She wept, trembling.

Shawn just sat there and ate what was in his fist.

He didn't even care that she was watching anymore.

He quickly became obsessed with eating them.

It stopped being about hunger after the third or fourth one.

He started eating them when he didn't really have to, often mere moments after finishing with one. With his belly full with little hands and scales and fins and heads, he'd cast a hand into the salty brine for more. He couldn't help it, they tasted good. Their creamy, stringy meat sweet, their innards sour with a tinge of spice. He'd taken to killing them beforehand so the twitch and shudder of their bodies didn't ruin the experience.

Sometimes he choked them until their little faces bulged, or he'd bash them hard against his kneecap until he heard a vital thing inside them snap.

He should have been wondering why Mia had stopped complaining, but he was well beyond caring about what she thought.

He became nervous and frustrated when the fish quit coming in.

He thought that perhaps they were addicting or some such nonsense.

Without them Shawn felt tired and uninterested. He started sleeping, and oversleeping. His dreams were about wet bodies darting in night-colored water.

"There, there," he heard Mia saying, "I'm not going to let anybody get you. You're the most special one of all. You're nothing but a wittle' baby."

Shawn stirred awake, and she whispered, "Shhh, quiet now, he's awake."

A rustle of fabric, movement.

Shawn blinked his eyes open. Mia was obviously trying to act casual, picking at her fingernails with an unnecessary interest.

He searched the water for more fish and his heart deflated slightly when he saw nothing but murky ocean.

"There aren't any more." Mia informed him, "You've had enough anyway, you don't need that much, you're being a glutton."

"A big, fat, greedy glutton." She added, grinning.

"You act like I'm doing this for fun. I don't enjoy it, I'm trying to keep myself alive." He said but he was lying and Shawn knew that down to the bone.

She might as well turned her nose up at him given the tone she took. "No matter which way you cut it it's wrong."

"It's not wrong! Fish don't have any feelings! Haven't you ever heard that?"

"They're not fish!"

He snorted. "What are they then?"

"Mermaids." She said, this ludicrous grin on her face, "I've decided they're mermaids."

It figured she'd think an idiotic thing such as that, went along perfectly with her unborn fetus heaven.

His hands and jaws trembled for more of the delicious fish.

He turned and wheeled on Mia. Fists clenched.

"You've got one, don't you?"

She slapped his hand hard when he tried to grab her. "Stop it, you're being a lunatic!"

"I know you've got one, there's no mistaking that smell!"

He pinched and groped, getting frustrated and desperate.

"I don't have one, just leave me be!" but he saw her shirt quiver, saw the front ripple.

She fought him back, but he managed to get the piece of

clothing up and over her head before she kicked him directly in the ribs and sent him sprawling backward. There was no hiding it now, though, he'd seen the fin-Mohawked' head held snug between her bare breasts.

"You liar!"

"He's mine." She said, cradling that little abortion in a way that made him jealous, "And I hate you. We both do. We wish you'd just jump off this boat and drown."

"You don't meant that."

"Yes I do."

She winked at the squirming creature as if they were in cahoots together. "He told me that he thinks you're appalling, that you're just absolutely hideous and I agreed."

Shawn had had it up to here with her. She was gonna' have to grow up whether she liked it or not, he decided.

He ripped the fish from her, and shoved Mia down. He did not give her terrified expression a second's thought. Placing both thumbs over its small eyes, he curled and hooked them deep into its head, paying no mind to the snap of gristle, or the dig of his nails running through brain. Mia bawled as he began tearing what she believed was a baby mermaid into neat bite-sized strips.

He told himself this was for her own good, that he did it because he loved her and wanted her to live, but his heart knew the truth: he just hadn't wanted to be the only that had stooped so low.

She jerked her face from side to side, mouth folded in a tight line to avoid the pale pink cutlet he held pinched in his fingers.

"It's for your own good." He said, snatching the corners of her mouth hard enough to scrape the skin and drawn blood, "Your own damn good!"

He hadn't meant to shove it into her throat so hard, but felt oddly satisfied when she gagged.

She made a feeble attempted to spit the piece out.

"Hun-uh, no you don't, don't you fucking dare."

He held her nose and mouth shut so she'd have no choices other than suffocate or swallow.

He wasn't proud of himself when her spirit broke and she lay limply on her back, belly up, like a gutted fish.

She lay like that for a while, not moving.

Idly, Shawn wondered if he'd killed her.

He woke the next morning and found her exactly where he'd left her.

He poked her with his toe. "Mia."

Nothing.

He sighed. "Mia I'm sorry. I just didn't want you to die."

He'd never seen someone move so slowly, it took her half a minute just to get to the edge of the ten-foot lifeboat.

He'd be the first to admit this whole mess was his fault, he'd let things get out of hand.

But he was almost positive he could get things between them back on track. She was his Mia for godssake'.

"Bet that stomach of yours isn't growling so much anymore." Shawn tried to smile.

She gave no sign that she'd heard him, she traced the

surface of the ocean with her fingertips.

"I bet we're close to somewhere now," he said, being optimistic so she'd be optimistic too, "we'll be back home in no time. Back to those bagels we love so much."

He smiled at her again, and he really meant this one, and when she turned toward him and smiled back he felt so relieved that she was alright that he had to laugh, but he choked on that laugh like a fishbone halfway through because Shawn realized that her smile was ten thousand different kinds of insane.

"You really are a disgusting person," she said, grinning, "an extremely, extremely disgusting person."

He watched Mia lean backward and fall into the ocean. The last thing he saw of her were the pale bottoms of her feet and heels bobbing on the pale green surface before they were swallowed up.

He sat there several minutes expecting her to return, to come gasping up from the foam giggling and saying that she was just kidding, that she sure got him, hadn't she, but when Mia didn't come back, Shawn only shrugged and went searching for more baby mermaids to eat.

Shawn stopped bothering to chew. He guessed the ones he found now could be considered infants. Small, tadpole like, no bigger around than his finger. They were slick and wet enough to easily swallow whole and alive.

He didn't mind that they thrashed on the way down his throat.

Occasionally, he felt sad about Mia. He had loved her, after all.

He supposed that she was happy now in her vision of heaven, probably frolicking up in the clouds with all those curled unborn fetuses.

To calm himself, to entertain himself, he ate more of the infant fish, the baby mermaids. Swallowing them alive, smirking as he did it like it was some sort of trick you'd show at a cocktail party.

He let one stay alive longer than usual, holding up by its finned Mohawk. He brought an index finger to its lips. Shawn didn't think it'd open its mouth, he hadn't see one open its mouth before, and out of scientific curiosity he wanted one to.

His fingertip moved closer and, just when he felt its cold, undersea breath on the skin under his nail, the tiny mouth opened wider that should have been able to, and he saw the hundreds of round rows of circular-saw teeth.

A nasty shock of fear bunched the muscles on the back of his neck, and he quickly threw the fish away in disgust.

Revolted, Shawn wiped his hand where he'd touched it on his swimming trunks.

The worse pain he'd ever felt before overtook him then, a slither in his guts, several slithers in his guts. Spiky fins knocking his ribs, slick bodies darting through his small intestine. Shawn held the folds of his belly.

They were in there.

Alive.

He could feel them.

He really, really, shouldn't have swallowed them whole like that.

Panicked, he wondered if there was some way he could reverse that decision.

He tried to think rationally. Maybe it was alright they were in there, maybe nothing would come of it.

Just as he thought that, the first row of pointed teeth began chewing its way through his belly fat, soon followed by the others.

Shawn frantically looked around for something that might help him. That's when he saw her, pale, spherical head clung with wet blonde hair rising from the murky water.

She was opening her arms to take him. She whispered his name, and Shawn had never seen Mia look that gorgeous before, her flesh bloated and fish belly white, nearly blue. Her eyes gummed and glazed with seaweed.

"Heaven's under the sea," she told him, "it always has been. Heaven's under the sea."

Shawn liked that, he thought it sounded beautiful and poignant, a thing the Mia he knew and loved would believe in.

Shawn wanted to see heaven under the sea.

She took him in her sea-water smelling arms, and opened a mouth filled with a hundred rows of round circular-saw teeth.

## Sky Demon

Jeff Brigham

9:15am

The creature had a wingspan comparable to a four-seat, twin engine airplane. An uneven row of curled, jagged fangs zippered the length of its extended snout, which looked to be an odd blend of crocodile and kingfisher. It had unblinking obsidian eyes, tiny claws at the front-most tip of each wing, and a trailing point on the back of its head. Featherless, with membranous, seaweed-green skin stretched taut over a sleek skeletal frame, the Mesozoic beast resembled a bat more than a bird.

It soared close to the tree tops, stealthily, no higher than twenty feet above the bike trail. Two, three seconds, max, and it was gone.

"Did you see that!" Charlie said, squeezing the break handles on his bike.

Lewis searched his pockets for his cell phone. When he found it, he acknowledged Charlie, who was a good distance ahead of him. "Yeah," Lewis said. "I saw it. Maybe we can get it on video!"

"It's gone."

"It might come back."

Charlie's head tilted skyward. Tall trees and thick underbrush flanked the trail as far as the eye could see.

To Lewis's right, an orchestra of crickets improvised a symphony in the field of wild grass. A woodcock buzzed somewhere nearby. A mosquito landed on his ear and he slapped it.

They waited.

Nothing.

Then a preternatural quiet seized the area.

The woodcock hushed and the crickets went silent.

A squirrel bolted up a tree.

Something felt off. Lewis watched Charlie turn to him, almost in slow motion; his gray tee-shirt and jeans, his mop of curly, chestnut hair, his tennis shoes that had seen better days, his trusting, loving smile—all the unwavering characteristics of his son—charged him, possessed him, and kissed him goodbye. Lewis wanted to vomit.

Charlie started. "That bird looked just like a dino--" But

didn't get to finish.

From somewhere close, somewhere just beyond the visible forest, a scream, thunderous and frightful, tore through the quiet. It ripped through Lewis's body like high voltage electricity.

Charlie covered his ears.

Lewis dropped the phone.

Swiftly, a giant shadow fell over Charlie.

Lewis watched in horror as the flying creature reappeared, dropped down into the space between the trees, extended its long, grotesque snout, and chomped down on his son. Its marble black eyes regarded Charlie not as a human being, but as a rodent or a fish; the beast did not recognize Charlie as a person; Lewis understood this with absolute clarity. It was only seeing prey. Its enormous bat wings beat furiously, tearing into the underbrush, kicking up clouds of debris, producing a tempest that ripped leaves off branches and branches off trees.

Lewis mounted his bike and raced to his son.

Charlie kicked and screamed, pounded the blunt end of the creature's snout with his fists while dozens of jagged teeth dug into him, impaling his tiny body, making escape impossible. Blood soaked the creature's maw.

"Nooo!" Lewis cried.

Charlie was hoisted off the ground, and his mountain bike came with him; one of the pedals snagged the cuff of his jeans, and it dangled loosely at the corner of the creature's jaw.

Lewis stopped just below Charlie and watched helplessly. His son was too far out of reach. He screamed, "Let him go! Let him gooo!"

Charlie reached for him; blood coursed down his arm and spilled out onto the breeze. It be-speckled Lewis's face and drizzled to the earth around him.

The creature gained height, taking Charlie above the trees. It shook its head in attempt to lose the unwanted bike, thrusting Charlie side to side. A few sharp jerks did the job and the bike dropped. Then the beast flew off.

A wink, and his boy was gone.

In that moment, come hardship or hallowed ground, Lewis vowed to find his son, and to bring vengeance onto the flying creature that took him.

2:00pm

[The following is a transcription excerpt from the interview of the witness and father of the missing child, Lewis Conway, by Lieutenant Dom Wellford, conducted at the

Sheltonville Police Department.]

LC: I didn't see anyone else, no.

DW: How long, would you say, you and your son were on the trail?

LC: About an hour.

DW: You didn't see anyone else that entire time?

LC: I told you, no.

DW: What was your son wearing?

LC: A gray shirt and jeans. And a pair of old white tennis shoes.

DW: Did he have a wallet?

LC: No, I don't think so.

DW: ID?

LC: He's nine.

DW: A library card or anything of the sort?

LC: No. Do you have a helicopter?

DW: Excuse me?

LC: To search for him. You will need a helicopter. Are you searching or just questioning me?

DW: We are doing everything we can, Lewis.

LC: Are you sure? 'Cause it doesn't feel like it.

DW: Yes. We are doing everything we can. Right now, I

need your side of the story.

LC: I'll tell you anything you need to know. Just find my son!

DW: Why are you covered in blood?

LC: It's Charlie's.

DW: How is it you have Charlie's blood all over your face and clothes?

LC: Charlie was above me. The creature had him up in the air, in its beak. Its teeth shredded him.

DW: Could you describe this creature to me?

LC: I already did.

DW: Maybe you forgot something. Sometimes more details come out.

LC: It was large. Its body was tiny but its wingspan was enormous. Its skin was bat-like, a blackish green. It had a long, pointed snout with sharp teeth. A head that came to a point. Did you ever see a picture of one of those flying dinosaurs? That's pretty much it. I know how it sounds, but it's true. I swear it.

DW: How does it sound?

LC: You know.

DW: Why don't you tell me.

LC: Fucking crazy, that's what. It sounds crazy.

DW: Yes. Well, it's quite a fantastic story.

LC: Do you believe me?

DW: I'm just getting your statement.

LC: Yes, but do you believe me?

DW: I'm not sure what I believe.

LC: Do you think I'm crazy? Do you think I did something to my son?

DW: I'll tell you what, Lewis. I don't think you're crazy. I'd like to think that if you had done something, you'd at least make an attempt to clean the blood off your face. Your alibi is off-the-wall ridiculous, and doesn't sound like an alibi that a guilty person would come up with. Besides—the bike.

LC: What about it?

DW: Your son's bike, Lewis. We found it in the upper branches of a maple tree, some forty odd feet above the ground. The department is currently trying to wrap its collective brains around that one. I guess I'd be more interested in hearing an explanation from you.

LC: The bike snagged on Charlie's pants cuff. When the sky demon took him away. It dropped onto the trees.

DW: Sky demon?

LC: Yeah.

DW: Did you just make that up?

LC: I did.

DW: Ahem. Yes. Thank you. Why don't we start again? Take me back a bit earlier this time. When did you wake up this morning?

LC: My wife woke me up at about 7:30.

DW: What's your wife's name?

LC: Flora.

[End of transcription excerpt.]

3:45pm

Lieutenant Dom warned Lewis not to travel, that the police would be in touch soon, and escorted him to the police station waiting area, where his wife, Flora, sat on a hard, plastic chair next to the magazine table. Her long brown hair was disheveled; her face was pale and makeup-less, and her eyes were swollen and red from crying. A small brown purse sat on the floor at her feet and a white handkerchief lay twisted on her lap. Her countenance did a landslide when she saw him. She stood and grabbed him, collapsed into his chest and sobbed.

"Where's Charlie? Where's my boy?"

"I don't know," Lewis said.

"What happened?"

"Something terrible. Let's get out of here. I'll tell you about it in the car."

"Tell me now!"

"The police are handling this. I need to wash up."

Flora beat his chest with her fists. The white handkerchief tumbled from her hand to the floor. "Where is he, goddammit? Please. Please. Oh, please…"

Lewis hugged her, squeezed. "Let's go home."

4:05pm

The car ride home was fraught with stop lights that took forever, pedestrians that didn't pay attention to where they were walking, roads that needed fixing, and other goddamn asshole drivers who needed to learn how to drive or get the hell out of the way.

Flora exacted her own interrogation, not unlike the one at the police station, except that she was, at certain moments, hysterical. But understandably so.

Lewis: Yes, that's what I said, a prehistoric flying creature.

Flora: Oh, lord in heaven, Lou! Do you know how you sound right now?

Lewis: Of course, I do.

Flora: Oh God—the blood on your face… Charlie's

blood?

Lewis: Yes. Charlie's.

Flora: And what about you? Are you hurt?

Lewis: No.

Flora: The bird took him away? Into the sky?

Lewis: Yes.

Flora: To eat him?

Lewis: I don't know.

Flora: Of course, you don't know. Why did you let him out of your sight anyway? You were supposed to protect him! You're his father!

Lewis: He wasn't ever out of my sight. Just a little ahead of me. This thing came out of nowhere. How was I supposed to know? I had no idea anything like this could happen. In real life. To Charlie. To us.

Flora: A flying dinosaur?

Lewis: Jesus, I didn't believe monsters were real. It didn't come out of the closet. It didn't come from under the bed. It came from the sky, from somewhere in that forest, and it had wings.

Flora: Did you do something to hurt him? Lewis?

Lewis: Of course not.

Flora: Because if you did we could figure something out, Lewis. We could. I just need to know. I mean, I don't think you would but I need to know.

Lewis: I swear to you, Flora, I did not hurt him. And if you think I did, the bike, Flora. What about the bike?

Flora: Yes. There's no explanation that makes sense.

Lewis: Charlie's bike is so high up in that tree it might stay there forever... Unless they chop the whole damn thing down.

Flora: So, what now?

Lewis: I'm going to go home, get cleaned up, pack some supplies and head back to the bike trail, to the place where he was taken.

Flora: What about me?

Lewis: You need to stay with Patrick.

Flora: But I want to help.

Lewis: He's a puppy. He can't be left alone for an extended period.

Flora: The neighbors can take care of him.

Lewis: We've only been living here for a year, Flora. We don't know any neighbors. More importantly, they don't know us. Why would they want to take care of our dog?

Flora: We'll leave him food and water. He'll be fine.

Lewis: I don't need your help. I can do this on my own. I'm not coming back, Flora. I'm not coming back until I find our son, period. We're talking a pretty large area of wilderness here, thousands upon thousands of acres.

Flora: You'll find him? No matter what?

Lewis: Yes.

Flora: Well, I don't know.

Lewis: You don't know what?

Flora: Lewis, I need to tell you something.

Lewis: What?

Flora: Oh, Lewis…

4:45pm

After taking a shower, after washing Charlie's blood off his face and out of his hair, Lewis grabbed a backpack from the top shelf in the bedroom closet and began gathering supplies. A box of wooden matches and a lighter, a compass, bug spray, a canteen filled to the screw top with tap water, canned sardines and a handful of granola bars. Second guessing himself, he added a small vinyl tarp, a flashlight, and a weathered, coffee-stained copy of Moby Dick.

All the while, 'Lewis, I need to tell you something'

slithered within the shadows of his mind. It haunted him that she couldn't just say it, that she had to make the announcement, without coming right out to say what it was. But he felt he already knew somehow anyway. Even amidst the grief over the loss of their son, her words chilled the marrow of his bones.

She sat on the edge of the bed while Lewis fiddled with the shoulder straps of the backpack, looking down at the tissue in her lap, her face streaked with drying trails of tears.

Her voice spilled remorse. "Remember the day we took Charlie to the Historical Society and it rained so hard and he stepped in that puddle and got his shoe wet?"

"Sure. We drove to the store just to buy him some dry shoes. I damn near had a heart attack because I couldn't find my credit card, then you paid cash," he said.

"That night. I went away."

"Yeah. You left to help your mother. I put Charlie to bed and got drunk."

She paused. The bedroom air was charged with her silence.

"What about it?" Lewis nudged.

"That night," she said. "That night. I wasn't with my mother. I was…"

She paused again, testing his patience. Lewis just wanted her to be out with it. He turned his back to her, pulled the sock drawer open, and pretended to search for a pair. "You were what?"

"I was with Gary."

He stopped. Facing the mirror, he didn't have to turn to see her. She was looking at him.

"Gary Washburn?

"Yes."

"You slept with my co-worker, Gary Washburn?"

"Yes."

"You fucked him?"

"Yes."

Lewis rubbed his temples. He paused, a thousand questions reeled through his mind but he wasn't sure what to ask. "How long?"

"That night?"

"No. I mean how long was it going on. Between you and him?"

"A couple weeks."

"How many times did you fuck him?"

"I don't know exactly. Maybe five."

"Why are you telling me now? Christ sake, Flora? We just lost Charlie to some flying monstrosity, and you choose to tell me now? Why not last week? Why not last year?"

"I tried, Lou. I really tried. I wanted to but couldn't. The time wasn't right."

"And now it is?"

"I should have told you sooner. I owe it to you to tell you. I don't want to lie to you anymore. I feel like I'm lying to you every time you look into my eyes."

"So, you're off the hook because of a larger pressing issue?"

"No," she said.

"Any other secrets? Any other men you've been screwing behind my back?"

"No, Lewis. None. For heaven's sake."

"How the hell did you get together with Gary, anyway?"

"He called one day when you weren't home and we just started talking and I think I was feeling a bit lonely. He invited himself over."

"Oh, so blame it on him! He invited himself. It was all his fault, not yours."

She sat quietly, peering down at her lap.

"Was he good?"

She gave it thought. "Yes."

"Really? That's your answer? Yes?"

She nodded solemnly.

"What the fuck, Flora? Seriously. What is that supposed to mean—yes?"

"It means," she said, "I'm not sure I love you anymore."

Lewis turned to face her. He folded his arms, then unfolded them, shifted his weight and folded his arms again. He poked his cheek with his tongue and cleared his throat.

Patrick ambled into the room, name-tag jingling, sniffed at this and that, then jumped up onto the bed and nestled into Flora. He watched Lewis with curiosity.

"Lewis?"

"What?"

"If you don't find Charlie what will you do?"

Lewis thought about it. There were several ways of answering her question, but he didn't feel like trying.

He felt like finding Charlie.

6:10pm

He looked at his watch. Two hours had passed since the police released him, four since the search officially began.

Everything set to go, he checked his phone and saw it was only about half charged. He'd have to wait slightly longer. Every last bit of juice was going to help. He'd only use it once a day and, if he found Charlie, he'd use it to phone Flora.

(No, Lewis, not if… When.)

The phone blinked, alerting him to a call or text. He hadn't heard it ring. The phone wasn't silenced. The amazing brain-farts of modern technology never ceased astounding him.

No one important had called. No family members (not that he had any to speak of—his aunt in Tennessee hardly counted.) No calls from the police.

Lieutenant Dom Welford said he'd call either way.

Either way.

His exact words.

It meant the police would call if they found Charlie dead or alive.

Lewis swallowed.

While waiting for his phone to charge, he fired up his desktop and checked his email. Nothing important. Nothing he cared about. He logged onto Facebook and noticed a large number of personal notifications. He went to the home screen and saw a gazillion condolences. He browsed them. I'm so sorry for your loss. Terrible things happen to good people. Praying for Charlie. Praying for your son, praying that he comes home safe. Prayers for you and your wife during this time of great difficulty. Praying for you in your time of need.

Lots of praying apparently.

Even Gary wrote on his wall. Thinking of you, Buddy. Thinking of your family and wishing you best of luck in the search for your son. Tried calling but you didn't answer. If there's a way I can help, let me know.

Yeah, Gary, Lewis thought. There's a way you can help. How about you have a good sit-down with your wife and tell her how you boned my Flora five times in the span of two weeks? Take a picture of her face and post it to Facebook. I'd really like to see it about right now.

In his newsfeed, he noticed a picture of a dinosaur (specifically a Tyrannosaurus rex) brandishing a bloody butcher knife, with a photo of Lewis's face super-imposed over the dinosaur's head. Some cocknocker by the name Bobby Ray Mathers posted it, not that it mattered.

The word was out.

He searched for the television remote, gave up, then manually turned the TV on. Breaking news was covering the disappearance of Charlie, with at least two reporters on the ground and one in the sky. He watched live footage of a helicopter shadow rippling over countless acres of green foliage.

Another channel broadcasted a sketch of the sky demon. The caption below the sketch read 'pterosaur: myth or mugshot?'

He slipped away from the television and checked the living room bay window for news vans outside. To his relief, he didn't see any. But he did notice a parked four-door sedan with a driver behind the wheel. It passed as the type of car the police might use to remain unnoticed while watching a suspect. As he studied the suspicious vehicle, Flora came up behind him and placed a hand on his shoulder. He shrugged her off.

When it was time—his cell phone was charged most but not all the way—he grabbed it and slipped it into his pocket. He made sure he had his keys and exited to the garage, retrieving the machete from its hook on the wall.

7:30pm

He arrived at the gravel lot that gave passage to the bike trail. The suspicious four-door Sudan did not follow him. So much for paranoia, he thought.

Unlike that morning, parked tightly into a few makeshift rows, were a dozen cars (probably volunteers to the search party,) two police cruisers and a news van. A helicopter droned somewhere in the sky out of sight.

He donned the backpack and stuck the machete under his belt. He pushed a pair of dark sunglasses onto his face and slapped a ball cap with the Arizona Cardinals football team logo over his head.

He hurried through the gravel lot to the edge of the forest, tore into the brambles, and disappeared. In no time, he was alone with the trees and the wind and the dirt under his feet.

He never felt so alone in all his life.

Day 1

When night brought out the stars, after making a fire and tearing into his sardines and jerky, he called Flora, only to confirm what he already knew, that Charlie had not been found. He also learned that the police were very interested in where he went, and in finding him.

Day 2

Lewis chanced upon a waterfall and bathed in it. Naked, with his clothing hung over a nearby branch, he spotted a large black bear with her cubs enjoying the cold river water a click or so downstream. He watched them from inside the cascade. They either didn't know he was there, or didn't care.

He would have felt better with a gun.

But Flora didn't believe in firearms and wouldn't allow him to have a gun in the house.

C'est la vie. The machete was what he had for protection, and it would have to do.

Day 3

At sun set, Lewis finished the last of the sardines, tossed the can into the fire, and watched the flames lick helplessly at the metal. It was the third day and his search so far had produced no result. His son was still lost, somewhere out there, alive or dead.

Either way.

Lewis clawed his ankles. He'd walked through poison ivy at some point, probably early that morning while stomping a path through the dew-drenched wild grass. He removed his socks and shoes, wanting to keep them dry. Big mistake.

The battery on his cell phone was at 45 percent power. Not bad. The charge was holding longer than he imagined.

When he called Flora, she begged him to come home. She told him she was sorry and that he had every right to be mad as hell and that she missed Charlie (so apparently the search team hadn't yet found him, telling Lewis everything he needed to know) and that she couldn't sleep at night because Patrick kept barking at the wall in the hallway.

Before falling asleep, he tried reading Moby Dick by firelight but couldn't stay focused. He gave up and, too exhausted to wedge it in the backpack, placed it on a large, flat rock close to where he lay.

Day 4

A morning shower woke him from a deep sleep. He crawled out from underneath his tarp. The rain had drenched his backpack, and transformed his copy of Moby Dick into a bloated, rounded pile of paper mush.

He scooped up his belongings and hurried to the nearest tree for cover.

Waiting for the rain to abate, he spotted a figure in the mist, one having every characteristic of a nine-year-old boy. It darted across a path, through some heavy nettle and ducked behind a tree. This figure had every nuance belonging to Charlie, but if Lewis had seen correctly, that is, if his eyes were not lying to him for the lack of proper sleep and food, Lewis saw that the boy was semi-transparent, like an apparition.

"Charlie!" Lewis called. "Charlie!"

Lewis watched, steadfastly, not daring to blink.

"Charlie!"

Getting no response, he jumped to his feet and sprinted. The space behind the tree was empty. Lewis groaned.

"This way, dad…"

Lewis looked up. His son was visible again but his position had jumped; this time he appeared in the east, through a grove of tamaracks. He saw his boy much clearer now. He looked just as he did the day he disappeared, same clothes, same shoes, same mop of chestnut curly hair. Minus the blood. If Charlie had been a figment of Lewis's imagination, he'd surely have blood. No matter how hard Lewis tried, there was no shaking that final image of Charlie from his mind.

Charlie scooped air with his hand, motioning for Lewis to follow.

"Is that really you, Charlie?" Lewis asked. A tear gathered in his right eye and spilled down his rain-wet cheek.

No answer.

Charlie just smiled and turned. He took a few steps and melted into the thicket.

Lewis followed.

Day 5

The mosquitos were terrible on day five, worse than all other days combined. Maybe the rain showers had brought them back to life.

Lewis emptied the can of aerosol bug spray, giving his head and ears a good, last douse, and pitched the can as far as he could throw. It smacked into some random tree, startling a dozen or so crows into flight.

He pulled out his compass and confirmed he was still headed due east, the direction indicated by his son (or by the apparition of his son.) The morning was still young and the sun filtered onto the forest floor through the generous gaps of tree leaves in this neck of the woods.

He powered-on his cell phone to check the battery, but it didn't start. Dead, no doubt, but that was okay. He didn't need it anymore. He chucked that too, like the aerosol bug spray. One less item to carry around.

He didn't have much use for God these days.

But faith had returned to him.

Faith disguised as a manifestation of his son, guided him to the lair of the sky demon.

Day 6

There was no fire for Lewis the night prior. His matches were damp and didn't work, and he had lost his lighter somewhere along the way. He hadn't gotten much sleep, and he was developing a migraine. Hunger gnawed at his gut like a rat at a head of cabbage. His feet throbbed from walking with an erratic gait, because his shoes were falling apart. The skin at all ends of his body ached from welts and insect bites. He stopped by a tree on his journey east and turned it into a scratching post, getting that maddening, unreachable spot on his back.

And every so often he'd catch a glimpse of his son, in spectral form, silently urging him forward. Follow me, the ghost said with its eyes.

And Lewis did.

At noon, Lewis crested a foothill and found himself standing before a giant lake. The wind licked up tiny waves, not even whitecaps, and its water shimmied silver in the midday sun. The lake was nestled into a titanic hillside, a massive, steep slope, disfigured by burnt and broken timber, scarred by crevices and fissures and scattered clusters of foliage, brown and long dead. Boulders sat awry and crooked rocks jutted from the soil like rotten molars in diseased gums. Far up on the hillside, about a thirty-minute climb for Lewis, was the mouth of this marred landscape: a cave opening large enough to accommodate a four-seat, twin engine airplane. The ground of the hillside preceding the cave was discolored by giant, wan streaks that Lewis guessed to be guano.

He set forth and climbed.

He reached the cave and hoisted himself up.

While catching his breath, he peered inward. His eyes adjusted from the brightness of the afternoon sun to their new darkened surroundings. Squinting, he became aware of a putrid odor, the stench of cadaver.

He heard the buzzing of flies.

The cave went back roughly forty feet or so. Only half its length was illuminated by daylight; the other half remained shrouded in darkness.

Back there, in the deep dark, something moved.

Lewis had the sensation of being watched.

He dropped his backpack and fished around for the flashlight. He readied his machete and switched on the light.

Piercing the darkness with the beam, the limestone and mineral deposits sparkled in the luminescence. Lewis did not see a demonic prehistoric bird, but at the cave's deepest point, he did see what appeared to be a nest.

He advanced carefully, machete poised to strike, ready for anything that might jump out at him.

His face broke a thread of cobweb and he brushed it off.

(Oh God, Charlie, please don't be in here.)

It was funny how he wished to not find his son, considering all he'd been through to do just that. It's also funny when you tickle your tonsils with the barrel of a shotgun. Funny can be a funny word.

He passed through the area of the cave lit by day, then crossed into the other half.

"Charlie?"

No response.

His foot brushed against something leathery, an item that felt like it did not belong in a cave. The buzz of flies had grown frantic. Lewis side-stepped and aimed the flashlight downward.

It was a blood-stained tennis shoe.

"Charlie!" Lewis called.

No answer.

Searching for more, he swept the beam across the floor and spotted fragments of a gray tee-shirt. Lewis knelt and plucked them off the ground. He regarded his find as a gut-wrenching confirmation. After tucking the fabric away in the back pocket of his jeans, and upon closer inspection of the area, he noticed that the shallow pits and fissures at his feet contained varying amounts of a bluish-green substance, sticky to the touch. Was it the blood of his son, six days cold, or bird shit? He examined his finger by light; a tiny black fly landed on the tip, tasted it, then flew off.

Crouched, with knees aching, Lewis fell backward to sit, but instead of landing his cheeks on a rocky surface, he came to rest on a smooth, balanced stone about the size of a cantaloupe. It wobbled under his weight. It seemed hollow and, after careful consideration, didn't feel so much like a stone after all. Lewis's attention, which had been wholly fixed on his finger, now shifted to the object on which he sat. An icy cold, creeping horror danced up his spine. He jumped off and aimed the flashlight at it, revealing its identity.

A decomposing skull, teeming with maggots; strands of curly, chestnut brown hair, wet-stuck to the bone.

Lewis had found his boy.

He sat down Indian-style, back straight, sighed and studied the skull by flashlight. Memories of his son fluttered in his mind like butterflies in a jar. His first haircut. Learning to ride a bike. Swimming at Beachford Park. The way he roughhoused with Patrick. His laughter.

After a long, hard moment, he collected Charlie's head and got to his feet. He brushed off the maggots as thoroughly as possible, then dropped the remains into his backpack.

He still had work left to do.

Lewis advanced to the nest, this time watching the ground to make sure he didn't step on or trip over anything else.

The nest, made up of sticks and down and branches and plant roots, looked somewhat like your average bird's nest. Except, of course, that it was much larger—about the size of a plastic kiddie pool you might find at any given department store in the start of summer.

Inside were two large, white eggs the size of beach balls. He poked one with the tip of his index finger and the shell gave way slightly; unlike chicken eggs, these eggs seemed to be soft, pliable.

"You've got kids, eh?"

Lewis swung the machete down on one, splitting the egg in half. He plucked half the fetus from its shell (the half with the tail and lower legs, still twitching,) and pitched it at the cave wall. It made a dull, wet smack, and stuck for a few seconds before sloughing down. He peeled the other half from the shell, took a few steps to make room for himself, then kicked it toward the entrance of the cave. It was a lopsided kick, not centered as Lewis had intended. As a result, instead of soaring out the entrance of the cave with all the grace of a football flying through a goal post, it angled off his foot and tumbled across the floor.

He bent to scoop up the second egg. It quivered before he touched it, like a short-lived Mexican jumping bean. Did it know its fate? Was it aware of what was coming? As Lewis picked it up, he hoped so.

He carried the egg to the mouth of the cave, where he stopped and took a seat. The sun became hot on his face as he took in the sights and sounds of the wilderness, and the view of the lake below. He watched a bald eagle hunt the shoreline and spotted a herd of deer moving under the trees. But the sky demon was nowhere in sight. She would be returning to the cave at some point, Lewis figured. He just needed patience.

Enjoying the view, he played with the egg in his lap—popping it left and right, turning it over, tossing it, catching it. When he was done playing, he raised the egg to his mouth and took a bite. The shell tasted chalky, but the egg's casing was not inedible. To boot, it was easy to chew.

The fetus inside squirmed.

Lewis took another bite and tore into the wing. The bat-like skin, drenched in amniotic fluid, tasted like the viscid slime on a shore-washed fish, or so he imagined.

Charlie sat next to him, hands folded in lap, feet dangling over the edge.

"I'm bored. When are we going home?"

"Soon," Lewis said. Pink birth juice leaked from of his mouth and bubbled down his chin. He chewed hard, swallowed hard, belched and went in for the next bite.

"Why are we still here, dad?"

"We're waiting."

"For what?"

"You know for what, Charlie."

With the machete by his side, Lewis waited.

## Something in the Strawberry Fields
Eric J. Guignard

The heat was monstrous.

Workers toiled beneath a high sun like figures of clay that harden and crack. They wore old, long-sleeved cotton to protect from the scalding rays. Sweat streamed down their foreheads and necks to soak at the collars. Muddy sneakers wrapped their feet, stained gloves covered their hands, and faded headgear bound their heads. Passersby, looking across the fields, might see only bobbing Dodgers baseball caps or wide-rimmed cowboy hats with twisted, frayed edges, dipping up and down over the strawberry plants like little boats in a sea of red and green.

Like the others, Luis did not speak as he labored, but silently cursed and blistered and endured. The sun stole his energy, slowly, like a canny pickpocket, so he did not notice the loss until it was too late. His back and knees became a cold black iron, heavy and without feeling; in the morning his bones howled in complaint as he crouched for hours and hours, but by afternoon he felt nothing, just a metal fusion of stiff bolts and beams. He picked strawberries from the ground and placed them into a large bushel. Then he stood with a mighty creak and carried the bushel to the counter and had it weighed. He brought his empty bushel back to the fields and picked from the ground again. He performed this routine from seven in the morning until four in the afternoon. The harvesters worked six days a week with only Sundays off. Luis made little money, but he had few responsibilities either, so he got by. Some of the men had families to support, and Luis could not imagine how they provided the means to raise so many *niños*.

His thoughts drifted as he plucked strawberries, one by one. Lost in thought, Luis reached down and pulled one, and he felt the plant grasp his hand and pull back, trying to yank him into the worlds far underneath the earth. Startled, he let go of the plant and fell backwards shaking his head.

"*¿Qué paso?*" Joe, his cousin, called to him from the next row.

"*Nada*," Luis muttered back. "The temperature is getting to me."

He stared at the plant, then quickly grabbed the same glimmering strawberry and pulled it again. It popped off its leafy stalk with ease, as had all the thousands of others Luis had picked that week. *Heat plays funny tricks on a man*, he thought. Joe went back to working, and Luis glanced at the other men around them, quietly harvesting at their own patches of strawberry heaven, bent rigidly over on hands and knees.

Luis resumed plucking under the summer sun and soon fell back into his methodic routine. His muscles were knots of cramped stone toiling dully, replaying the same motions. His bushel measured only half full.

He let his mind drift again, this time to the Chupacabra...

Luis had moved to Portero, at the bottom of California, four weeks earlier. He had only recently obtained work harvesting strawberries through Joe. The two of them grew up together a few miles across the Mexican border in Tecate, east of the crossing at Tijuana and San Diego. Joe had lived in Portero already for several months and he told Luis of strange events that began to transpire. In recent weeks, neighboring farms were discovering livestock slaughtered and drained of blood. Goats and cows, limbless and lifeless, were uncovered under shallow mounds of dirt and crops. The laborers spoke solemnly of signs and superstitions, and more than one man shared tales told him long ago from an *abuela* in her rocking chair that the

Chupacabra had returned.

The Chupacabra was a story Luis knew well, having heard them since his boyhood. The creature was said to be a spirit in the form of an upright creature, described as a coyote that walked like a man with spines erupting from its back and giant black eyes like saucers of ink. Like all mythical creatures, its physical characteristics varied greatly according to the storyteller, as did its ferocity and unnatural powers. Some thought it to be a misplaced soul while others claimed it a vengeful demon. The Chupacabra could carry children away in the night or it could punish the ungodly or it could attend any deed that people imagined, those people being parents and preachers who spoke of the creature in low voices, prophesying by candlelight.

In its latest manifestation, the Chupacabra seemed to be haunting the lands outlying Portero. Last night it emerged again and fed on two sheep, which were found on a neighboring farm down the road. Their animal carcasses were discovered, wooly bundles of visceral gore buried under stalks of asparagus. One of the workers said the Chupacabra was searching for something. To Luis, the Chupacabra was only Mexico's vision of Bigfoot.

The afternoon grew late, and Luis continued picking strawberries, rows and endless rows of the leafy flora. His eyes began to burn with visions of ruby-red fruit speckled by yellow-black seeds. Again, a leafy plant seemed to grasp his hand when he was not paying attention and try to pull him under the earth. He gasped, but then a sudden shout rose through the searing, still air followed by a cry of "*¡Madre de dios!*" Excited voices clamored, and Luis joined the laborers rushing to an unpicked patch of the strawberry crop a quarter acre away.

Another corpse had been found, buried by mounds of leafy vines. However this was not the corpse of an animal, but the skeletal figure of a man, stiff and desiccated, strawberries growing out from his hollow eye sockets.

One of the harvesters pulled off the clumped plants, trailing heady brown roots. The cadaver was fully revealed, a mid-size man, fleshless from rot. Matted black hair ringed its withered skull, and one lower tooth gleamed of gold. The body was dressed in denim pants and denim jacket, a 'Texas Tuxedo,' which were rancid with decay and dirt. The dead man wore also white-spotted cowboy boots—snakeskin—with silver metal tips across the toes and large silver buckles over each instep. The buckles had initials engraved in calligraphy upon them: the letters *M.G.*

Luis knew those initials well... *Miguel Garcia*, the man he killed.

The police allowed the harvesters to leave. None of them were suspects, but were lightly questioned. Did anyone know the dead man? *No.* Did anyone notice anything suspicious? *No.* The police closed the strawberry fields for forty-eight hours to search the grounds for evidence.

Joe and Luis and several of the other workers walked to the nearby Burger Grille.

"*Fue el Chupacabra,*" one of the men announced quietly and performed the sign of the cross over his chest.

Luis nodded and looked around at Joe and the other harvesters. "*Si, si,* it was *el Chupacabra.*"

Joe shook his head. "No, that was no Chupacabra. Luis, I thought you didn't believe in such things."

"I believe in what I see," Luis replied, feigning sincerity.

"El Chupacabra is angry," one of the laborers said. "He is not satisfied with animals now and is haunting people."

Joe disagreed. "*¡No seas tonto!* That was a skeleton. You all saw it. Whoever he was has been dead for a long time."

"I'm saying only that I don't think it's a coincidence," the laborer said. Other men murmured and shared tales of the creature's lore.

They arrived at the Grille, and Luis excused himself. "Hey, Joe, I think I'm going to head home instead. I don't have much appetite right now."

"*Te comprendo.* I don't either, but we should eat something," Joe said. "It's been a long day."

"Nah, I'll see you back at the apartment."

"*Esta bien. Adios.*"

"*Hasta luego.*"

Alone at the apartment, Luis thought of Miguel Garcia, a festering skeletal corpse in the strawberry fields in Portero. A man who appeared to be dead for many years. A man Luis encountered last, only a month ago, while at home in Tecate.

The man was a stranger when Luis first met him. He had knocked politely at Luis's door and spoke with a genuine sincerity in his voice, inquiring, "Luis Fernando Castillo?"

"*Si, yo soy.*"

"Are you okay? Are you feeling well? Has anything happened to you?"

Luis answered, confused. "Yes, I'm fine. Who are you?"

"I was very worried about you, Luis. I thought surely

something must have happened to you. I thought, I should say *we* thought, perhaps Luis fell down the stairs and broke his legs. Or perhaps Luis' car caught fire while Luis was inside. Or perhaps Luis' fingers were cut off by gardening shears, and he could not use the telephone any longer. You never know when such an accident may befall."

"What's this about?" Luis demanded. He tried to make his voice sound tough, but spoke too quickly and spilled his bluff through his words.

"My name is Miguel Garcia," the man said. "I work for Don Delgado. Consider me like an account manager. I maintain relationships with Señor Delgado's clients."

Luis's breathe froze in his throat, and his heart plummeted to his feet. He didn't know what to say and stared dumbly at the well-groomed man standing before him.

The corners of Miguel's lips curled up in a malevolent smile. "You do not seem so happy to see me. You are not difficult to find. This is only Tecate after all. Don Delgado asked me to call upon you. He is worried about your well-being, and you know why he is worried, don't you?"

"*Sí.*" Luis spoke softly. His eyes dropped down and fell upon Miguel's white-spotted snakeskin cowboy boots.

Luis had placed wagers with Don Delgado's bookies, wagers he lost and could not pay back. The most sensible thing Luis could think of was to bet again with the bookies and use those winnings to pay back his previous losses. He had a tip on the Cortez-Silva middleweight bout. Cortez would pull a T.K.O. in the ninth round.

His tip turned out to be bad.

Silva landed an uppercut that knocked Cortez over the ropes in the first. Luis then owed much more. He approached Don Delgado full of bluster and promises. He was a hard worker, he said. He could make *mucho dinero* and pay *el Don* back very soon.

Señor Delgado had nodded at that and added, "With interest, of course."

"Of course," Luis replied. But instead, he fled and hid. Luis moved secretly to live with a friend and never repaid a *peso*. He feared this day might arrive, and the day did not leave him long in waiting.

Miguel placed one hand on Luis's chest and pushed him gently backwards from the doorway into the hall entrance. "May I have your permission to enter?"

"Yes, please." Trepidation shadowed Luis's insincerity.

"*Gracias.* I feel like a bible salesman standing at your door for so long."

It was nine in the evening. Luis lived in a small side street apartment with his friend who was away working the night shift. The apartment entrance opened from the crux of a short alley bordered by brick high rise complexes. Little light shined down in his home and, as Miguel entered, shadows played across his features. Miguel led Luis through the apartment as if he had been there before and sat him down at a dining table.

Luis finally spoke to his defense, impulsive words, and words he immediately knew Miguel had heard ten thousand times before. "I'm working on getting the money to pay back Don Delgado soon, I swear. I just need more time."

"Shh, Luis. Don Delgado is not worried about that. He knows he will get his money from you. He is only worried about your health. If you should vanish again or have an accident, he would like to feel more secure knowing he is protected."

Miguel opened his denim jacket and pulled out a set of documents, folded and bound under two binder clips. The papers were carefully opened, laid out before Luis, and a slender gold ballpoint pen set on top. Luis swallowed instinctively as he read the heading: *Life Insurance Policy.*

"And if you will sign where indicated," Miguel said. "You may feel gratified knowing we value you at half a million American dollars."

Luis felt himself breathing faster and harder, tendrils of cold alarm seeping wrapping his senses. He touched the policy, immediately noting that Señor Dominique Delgado was the sole beneficiary.

"Please, Señor Garcia, I don't think this is necessary."

"It's not an option. Please sign on the lines where notated."

The policy was already filled out, including Luis's personal information neatly typed in and followed by a signed notary's stamp. The policy was backdated to three months earlier. Luis pointed that out to Miguel with a shaky finger.

"It is only a little oversight. *Mi hermana* is the agent." Miguel shrugged his shoulders. "So she will have all the dates corrected. You needn't worry at all, *amigo*. She is very good at what she does."

Miguel leaned in close, and Luis could smell the slight tang of *habaneros* on his breath. He took the ballpoint pen off the policy and forced it into Luis's hand. As he crouched to do so, Luis saw his denim jacket brush open and reveal the black grip of a Magnum revolver.

Luis whimpered and shook his head.

"*¡No me jodas!*" Miguel said into his ear. "I can make this much worse for you."

Luis was not a violent man, but he was brash and young, and panic took hold of him. At Miguel's words, he abruptly swung the ballpoint pen in his hand and plunged it directly into Miguel's eye, thrusting it so deep that only the gold band of the rear cartridge remained sticking out.

Miguel shrieked, a drawn out letter *E*. The sound lasted scarcely a moment, and Miguel fell backwards, his face a paralyzed cartoon with jaws wide apart and tongue lolling out. He died immediately. The pen rose from his deflated left eye like a crooked nail driven in almost to its head. It had passed through the socket and plunged neatly into the brain's delicate frontal lobe; a viscous trail of blood and aqueous humor leaked out.

Luis stared at the body for too long. He then packed his meager possessions and loaded them, along with the limp corpse, into Miguel's car which he found parked outside the alley. He buried Miguel in the desert, just outside of Tecate, and fled to America, never to return to the homeland of his birth.

Luis remembered all this as it had occurred.

He now stared at himself in the bathroom mirror, He splashed water across his face. He expected the one-eyed corpse of Miguel Garcia to seize him from the other side of the glass.

He had buried Miguel deep in the sandy desert outside Tecate. There had been only saguaro cacti and scorpions for witnesses of the interment. Yet now in Portero Miguel's body, which should be freshly festering, appeared as a skeletal mummy nearly in Luis's hands.

Chupacabra or not, Joe was right when he said that strange things were transpiring here.

In the morning, Luis fried up eggs and tortillas for himself and his cousin. They ate, drinking bitter coffee while the small television crackled nearby.

"It's nice to get some extra time off," Joe remarked.

"Yeah," Luis agreed, his voice distant.

"You should have stayed with us at the Grille. Manny and I scored double dates with the two waitresses there. That could have been you instead of Manny. His date is only going because mine asked her to. I'm sure she would have preferred you. She's a fine little *mamacita*. You know the one with the dark blonde hair?"

"Sure."

"Hey, Luis, snap out of it, *carnal*. You've been moping around since that body was found. Did it really bother you that much? It was probably just a transient or something. An old *vato* without any family."

"You're right. I shouldn't let it get to me."

"Speaking of family, how is yours? *Tia* Lupe was always a favorite. You should call them."

"No," Luis answered quickly. "I'll write. I'm going to send money anyway, but I didn't really leave on good terms. I need some time to pass, let things cool over, *sabes?*"

"*Si, claro.* If you need to talk, my door is next to yours."

They finished eating and sat watching the small television. Newscasters spoke in monotone, feigning interest in politics and business. The air conditioner creaked on and a sad hum sang through the small apartment.

Luis was grateful for Joe's benefaction. He had appeared unexpectedly at Joe's doorstep last month, and Joe took him in with a warm "*Mi casa es su casa.*" He fed Luis and helped him get hired on to harvest with him. Luis wanted desperately to tell Joe everything... The skeleton in his closet had let itself out, and Luis did not know how to put it back inside.

Two days later the strawberry farm reopened, and the laborers went back to work. Luis felt apprehensive about returning to the fields, so close to where Miguel's body had mysteriously appeared. However, his first thought was that it might appear suspicious if he were to suddenly flee. Besides, he also thought there was some logical reason the corpse emerged at the farm anyway, and he chided himself for being superstitious. After all, the two cities were only four miles apart, across the national border. Perhaps coyotes had dug up the decaying man and dragged him along, feasting on the flesh as they moved in pack. Perhaps sandstorms relocated it. Perhaps immigrants crossing illegally were using it as a dupe, to draw attention from where they travelled. Luis was creative and could imagine a dozen reasons and scenarios, although he admitted that each was ridiculously unlikely.

The harvesters arrived in the morning on foot and in dusty pick-up trucks. They spoke of their adventures during the time off, of ball games and *novias*. Their conversation eventually turned to the Chupacabra. Another goat had been found dead and drained, and one of the men had gone missing during the night. Some ventured the Chupacabra was involved with the disappearance, while others spoke that the man simply found a better opportunity elsewhere; such was the life of a migratory farmhand.

Loudspeakers hung high on splintered posts announced the time for work to begin. Luis and the others spread out into the field, each claiming his own lot of land like homesteaders on a prairie. The early morning sun rose high in the sky and the land simmered underneath. Luis sweated and toiled, and the hours passed. He tried not to let his mind drift away. He focused on the fruit at hand, picking each strawberry grimly, but he imagined Miguel Garcia leaning over him at every moment. *An eye for an eye*, Miguel would say, and swing the slender, gold ballpoint pen.

The morning melted away, and eventually the men broke for lunch. Luis and Joe sat under a faded vinyl awning with Manny.

"*Ay chinga*, it's hot out here today." Manny was huskier than the other men, and pools of perspiration soaked his shirt.

Luis agreed. "And I thought Tecate was hot."

"At least there's a breeze blowing out there. Up here, we just cook like *churros*."

Luis nodded and confided to the other men, "I don't know how much longer I can work out here on the farm."

"It'll get easier. Your body is growing accustomed," Joe said.

"It's a good job," Manny added. "Work is hard to come by right now."

"I know, but I've been having these nightmares about the fields…"

"It's the dead man we found," Joe interpreted to Manny. "Luis was spooked by it."

"I've seen dead men before," Luis said. "But this one was… unexpected. Maybe it's the superstitions I hear from the others—I don't know." But as he spoke, he *did* know. What he could not say was that his fear grew, a horrible suspicion he had not seen the last of Miguel Garcia.

"Death is unexpected, *mi amigo*," Manny told him, shrugging his shoulders. "Whether you believe in God or the Chupacabra or whatever else, something will come for us when it's our time. We pull strawberries from the ground. We don't think about each one, we just pick them because it's our job to do. We pull fruit from the soil, one after the other, and when the time comes, something will pluck us from our lives just the same."

After lunch, Luis returned to his patch of crops, crouching down on numb hands and knees, working to fill another bushel. He crawled from plant to plant, dragging the bushel after him. The temperature crawled too, mimicking him, as it grew ever hotter. Minute by minute, the heat seemed to increase. Sweat formed on his brow and dripped over the strawberries as he picked them, forming wet, glistening sparkles that flashed like silky pricks of light. He found the sparkles mesmerizing and allowed himself to drift away on their gleams, dreaming of his younger years.

Luis caught glimpse of something in the strawberry fields far from him, watching.

It was distant and not more than a dark shadow, fuzzy under the sun, with spines that swayed like summer grass upon its back. The creature crouched, but appeared to have the ability to stand upright. Two dark eyes glowed like briquettes of fiery charcoal, gazing intently upon Luis. The other workers in the field toiled diligently, all with heads bowed deep and filling their own bushels, unaware of the specter's presence.

Luis's sweat turned cold. He blinked and rubbed unbelieving eyes, and the shadow beast was still there, tense and crouching, preparing to pounce should he dare look away. Luis would not dare; he locked sight with the thing and started to rise from the ground. A wiry vine sprung from the strawberry patch and wrapped around his wrist, yanking him quickly back to the dirt. He shouted in surprise and another stalk, this one sprouting many leaves, thrust into his mouth, chocking him as it climbed down the back of his throat. Luis threw himself backwards with all his might, tearing the vines out of the ground and coughing the leaves from his mouth before screaming in panic.

The other harvesters dropped the fruits of their labor and ran to Luis, expecting him to have found another corpse. Instead, he stood merely gasping and shaking his head.

"What is it?" Joe asked in concern, rushing to his cousin.

"Something attacked me, it choked me!" Luis spit out a thistle from his tongue and pointed to where the shadow had watched him. "There's something over there, beyond that patch."

Several of the men went to investigate and shook their heads quietly when discovering nothing but guiltless plants. The field foreman shuffled over, a sunburned old farmer with a gut set to burst the seams of his britches.

"What's going on here?" he asked. "You didn't find another rotter, did ya?"

"There's something in the strawberries. It grabbed me." Luis held up his wrist, encircled with a scarlet-colored welt like the imprint of a hangman's loose. The foreman was not impressed.

"Sonny, I think you're gettin' the heatstroke. Why don't you take a rest over yonder." He pointed to the exact spot where Luis had seen the shadow creature watching him.

Luis startled in surprise at the foreman's proposed resting area. Why had he told him to go there? There were no trees or other shade at that location to suggest any place of respite. He looked incredulously at the foreman, searching for a sign he was in on some master plot to entrap him. The foreman stared back, balking under Luis's accusing glare.

"*No, ya termine,*" Luis muttered. "I'm done, I'm out of here." He left his upturned bushel lying on the ground and walked quickly away with Joe chasing after him.

The foreman's voice trailed behind. "You don't get pay for half days, sonny."

Joe grabbed Luis's shoulder. "Hey, *carnal*, wait up."

"I'm sorry, Joe, I'm leaving. I mean, I'm leaving Portero. I never should have brought my troubles to you."

"What troubles? It's great to have my little *primo* stay

with me."

"*Gracias*, Joe. You've been great to me, really, but I can't stay here anymore."

"Are you going back home?"

"*¡Dios no!* I've got to get further away."

"Will you wait to leave until I get home tonight? We can talk some more."

"*Sí*, I'll still be there. See you back at the apartment."

Luis finished packing. He did not claim ownership to much, just a dented beige suitcase and a couple duffel bags filled with clothes and personal effects. He had some money saved from working in the fields, too. It would pay for bus fare and several nights at cheap motels. He decided to leave in the morning.

Thoughts of his future roamed feral through Luis's mind, the bleak prospects of running ever further away. He had no destination to strive for, knowing only that Portero was too close to Tecate. He vaguely decided he'd follow the coastline as it sprawled northward, away from the heat and the nightmares incurred by Don Delgado. Some day, he thought, he would be far enough away from Tecate that he would settle down and start his own *familia*.

Something dropped on Luis's head and bounced off, landing with a spongy thud. He looked down and cringed. A single heart-shaped strawberry lay on its side, sprouting a small green crest of leaves. He looked up to the ceiling in alarm, then around the room, finding nothing out-of-sorts. He cautiously walked out the bedroom and down the short hallway into the living room. It was empty. The entire apartment was empty. Maybe the strawberry had gotten flung up by him as he packed... he could think of no other explanation.

Luis began to turn back and stepped on another strawberry. It flattened under his foot in a wet smoosh. He looked down and saw several more of the fruit lying scattered across the floor like ruby turds.

"*¿Que diablos?*" Luis murmured. His heartbeat quickened, and he felt a tingle claw up his spine. He paused, sensing the room around him, waiting for another strawberry to fall or mystically appear. He stood there some minutes, eventually feeling almost disappointed in the anti-climax of events.

He'd tensed in anticipation and found himself still holding his breath. Luis sighed and tried to relax. His head throbbed with a dull migraine ache and he swore at his fright. *He caused himself a headache from his nerves.* He and Joe brought home strawberries every day. One of them must have just knocked over a bowl of the fruit as they passed by. Still, Luis would not feel safe until he was on the bus out of town.

Walking back down the hallway toward the bedrooms, Luis turned into the side bathroom to get a bottle of Tylenol. He opened the door and screamed.

Miguel Garcia was climbing out of the mirror. His face gleamed with red streaks, a cocktail of blood and strawberry juice. The gold pen stuck jauntily out from one eye.

"You left something back in Tecate," Miguel spoke casually. He held up the life insurance policy and grinned. Maggots squirmed between his teeth.

"No, no!" Luis cried. He backed away from Miguel into the living room, stumbling over strawberries. The front door leading outside was only several steps away.

"You do not seem so happy to see me," Miguel said. "You are not difficult to find, Luis. This is only Hell after all. El Chupacabra asked me to call upon you. He would like for you to join us in the strawberry fields." Miguel reached up to his face and grasped the pen, pulling it out of his eye with a sickening hiss like a deflating tire. He offered it generously to Luis.

Luis turned and ran to the front door. He flung it open but froze just before passing through. The door opened to a dark land of strawberry fields stretching endlessly to the horizon and then curling impossibly upwards into the black sky, as if looking up at the crest of a wave about to crash down. The fruit plants were large and full and alive. They rustled about on the ground, scratching into the soil.

Corpses of livestock littered the strawberry-infested land. Rotting skeletal carrion of cows and sheep lay on their backs with stumps of severed limbs pointing askew. The animal husks were shriveled and dry, drained of fluid. The weedy fruit covered the carcasses, sucking up their moisture.]

A mixture of cries and pleas and curses fell from Luis's mouth all in one soft syllable. He turned and looked back at Miguel who stood in the living room, laughing.

"An eye for an eye," Miguel announced, and his eyelid winked over the wrecked hole where an eyeball had once been.

Luis looked again through the door into the strawberry fields and sank to his knees. He saw a dark shadow peering at him from the distance, the same fuzzy image he had seen watching him at the farm. The distant black shape crouched in the field, preparing to pounce. It looked as if an etching of charcoal was brushed across the horizon, with black eyes like saucers of ink, glaring in judgment upon him. Luis knew, then, the Chupacabra for what it was.

Creeping vines snaked through the doorway and lashed onto him. Luis did not resist as the strawberry plants dragged him through.

That evening, Joe arrived home to find Luis missing. He tapped on the bedroom door. It opened with a slow creak from the push of his finger. He saw the packed luggage stacked in the corner, so did not worry immediately at his cousin's absence. What struck him as odd, however, was the single plump strawberry set on top his pillow. Joe shrugged it off. He sat on the couch and ate dinner while watching television.

Hours later, Joe felt drowsy, even while he began to worry about where Luis could have gone for such a long time. He wrote a note for Luis to wake him and say goodbye before leaving, then laid down on the couch to rest. He quickly fell asleep and dreamt a terrifying vision.

The night was black, an unworldly sky with no stars or moon to interrupt the darkness. Around him, strawberry plants crouched and hissed in warning. Joe knew this was a land which the living were not to traverse. He heard moans and sounds of rustling nearby. His dream body led him to the commotion, seemingly against his will. Joe sensed he must flee, but there appeared nowhere to abscond. The land was strawberries—*all strawberries*—growing wicked in the sunless soil. As he drew closer, a mound appeared before him, writhing in shudders. The fruit vines coiled and grew over a figure that Joe recognized immediately: *Luis.*

Joe leapt to him. He reached through the crawling flora and grasped Luis's hand, pulling it quickly. Luis hand snapped free like a loose tooth popping from gum line. Joe looked down, and the hand became into a cluster of fresh strawberries on a leafy vine. Luis thrashed beneath him and let out a choked wail. He squirmed and kicked under the strawberries. Joe frantically reached through the plants again and grabbed hold of Luis's leg, trying to drag him out from the suffocating mound. The leg tore free, and Joe fell backwards holding a thick bush extract. It was a long plant with the biggest, reddest fruit yet, trailing dirty tangled roots back down to the ground.

Joe screamed. He somehow found the strength to clamber back into the strawberry patch but, as more plants grew over him, Luis could hardly be seen any longer. He gradually became just a fluttering mass as if the wind blew through a pasture of wildflowers. Joe could see his cousin's face last as it vanished, peering from under the fruit. His staring eyes turned bright red with pupils of yellow seeds, glazing over as they ripened.

Something then came toward Joe from across the field. He saw the shadow approaching and, looking up, screamed again. It was the Chupacabra, and it rose above him, towering high, the guardian of the strawberry fields. As it came closer, Joe saw that its face resembled a coyote's with a snarling, pointed snout. Spines protruded venomously from its back like a porcupine, and its eyes glowed, burning black. It spoke an incantation, and Joe woke shrieking.

He bounded from the couch and went to Luis's room again to check if he had come back yet. The room remained empty. The lone strawberry on his pillow glared ominously at Joe, and he could see each yellow seed as a vision of Luis's fading eyes. Joe snatched the strawberry and hurled it against the wall. It splattered into soft, wet chunks that slowly slipped down the wall leaving red streaks. The fruit pieces landed on a set of papers, bound with a paper clip, lying atop a small table. Joe picked up the papers and stared at them in dread. It was a life insurance policy, speckled in drops of dark red. Whether the red drops were stains from a strawberry or were dried blood, Joe thought he did not ever want to know.

Joe never returned to work in the strawberry fields. He left Portero, telling no one of his fears. A month later, the harvesters found another body buried underneath the strawberry plants. It was unidentifiable. The corpse was drained like the others and withered to a sun-beaten mummy as if it had lain in the desert for many, many years. Had Joe been there, he would have known immediately who it was.

The fruit crop flourished that season. People remarked that the strawberries had never grown so plump or tasted so juicy before. They said it must be something in the fields.

## You Will Be Laid Low Even at the Sight of Him

Kevin Wetmore

On the fifth day of the expedition, sweat dripping from the brim of his cap, Brian began to question, if not his faith then at least the goodness of God. He was exhausted, frustrated, missed his family and there were blisters in the crevice between his thumbs and forefingers that formed on the first day on the lake and continued to bleed and not heal and yet he kept paddling from the rear of his canoe. He had known this would not be easy, but it was for the glory of the Lord and to bring the truth of Creation to atheists, nonbelievers, heathens and scientists, but he wished the Lord could have placed the object of their quest a little closer to home.

He looked over at Reverend Ezekiel who sat in the middle of the first canoe, two locals paddling him as he read from his Bible. The sweat gleamed on his head and turned his white, short-sleeved shirt translucent, so one might see the t-shirt underneath. Every once in a while, the Reverend looked up and around at his surroundings, then buried his nose back in the Good News, undistracted by the heat, humidity, movement of the canoe or the seemingly thousands of noises surrounding them in the marsh.

Brian, realizing his frustration, quickly asked the Lord for forgiveness, patience and the ability to endure this situation. Admittedly, he had volunteered (heck, he had given Reverend Ezekiel six thousand dollars out of his savings for the privilege of supporting the expedition and joining it) but he realized in hindsight he had not had any idea what was in store for him. Still, he reminded himself, the Lord asks nothing of us we cannot handle.

In addition, he had also seen Reverend Ezekiel paddle with a passion and a fury in the first days on the lake, driving the rest of the group with his model. His sincerity and devotion to the Lord were unquestioned, and Brian knew in his heart the Reverend was a good man. Brian would not have followed him all the way to Africa if the Reverend were not the real deal.

Six days earlier, after fourteen hours in the air, Reverend Ezekiel Wilcox ("Pastor Zeke" to his close friends if only one or two are around, otherwise "Reverend Ezekiel" - he preferred the formality of both the title and his full name) and his hand-picked expedition of twelve men descended from the plane into the heat and humidity of a Brazzaville summer morning. After a night in Brazzaville, they met their charter plane back at the airport to take them northwest to Impfondo Airport, and then spent the next forty-eight hours making their way via Land Rover to the village of Epena and then from there through the rainforest to Lake Tele. Their canoes hit the water and they began paddling towards the marshes south of the lake almost one year to the day after agreeing to fund and carry out this expedition.

A year ago, Reverend Ezekiel stood in front of their congregation in rural Ohio. It was a hot summer day, not as humid as here in the Congo, but Ohio can hold its own when it comes to humidity, as Reverend Ezekiel liked to joke. The fan blades were turning slowly, and members of the congregation were fanning themselves as the Reverend stood up at the pulpit and began preaching.

He surveyed the congregation slowly, as if really seeing them for the first time, a troubled smile playing about his face. "Matthew twenty-five, verses twenty-nine and thirty, he began. "'For unto every one that hath shall be given, and he shall have abundance: but from him that hath not shall be taken away even that which he hath. And cast ye the unprofitable servant into outer darkness: there shall be weeping and gnashing of teeth.' My friends, I had a word from the Lord. We are being unprofitable servants."

That pronouncement set the congregation all a flutter. They knew they were good Christians. Bible-believing Christians. Didn't the church actively work to bring the Good News to the unchurched all over the world? Did they not carry out every project the Reverend brought to them with diligence and zeal? If Jesus himself were here, he would praise them for being good and faithful servants. Had not the Reverend Ezekiel told them this many times over the years himself?

They genuinely believed they had an obligation to help others, even if others did not see it as help. God's word was Truth. Must we not sacrifice our time, our money even our very selves to bring others to the salvation we already have? If a ship sank and we were on a lifeboat, would we not have an obligation to reach out to those in the shark-infested ocean, even if those folks misguidedly thought they were just swimming? They knew their hearts were clear when they did the work of the Lord. So to be told they were failing at it was a grave thing indeed.

The Reverend could tell he had caused consternation (Brian knew that was his intention all along, it was a great way to start a sermon). He held up his hands for silence and smiled. It was the smile of a teacher who knew he had to bring children out of their ignorance and did so with humility and love.

"Does it not say in Genesis one, twenty-four, 'And God said, "Let the earth bring forth the living creature after his kind, cattle, and creeping thing, and beast of the earth after his kind: and it was so"'? And does it not say in Genesis one, thirty, 'And to every beast of the earth, and to every fowl of the air, and to everything that creepeth upon the earth, wherein there is life, I have given every green herb for meat: and it was so.'?"

The congregation gave their assent. It most certainly did say both things in Genesis.

"Brothers and sisters, it is clear that man and dinosaur lived together and co-existed at the same time. It was the Fall, our sin, the sin of Adam that first made the dinosaurs eat meat, and then it was the flood of Noah that killed them off. But not all of them. Oh, no."

With that, a slide came up, projected on the screen hanging from the wall of the church behind Reverend Ezekiel, right next to the large cross that hung behind the pulpit. An image of a large dinosaur on four legs in a swamp, eating leaves from the tops of trees.

"This is Mokèlé-mbèmbé." Reverend Ezekiel looked at

the image with the congregation for a moment and then let out a long low whistle. "He's a big one, ain't he?" The congregation let out a small laugh. "His name means 'He who stops the flow of rivers,' because he is so big." He looked at the image some more. "'He who stops the flow of rivers.' That's a lot of power. You know who has more? God almighty. Can I get a witness?"

The congregation loudly called out, "Amen."

"That's 'cause God created the rivers. He can stop the flow of rivers. If He wanted to, He could make the mighty Mississippi run backwards." The Reverend patted his face with his handkerchief to remove some of the sweat. He then pointed at the image.

"We know God created the dinosaurs on day six. We know this. Genesis one, twenty- four through thirty one. God spoke and 'every creeping thing that creepeth upon the earth' came forth, including Mokèlé-mbèmbé.'

He smiled again at the congregation, the sunlight glinting in his brylcreemed-back black hair. "That's a mouthful, ain't it?" They smiled back to show it was. "I'm just gonna call him 'Big Mickey.'" A small laugh rolled through the congregation at that as folks resumed fanning themselves. "Now a scientist would call Big Mickey an Apatosaurus, and that's just fine. A scientist would tell you he's a vegetarian, and that's just fine, too. But that scientist would tell you Big Mickey here lived millions of years ago. Now that's not so fine."

He touched a button on the pulpit and the image shifted to text. "The Bible," he solemnly intoned, "calls Big Mickey 'Behemoth,' and knows that he lived with us thousands of years ago. Job forty, fifteen to nineteen: 'Behold now behemoth, which I made with thee; he eateth grass as an ox. Lo now, his strength is in his loins, and his force is in the navel of his belly. He moveth his tail like a cedar: the sinews of his stones are wrapped together. His bones are as strong pieces of brass; his bones are like bars of iron. He is the chief of the ways of God: he that made him can make his sword to approach unto him.'"

The slide then switched back to the dinosaur. "Behold now behemoth, our good friend Big Mickey. His tail is like a cedar tree. I ask you what other animal could Job be describing? Big Mickey is the Behemoth of the Bible."

"As you know, every summer we send a small group of missionaries to the Congo for a week to evangelize the heathens and bring them to the Lord. Next summer, we will do something different. Something much greater for the Lord."

A new image, Reverend Ezekiel in Africa, his arm around

a smiling black man. "Our good friend in Africa, Alphonse Tam'si, who helps coordinate our mission there, told me about Big Mickey, who lives in a swamp next to a lake in the Congo. As soon as he told me I realized what Big Mickey was and why the Lord led me to him."

"Next summer, myself and twelve stout disciples of the Lord will go to this lake armed with cameras and recording devices. We will bring back incontrovertible proof that dinosaurs are not extinct, but that they still live in the Congo. The damned liberal secular evolutionists will not be convinced, but they are already lost to us, are they not brothers and sisters?"

The congregation nodded solemnly. There are none so blind as those who will not see and the damned liberal secular evolutionists, a favorite topic of Reverend Ezekiel, were clearly beyond saving.

"No, friends, we will save those who are not certain. Those who are on the fence. The lost children of God who, if presented with evidence, will leap into faith in the Lord and know in their hearts the Earth was made six thousand years ago. Maybe then, finally, the truth will be taught in our schools."

The congregation gave a loud "amen" and a scattering of applause echoed around the small church.

## You Will Be Laid Low Even at the Sight of Him

"The Lord gave me a word that this was our special role to play. He wanted our congregation to send a mission to Africa, not to save the heathen, but to save the whole world, just as His son did. We are, after all, children of the light: 'Ye are all the children of light, and the children of the day: we are not of the night, nor of darkness. Therefore let us not sleep, as do others; but let us watch and be sober.' First Thessalonians, chapter five, verses five and six. We will not sleep, brothers and sisters. We will not sleep, but will raise the funds needed for this mission, and next July, twelve volunteers, new apostles if you will, will go with me to bring back proof of Big Mickey and shine the Lord's light on the entire world." And the congregation smiled and began the great work.

And that is how Brian found himself in a canoe, paddling through the marshes south of Lake Tele in the Congo, looking for Mokèlé-mbèmbé almost a year to the day after he stood with the other men at church and said he would. Only one moment threw him. As they exited the airport, on their way to a combi that would take them north, an elderly woman, her skin so old and thin it looked like paper, her eyes sunk in her head but dancing with light, grabbed his hand. At first he thought she was begging for money, or distracting him from pickpockets.

But all she did was pull him close and whisper, "If you stay for a week, the spirits will bless you. If you stay for a week and a day, you will die."

He did not know why he said it, but he simply responded, "I will stay until the Lord shows me Mokèlé-mbèmbé."

She withdrew her hand quickly, as if his had become painfully hot. Her eyes grew sad. "The spirits will let you find what you seek, but it will not make you happy. Death awaits you on the lake…" With that she slipped into the crowd. It wasn't until ten minutes later on the road he realized he had not mentioned the lake.

In the lead canoe, Alphonse Tam'si consulted with the Reverend. They had been in country for five days, three on the lake and no sign of Big Mickey. Brian strained to hear the conversation. He was hot, sweaty, tired, and figured the expedition had not lived up to his imagination. Now that he thought about it, he realized he thought this would be like King Kong, the original one, not either of the remakes. He figured they'd be seeing monsters and huge animals every day. Instead, they had seen a number of large turtles (indeed, on the second day on the lake, some Boha villagers caught, cooked and served them turtle), various birds and this morning a pack of gorillas drinking at the water's edge. But no dinosaur. Tam'si seemed to be defending himself to the Reverend on this count.

"There is no guide to find Mokèlé-mbèmbé. The swamp forests around the lake are largely unexplored. We will have to look through the bogs to the south and pray for luck."

"You don't 'pray for luck,' Alphonse. You pray for God's help." The Reverend set down the Bible and pulled a book called No Mercy that he had spent the past year consulting. It was dog-eared, full of notes and the cover had been halfway torn off.

"This fella says it's found in the Likouala region. Why don't we go there?"

"There has been unrest in Likouala."

"This fella doesn't mention the swamps. He says the animal appears in the lake itself."

Tam'si smiled. "And how many times did he see Mokèlé-mbèmbé on the lake?"

Reverend Zeke frowned. "Well, none. But still, his guides seemed to think you could see it by sitting on the shore and watching the lake."

Tam'si smiled harder. "Yes, in theory you could see one by waiting on the lakeshore. In theory, you sit in your home and wait for lightning to strike you. Or you can go look for a storm if lightning is what you want to see. I am taking you to the animal's home."

The Reverend grunted his assent and they paddled on.

Brian looked around at the others. Jeff and Aaron seemed to be fading fast, Aaron already had a terrible sunburn and Jeff was out of shape, though he would never admit it. Bill, Don, and Marshall were holding up all right. Ray, Little Bob, and Wayne were in one canoe bringing up the rear and Mike and Big Bob were in the other. Little Bob wasn't as strong a paddler as the others, but he was there as the photographer and videographer, so while the other two moved the craft through the lake, he fiddled with his cameras, took pictures and filmed their journey. He would collect the evidence the men hoped they would find that proved the literal truth of Genesis. Lastly, Tate was in the front of Brian's canoe, a pile of supplies between them, right in the middle of the pack. All twelve of them and Reverend Zeke had spent a year fundraising, planning, and finally getting a long series of vaccinations and enduring the visa application process. At last, they were on the lake and all they wanted was to get off of it. All except Pastor Zeke.

Within the hour they were back on shore. Between

them turtle), various birds and this morning a pack of gorillas drinking at the water's edge. But no dinosaur. Tam'si seemed to be defending himself to the Reverend on this count.

"There is no guide to find Mokèlé-mbèmbé. The swamp forests around the lake are largely unexplored. We will have to look through the bogs to the south and pray for luck."

"You don't 'pray for luck,' Alphonse. You pray for God's help." The Reverend set down the Bible and pulled a book called No Mercy that he had spent the past year consulting. It was dog-eared, full of notes and the cover had been halfway torn off.

"This fella says it's found in the Likouala region. Why don't we go there?"

"There has been unrest in Likouala."

"This fella doesn't mention the swamps. He says the animal appears in the lake itself."

Tam'si smiled. "And how many times did he see Mokèlé-mbèmbé on the lake?"

Reverend Zeke frowned. "Well, none. But still, his guides seemed to think you could see it by sitting on the shore and watching the lake."

Tam'si smiled harder. "Yes, in theory you could see one by waiting on the lakeshore. In theory, you sit in your home and wait for lightning to strike you. Or you can go look for a storm if lightning is what you want to see. I am taking you to the animal's home."

The Reverend grunted his assent and they paddled on.

Brian looked around at the others. Jeff and Aaron seemed to be fading fast, Aaron already had a terrible sunburn and Jeff was out of shape, though he would never admit it. Bill, Don, and Marshall were holding up all right. Ray, Little Bob, and Wayne were in one canoe bringing up the rear and Mike and Big Bob were in the other. Little Bob wasn't as strong a paddler as the others, but he was there as the photographer and videographer, so while the other two moved the craft through the lake, he fiddled with his cameras, took pictures and filmed their journey. He would collect the evidence the men hoped they would find that proved the literal truth of Genesis. Lastly, Tate was in the front of Brian's canoe, a pile of supplies between them, right in the middle of the pack. All twelve of them and Reverend Zeke had spent a year fundraising, planning, and finally getting a long series of vaccinations and enduring the visa application process. At last, they were on the lake and all they wanted was to get off of it. All except Pastor Zeke.

Within the hour they were back on shore. Between

## You Will Be Laid Low Even at the Sight of Him

the sun and the heat the men were feeling exhausted and disheartened. For the third time, they pulled their canoes up out of the lake, unloaded them, and set up camp. Eight three man tents (Reverend Zeke had one to himself, the others were occupied by the twelve apostles and Tam'si and his eight men) were arranged in a circle on shore. It still unnerved Brian when the men pulled two Kalashnikovs and a sawn-off, single-shot twelve bore from the canoes and positioned themselves around the tents.

"Animals. Gorillas, guerillas, poachers, and thieves," Tam'si explained when he saw the Americans' looks of concerns. "And, of course, Mokèlé-mbèmbé might not be as happy to see us as we are to see him," he smiled.

That night, Jean, one of their porters, cooked a meal of fish caught from the lake and vegetables he had found rooting through the forest next to the shoreline. Brian thought it was the most delicious meal he ever had. As always the meal began and ended with a prayer. After they had all eaten, they sat around the fire and Reverend Zeke told them more about God's plan.

"The Bible tells us about dinosaurs. It was the first book to talk about dinosaurs. It says right there in the Book of Job, 'Who can open the doors of his face? His teeth are terrible round about. His scales are his pride, shut up together as with a close seal. Out of his mouth go burning lamps, and sparks of fire leap out. Out of his nostrils goeth smoke, as out of a seething pot or caldron. His breath kindleth coals, and a flame goeth out of his mouth. In his neck remaineth strength, and sorrow is turned into joy before him. The sword of him that layeth at him cannot hold: the spear, the dart, nor the harpoon. The arrow cannot make him flee: slingstones are turned with him into stubble. He laugheth at the shaking of a spear. Upon earth there is not his like, who is made without fear. He beholdeth all high things: he is a king over all the children of pride.'"

Brian listened as Tam'si quietly translated Reverend Zeke's speech into French to the other men and they spoke in low tones to one another.

"'A flame goeth out of his mouth'? Sounds like a dragon," observed Big Bob.

"Not a dragon," Reverend Ezekiel snapped. "Make no mistake, friend, there are dragons in the Bible. One awaits us at the end of time, so says Revelation. But Job describes a dinosaur. A large lizard."

"Dragon Devil," spoke Francois-Pierre, shifting the twelve gage as he looked at the lake.

## You Will Be Laid Low Even at the Sight of Him

"Pardon me, son?" asked Reverend Zeke.

"Dragon Devil. Is English version of name for large lizard here."

"Mokèlé-mbèmbé?"

"No. Ninki-Nanka."

"What's that?" asked Wayne.

The Reverend stepped in before Francois-Pierre could continue. "Another name for Mokèlé-mbèmbé, like 'Brontosaurus' and 'Apatosaurus' are names for the same thing. The important thing is that the Lord is bringing us to him and him to us. I had a word from the Lord. Tomorrow is the day. Let us give thanks, go to bed, and ready the equipment for tomorrow." He looked to Little Bob, who nodded. "Now let us bow our heads in prayer."

"Not the same" whispered Francois-Pierre quietly. Brian thought he might be the only one who heard.

Later, just before lights out, Brian went to Francois-Pierre. "I respect you, friend," he told him. "And that's why I tell you the Reverend may be a little rough, but he is a good man, a brilliant man. He knows whereof he speaks."

Francois-Pierre continued to clean his Kalishnakov. "He may well," he responded quietly. "But I tell you as a fellow

Christian, he has never been on this lake before; he does not know the beast he seeks. L'opinion de l'intelligence est meilleure que la certitude de l'ignorant."

"Come again?" asked Brian.

"'The opinion of the intelligent is better than the certainty of the ignorant,'" translated Tam'si, sitting nearby, blowing smoke from a cigar to keep mosquitos away.

"Are you calling the Reverend ignorant?" asked Brian.

"He pursues a prey he does not understand for his own purposes. He makes a great deal of noise and expects to see an animal rarely seen. Does he seek God's glory or his own?"

"Surely God's," came the reply.

"Le prudent voit le danger et se cache, mais le simple passe et souffre pour cela".

"Ha!" laughed Tam'si. "'The prudent sees danger and hides himself, but the simple go on and suffer for it.' Let us hope we do not suffer this trip, huh?" and Tam'si walked away shaking his head.

"That another African proverb?" Brian smiled at Francois-Pierre.

"Proverbs 27: 12." Francois-Pierre fell silent, and Brian eventually wandered to the tent he shared with Tate and Jeff.

That night the camp was awoken by loud noises. Hooting and growls were coming from the forest. When Brian emerged from the tent, Jean-Baptiste and Henri Obenga (Brian had made it a point to learn their names) stood between the tents and the trees, Kalashnikovs at the ready. He noticed all the men climbing out of their tents in states of excited nervousness.

"Praise God," said the Reverend as he struggled to put on his glasses, his Bible clutched in his other hand. "Mokèlé-mbèmbé has come to us."

"Not Mokèlé-mbèmbé. Gorillas. Perhaps two dozen." Tam'si lit a cigar and considered the noise. "Not usually active at night. Like us, they sleep then. Something has stirred them up."

"Mokèlé-mbèmbé," Ezekiel insisted.

"Perhaps," Tam'si smiled. "Or perhaps us. We may have landed on a beach they consider theirs. They can be very territorial. I suggest we go to bed and allow the men to stand guard. Keep your wits about you, everyone." With that he went over and sat next to Henri Obenga. They kept their eyes on the treeline as they talked in low voices and Tam'si blew smoke to keep the mosquitos away.

"I shall keep watch, too," announced Ezekiel, "The Lord

may send the dinosaur our way tonight." With that, he sat down in the camp chair in front of his tent and began to page through his Bible.

In twos and threes, the other men drifted away, back into tents to attempt sleep. It was a long time coming for most, and Brian wasn't sure he slept at all until he opened his eyes at dawn and realized he had been dreaming of large lizards and blood.

Most of the men were dragging from the heat and the excitement of the night which prevented good sleep. Still, they managed to pack up the tents, load the canoes, eat a quick breakfast and get back on the lake.

Before they pushed off, Reverend Ezekiel and Tam'si agree to head southeast into the swamps below the lake. If the going was slow on the lake, it was even slower in the brackish water with trees and shrubs growing out of it. The canopy grew thick. The canoes alternately grew close together to pass through narrow areas, and spread apart to make their way through difficult areas.

For lunch, they tied canoes together and the Americans distributed bottles of water, granola bars, beef jerky, and cups of fruit. Their Congolese compatriots shared their fare but also ate palm maggots. They bit the heads off, spitting them in the water and then ate the squirming body. Tate and Ray both looked green watching this process, and Wayne stopped eating and looked as if he were about to vomit. Jean-Baptiste offered one to Brian with a smile, expecting him to refuse. Out of pride as much as curiosity, Brian took it, bit the head off, spit it out and then swallowed the rest with very little chewing.

"Tastes like bacon," he told the others. That was when Wayne actually did lean over the side of the canoe and vomited in the water. The others laughed, but not hard. Jean-Baptiste slapped Brian on the back and said something in French. "You're one of us, now," Tam'si translated.

"Supposedly," the Reverend intoned, "back in 1960, a group of Pygmies slaughtered a Mokèlé-mbèmbé, carved it up and ate it with some European travelers."

"Mmm," affirmed Tam'si. "That happened in the North of the lake."

"What?" asked Reverend Ezekiel, turning red. "Why are we down here then?

"Mokèlé-mbèmbé has been seen all over the lake."

"We have not seen him."

Henri Obenga spoke up in a rapid string of French. Tam'si turned to the rest of the group. "He says the northern

Pygmies blocked the Molibos that fed the lake to the north because the Mokèlé-mbèmbés were using them to come out of the swamps and feed on the plants that grew where swamp channel feeds the lake."

"We're turning around," the Reverend said. "We're going to the Molibos in the north of the lake." His tone said he would brook no discussion.

Two days later they reached the northern shore and began to scout out the Molibos. They once again pulled the canoes out of the water on a berm of dry land where swamp emptied into lake. They chose this location because Tam'si believed they found Mokèlé-mbèmbé scat on the shore.

They set up the tents and Little Bob prepared the cameras, setting one up to watch the waterway slowly flowing past. He set a motion detector so that if something went past above the water level the camera would record it.

They prayed. They sang. They went to bed. Brian got some of the best sleep of his life and woke the next morning in the predawn hours, realizing it was the seventh day. They had been on the lake for a week. It was Sunday, so they decided to take the day of the Lord off. Reverend Ezekiel believed this was the day when it would happen. The tents stayed pitched and the men filled the hours and kept their eyes peeled after morning services were over.

The disappointment as the sun fell was palpable. They ate dinner in silence. Unspoken between them was the idea that they needed to return to the United States soon. The Congolese also seemed sedate. They were not saddened, but cautiously quiet.

As dinner finished they heard the sound of something moving in the forest beyond.

"Something is out there," Big Bob said. "Something big."

A dozen hands reached for guns and one for a Bible.

They heard the sound of branches cracking and something big moving through the undergrowth towards them. The earth did not quite shake, but they could tell a behemoth was approaching.

Little Bob grabbed the video camera. He quickly handed digital cameras to Wayne and Bill. "Make sure you get photos of the Reverend with the dinosaur," he instructed them. "We need him in there for size and as proof that man and dinosaur share the planet."

The others, including some of the porters, pulled out

cellphones and pointed them in the direction of the approaching creature.

Reverend Ezekiel struck a dramatic pose in front of the forest and gave the thumbs up to Little Bob, who began filming and cued the Reverend.

"Brothers and sisters," the Reverend began dramatically. "We are on the shore of Lake Tele, one of the most beautiful places in God's good creation, today doubly blessed as we are about to see Mokèlé-mbèmbé, a real dinosaur! As it says in Genesis, man and dinosaur walked the earth together. Proof is found here, in the Congo. Unbelievers, come to the Lord and admit your error. Praise the Lord! His will be done! This is it. Here is the proof that dinosaurs and man lived side by side!"

Just then, with perfect timing, the branches on the trees behind him bent forward as a large reptilian head burst through the trees.

"Brothers and sisters, I give you Mokèlé-mbèmbé!" and he turned and looked at what the Lord had sent.

It was huge, but did not look like a dinosaur. Three horns sprung from its mottled green, giraffe-like head, blood dripping from its mouth. As it opened its jaws to roar, the top half of a large male gorilla rolled out and fell next to the

Reverend. "It's at least thirty feet high," Brian thought, "so it has to be at least fifty feet long!"

It surveyed the group looking at it. In slow motion, Brian watched it dart straight ahead. He thought the body of the reptile resembled a crocodile with very long legs. "Wow. It does look like a dragon," he thought before screaming in terror.

Reverend Ezekiel held his Bible high and cried out, "Begone, you old dragon, you serpent of old, called the devil, who deceives the whole world!" The creature leapt onto him, dwarfing him both in size and power.

Before the Reverend could say another word the creature's claws penetrated his shoulder and abdomen, knocking him to the ground. The rest of the company stood there, stunned as the mighty head of the beast descended down to the Reverend's body. Ezekiel was screaming, both in pain and fear. As the head came down, Brian heard a few gurgling words which may have been a Psalm, but the beast's jaws closed around his head and shoulders, tearing. The Reverend ceased making noise.

Ninki-Nanka straightened up and began chewing, tossing part of the Reverend's torso into the air to catch it in his jaws and swallow. It ignored the rest of the party as it began to tear off and swallow the limbs off of the rest of the torso. The whole surreal event had taken less than ten seconds.

Brian looked over at the rest of the party, who stood there, shocked into speechlessness and inaction. Tears ran down Big Bob's face while Little Bob looked about to be sick. The others were all in various states of bewilderment as the head descended again and again, the ground beneath him and his meal becoming a muddy red.

As the monster gulped down the last of the Reverend Ezekiel, the Congolese opened up with the Kalashnikovs. The Americans broke and ran for the canoes, leaving all of their possessions behind.

The beast glared at the gunfire, picked up the rest of the gorilla and bound off back into the bush. After the sound of it running through the forest subsided, silence reigned.

"They found what they were looking for," said Henri Obenga.

"No," responded Jean-Baptiste. "They wanted Mokèlé-mbèmbé; they got Ninki-Nanka."

"They should have known better," added Theophile. "So should we have. Ninki-Nanka comes out at night and eats whatever lies in its path. Mokèlé-mbèmbé just eats plants and tastes of cattle."

"Let us not speak of this to anyone," said Jean-Baptiste. "Speaking of Mokèlé-mbèmbé is harmless, but to tell people you have seen Ninki-Nanka and lived is to invite death to visit you."

The others all nodded in agreement.

"Are you kidding?" laughed Tam'si, holding up his cellphone. "I know a man back in Brazzaville who will pay good money for such film and sell it to American television."

The men agreed that was a very good idea, but they would go back to Brazzaville by a different route, as they did not want to meet up with the foolish Americans, who would have to make their own way through the world, now that they had seen Ninki-Nanka, even if they thought it was Mokèlé-mbèmbé.

Gregory L. Norris

## O Christmas Tree

Gregory L. Norris

Gina handed Nick the money, two twenties, the bills laid open. "Get a nice one."

Nick folded the bills, tucked them into the right front pocket of his jeans. Like he'd intentionally pick something ugly, some spindly, skeletal dog of a Christmas tree full of gaps. He wanted to tell her to shut up, to trust his judgment, but even as the urge shuddered up Nick's throat, painful like a rush of invisible vomit, he was thinking that forty bucks in his pocket was a carton of cigarettes. Cheap ones, ones that would amount to the equivalent of smoking a dead skunk's ass. He no longer smoked for taste or enjoyment but because his cells demanded it of him, so he choked down the retort, and it was sourer than he'd expected.

"Sure, a nice one," he said, flashing a saccharine smile. "The nicest."

Since he was out of work, she paid for everything—the rent, the utilities, the food. The Christmas tree, too, the devil on his shoulder reminded. Nick snaked a hand down, scratched at the money in his pocket. His fingers walked lower, found their other target, adjusted. His genitals were still there, but Gina was in charge now. Before long, she'd be ordering him when to come and how hard.

The Christmas shopping for the kids was done, she'd proudly proclaimed, and another stab of guilt jolted through his guts. That, too, had been all Gina. Nick's lungs seized as the voice in his head reminded him of the conversation that had followed after a space of tense seconds that passed mostly in silence.

"There's only one thing I want this year," she'd said as though reading his mind. "I want you to quit smoking. It's a disgusting habit. And expensive."

She didn't mention his health in the laundry list of reasons why, and how smoking was going to land him in the ground. Her sons, she'd reminded him enough times, looked up to him more than the biological sperm donor who'd done the deed. That hadn't come up, either, in the bargain. She was in control. He'd become her property, totally dependent upon her benevolence, which she was doling out with less frequency. A nice Christmas tree. Sure.

Nick's last job had been on a new construction site in northern Cherryvale—battleship-sized McMansions going in at the periphery of a one-time tree farm whose acreage was being chopped up into significantly smaller house lots. The site shut down halfway through the construction on the first unit, the start of his spiral toward this present night, which found him driving through the early December darkness, headed north. Luckily, Nick's inner voice reminded, he had rope and a handsaw in one of the toolboxes strapped to the bed of his pickup. She'd filled his gas tank two days earlier. Forty bucks. A carton of coffin nails. He promised her he'd quit for Christmas, but Christmas was still more than three weeks away.

Tonight, he needed a smoke. And a nice Christmas tree.

The shell of the house sat dark, its vacant windows cloaked in sheets of plastic that crunched and clacked whenever the breeze gusted. Three men had died on this job site, Nick's bosses, the fine folk at Armstrong Brothers' Construction, went belly-up as a result. The new neighborhood sprouting inside the dense green thickets of the old tree farm hadn't materialized as planned and might never.

He parked the truck, shut off the engine, and pulled a flashlight and the handsaw from the toolbox. The air smelled cold and green. Nick lit one of the unsmoked cancer sticks in his chest pocket and smoked it down to the filter, aware of its foulness, its wrongness, but suffering through anyway, like this idea which seemed a bad one once it was in motion and Nick was trudging through the dark woods.

The old manor rose through a break in the tight wall of tree branches. Nick tipped a glance at the gabled roof and circle tower—the fucking house from *Psycho*. Its windows tracked his progress, like dark eyes. Farther along, dozens more watched him, the panes of a greenhouse, except where the windows were shattered, the eyes poked out.

Brittle grass crunched under Nick's old steel toed boots. He felt the ice as it cracked and shivered. Back. He should go back. Give up the cigarettes. Be happy they were afloat, living in the decent ground-floor apartment of a neat old Victorian. He'd land another job, eventually regain some of his authority, his *balls*. Give up the cancer sticks, the expense, the foul taste.

The full moon gazed down from a sky stained by charcoal-colored clouds edged in silver. The scent of balsam and pinesap thickened in concentration, drifting in the air to the point of where it was almost sickening. Suitable trees appeared beyond a farmer's wall of ancient lichen-covered boulders, the source of the hypnotic fragrance. Lots of them.

Nick aimed the flashlight and saw the nearest tree.

It was a very nice tree.

The road flashed ahead of him through the windshield, lit by his headlights. Skeletal trees and the occasional street sign appeared in the pale white glow fighting against the broken silver cast down from the moon.

Nick slammed on the brakes. Rubber bucking pavement sent him forward into the wheel and then back against his seat. He sucked in a breath, held it. His body ached for a cigarette. He tipped a glance at the rearview mirror. Thick green branches filled the bed of the truck, gilt in silver from the moon and a pop of blood red from his brake lights.

"What the *fuck?*" Nick grumbled.

His fingers gripped the steering wheel, sticky from what he assumed was pine pitch. Suddenly, he struggled to breathe, unsure of how he'd gotten from the meadow beyond the old greenhouse to his truck, a few snapshot images flashing through the void: him on his knees, sawing; ripples of movement around him, sending his heart into a gallop; sap, flowing over his fingers, thick like syrup. Like blood.

Eyes still aimed at the rearview but seeing other things

through his fractured memory, Nick blinked. Movement reflected in the mirror, shocking him back to the moment. A branch shifted in the wind, moving as though from its own power. Only the wind, he told himself.

Nick swore again and resumed the long drive home.

"What kind of tree is it?" Gina asked. Of course she did. Gina the control freak, guardian of knowledge, keeper of all power.

Rage briefly ignited, fueling the lie. "I don't remember, but the dude at the tree lot said it was from a farm in Vermont where they plant three baby trees in the spring for every one they chop down at Christmas."

The lie put a smile on her face. "That makes me very happy," she said, arms folded, eyes aimed at the towering, lush specimen bolted to their tree stand, aligned perfectly in front of the living room's two tall windows. "It smells so sweet. Almost like cedar instead of pine. Not quite."

She drew in an audible breath. Nick knew instantly that her wheels were turning, attempting to put everything in order, round pegs into round holes, square ones into square. Something other than what she'd expected, *demanded*, had entered the Realm where she ruled supreme as el Presidente and Evil Queen alike. The tree was not from the very specific brackets she'd put forth in her Christmas memo. Nick felt his face flush with guilt. He'd been found out and tried not to hate her.

"So?" the liar within asked, owning his lips. "Do you approve?"

She opened her mouth, the start to an answer. Only he couldn't remember her responding. His next conscious memory was of those lips, which he'd grown to despise, between his legs, showing him a level of respect they'd denied since he was laid off from Armstrong Brothers' Construction. The expected result launched itchy, concentric ripples through his entire body, unleashing pinpricks from his throat to his toes.

Hours later—or it could have been days, a voice in his thoughts worried—he staggered out of bed to drain his bladder. A glance at the alarm clock on Gina's side of the bed didn't help reestablish the time line. The digital numbers blurred into a smear of red color; red, like the brake lights when he'd sat behind the wheel in northern Cherryvale, staring into the rearview.

Dull aches raced up his legs and both sides of his lower back. Nick's head pulsed in concert. After great sex, which any sex these days qualified as, he expected to be sore. But the badges of honor and battle wounds in this campaign didn't match the usual destinations. He stood. Pissed. Grunted. At some point in that long, painful pose, he noticed the lights oozing across an otherwise dark apartment and slowly tipped his head toward the direction of the living room.

The Christmas tree glowed from the strings of tiny white and red lights draped around its branches. Gina's angel, a relic from her childhood, was bound to the pinnacle in a hank of thick golden ribbon. Red lights coiled around the hem of the angel's lace petticoat lent, for a moment, the image of a prisoner tied to a tree trunk and set on fire.

Nick padded out of the head, past the door to the room Daniel and Henry shared. Daniel and Henry, however, weren't in their beds. He found them sitting cross-legged on the antique hardwood floor, their eyes lost in the lights and decorations. *Decorations*—he didn't remember them decorating the tree. Clearly, they had. A platoon of clothespin soldiers with black pompons for bear fur beefeater hats were clipped to boughs, along with glass bulbs and ones made out of Styrofoam and a bunch of plastic Santas and stray ribbons Gina had collected over the years. The soldiers…like the angel, he saw something perverse in their presentation, their clothespin legs straddling branches, their nonexistent clothespin balls stolen in the figurative sense, as Gina had robbed Nick of his.

The boys didn't look up when he entered, only stared at the tree.

"Henry?" Nick croaked, his voice barely above a whisper. "*Daniel.*"

The boys glanced over, both blinking rapidly, their trances broken.

"Dad," Daniel said.

It was late. Or early. Too late or early to correct the boy or consider the pressure his statement forced on Nick's shoulders. Instead, he scooped the younger up and took the hand of the older and shepherded them into their bedroom, aware of the thick green fragrance that clung about their bodies.

As he lowered Henry into his bed, another sting flared, this time at Nick's throat. Reaching up, he found it was a pine needle, one of several sticking out of the collar of the boy's pajama shirt. Or something that looked like a pine needle.

Gina sipped her coffee. Her eyes drifted toward the living room. "Be sure that you water the Christmas tree."

"I will," Nick said.

Then she started to unroll the long laundry list of duties she expected him to perform: wipe down the kitchen, sweep and vacuum, make sure the kids ate a healthy snack after he picked them up at the bust stop. "*Healthy*," she stressed.

"I know."

"Don't spend the day in front of the idiot box. And make sure you water the tree."

He thought about calling her out on repeating herself, but figured giving her any lip as Gina was on her way out the door would delay her exit, and so he choked down the urge. Best to let this battle fade, un-won.

Instead of doing anything she expected, he sat on the sofa in the living room and stared at the tree, his head filled with foggy images. In the deep woods of Cherryvale. Sawing. Sap flowing over his fingers, *pouring* like gouts of green blood. A fine tree, yes. From a strange abandoned place.

It was after twelve noon when he realized the boys were seated on the floor, dressed in their school clothes, staring at the lights. Blinking, he saw Gina from the periphery at the opposite end of the sofa. The sweet fragrance of the Christmas tree intensified, a narcotic blend not quite pine nor balsam; at times, it took on notes of vanilla, gingerbread, and peppermint.

Oh yes, it was a fine tree.

It wasn't a tree, not in the usual sense.

The idea that he'd actually cut down something that wasn't a conifer, a fir tree, struck Nick at some point in the clouded days that followed when, from the corner of his eye, he saw its wavy green branches undulating, reaching, like underwater sea kelp moving with the tide. Only there were no waves, and yet the tree still moved, producing a musical clink as bulbs chimed together and the occasional clank as some fell, smashing on the floor. Clothespin soldiers, their balls missing and inner thighs chafed raw, jumped off branches.

Not a Christmas tree.

He remembered the list she'd left him, untold sunrises and sunsets ago. Water the tree. Nick also thought back, way back, to that construction sight in Cherryvale. Cataldo, Grolier, and Anthony J. talked about it during a cigarette break.

"Going up to that old house, seeing if there was anything valuable in there," Nick whispered aloud.

Antique architecture that could be removed and resold, like Newell posts or decorative tiles or exotic wood fireplace mantels. If not, pipes that could be copper-mined and sold to a scrap dealer. Only…

Only Cataldo, Grolier, and Anthony J. had instead taken a dirt nap up in those remote woods. Near that house. Near—

Nick blinked. They were back in bed, he and Gina. In bed, naked and perspiring. Her sweat was cloying, piney-sweet, as nauseating as arousing. The pain in his legs returned, sharp and deep, stinging him down to the marrow. He ignored it and pretended to enjoy her affection.

In the woods.

Their bodies, not found for months, were in pieces. Animals had gotten at them, that was the popular belief. Suddenly, Nick wasn't so sure that was the case. Eaten by something in the woods. But not animals.

Pain, at his leg. Nick came out of the fog long enough to realize he wasn't in bed being pleasured by Gina. Constellations of red lights and little white ones formed before his eyes. He was back in the living room, sitting in his underwear. It struck Nick that there was a good chance he'd been there all along, maybe from the moment he'd brought the Christmas tree into their home.

He reached down. Wetness flowed through the hair that covered his muscular calf. Higher…

Nick recoiled as agony seared his fingertips. A branch bristling in pine needles had attached to his flesh, just beneath the knee. He drew back, yanked his leg away. A wet sucking sound glutted around him. The branch detached. Through his revulsion, Nick saw that its tip, ringed by a corona of sharp green needles, was filled with sharper ones. Green needle teeth stained in fresh liquid red.

A scream built in his guts, powered steadily up his throat, only what finally emerged was a wheezy moan, pathetic even to his ringing ears.

Not your typical tree, Nick now knew for sure. A pitcher plant or some exotic flora that had gotten loose from that ancient greenhouse; an abomination able to adapt, to lure its victims closer with the sweetest of scents. A green chameleon capable of blending in with the surrounding green space. The summer before, he'd read a book of Greek mythology with Henry as part of a library summer program for kids. The Hydra. Maybe that's what he'd found and brought back from Cherryvale. What had found him. Then his racing thoughts accessed a bit of junk from the idiot box he watched for hours that so offended her—one of those shows on mythological beasts believed to lurk in the world, in remote rain forests and the vast, turgid lake at Loch Ness. In that moment of stark clarity, he remembered its name: *Ya-te-veo*, the Man-eating Tree. There were others, according to the show—the Nubian Tree, the Madagascar Tree, the Vampire Vine, all of them hungry for flesh, thirsty for human blood.

Christmas bulbs clinked. Branches swayed, slithered. Nick brushed the back of his wrist over his nose. Blood—that's all he smelled now. The fucking thing was feeding on him!

His energy spiked, making it easier to see the horror for what it was. Nick reached beneath the bottom branches, toward the tree stand. His only mission was to get it out of the apartment and away from the family. Only when he yanked, the tree remained rooted to the spot, anchored in place.

It had cracked the tree stand and new roots now clutched at the floor, the walls. Nick exhaled a breathless expletive. The handsaw. He'd cut the thing down once, in those woods. He'd get rid of it the same way, only this time in smaller pieces.

One of the new roots, he saw, had snaked out of the fractured tree stand and into the hardwood floor, cutting through what looked like a hillock en route. The misshapen lump drew his focus and siphoned off his resolve. Nick blinked again and for another second or two the hillock's real identity didn't register. A root, drilled through a desiccated husk.

Right before the tree lunged at his spine, Nick saw the second and third lumps, placed on the floor beside the first, and the scream finally emerged, freed and at its loudest.

## The Basin

Lauren Childs

We went down into the basin with the intention of finding a thief.

The woods here go deep. Just across the expressway the bristly carpet of pine rises in a misshapen hill, looking like something hastily shoved under a rug at the sound of a car door. But on our side the slope goes downward. Not quite a sink hole--more of a depression with a town built along the high ground, white houses perched like oyster crackers on the rim of soup bowl. We learned in science class that the land used to be shaped like a V, millions of years ago, but a glacier sunk it down into the shape it is now. There used to be houses built further down the slope, but people learned fast.

It was right at the end of the dry season, like always, that things started going missing. It was always the most exciting part of the school year. We waited for the first story to drop, a spot of rain on the blacktop. Then the second, the third, and in came the downpour. We swapped stories like trading cards. The biggest thing this year was Mrs. Goulding's television set, an old black box that still played DVD and VHS. One of the third graders heard her complaining about it in the teacher's lounge, how she always made sure to lock her door and it never made any difference. She'd had something taken six years in a row (though I think she might have made up the fourth year to maintain the record). Our parents reminded us, again, to never go downstairs if we heard something at night. We were made to promise, again, that we wouldn't be intrepid. We promised with our fingers crossed, flashlights under our pillows.

It was Lamb's idea. Lamb is my neighbor, a quarter mile down the rim, a boy but otherwise not bad. He gets picked on for his name, but he's tough--every few weeks he comes to school with bruises on his arms, or a bloody lip, from picking fights with the middle schoolers. I've never been to one of his fights, but he says they're epic and I'd faint if I saw him throw a punch. It was his idea to go into the basin, to find the stash, everything that had been stolen since before we'd been born. Since before our parents had been born.

"We'll find the thief and give him to the cops, and we'll be heroes." He said it looking down at me, standing on the top of the wall between the school and the road. The sun was at his back, and he spread his arms out like wings. The middle two fingers on his right hand were bound together with bandages. He looked like an angel.

"Or we'll find all the stuff, and we'll be rich!" I shouted back at him, laughing.

You never know how dark the woods are until you've gone down.

I lay awake in bed, my heart pounding through the feathers in my pillow, waiting until I could hear the gravel-crunch of snoring from the end of the hall. I snuck out to Lamb's house after midnight. He slammed the door behind him, and I tried to smack him on the back of the head, but he ducked. His reflexes were crazy. I always wondered how the middle schoolers managed to land a hit on him.

"You'll wake up your parents," I hissed.

He just shrugged. "They're awake."

I asked what he meant, but he didn't say anything else. I'd never met Lamb's parents, only seen the back of his father's head through the picture window, a round silhouette made by the light of the TV. The TV was on that night, too.

"How do we find the stash?" I asked, assuming that, as always, Lamb had a plan.

"We go down," He grinned, teeth shiny and blueish in the moonlight. "Until we hit the bottom."

Once or twice someone went down into the basin during the rainy season, usually kids like us, and died; they couldn't get out of the mud, or the rainwater rose too high and they got caught on a branch and went under. It didn't take much. Plenty of the trees this far down had water marks higher than my head. We weren't allowed to go into the woods after a long rain, but I'd seen pictures; swamp water coated with a thick layer of leaves and pine needles, sometimes with chipmunks and birds floating on the surface. At the rim, by the church, there was a big stone cross where they etched the names of people who'd died in the basin. There were always stuffed animals around it, even during the wet season, when they got waterlogged and moldy and swelled up like drowned corpses.

It felt like we'd been walking for an hour, but the ground was still declining steadily downward. The pines leaned on each other, clung together like velcro, blocking out the moon completely. We both carried flashlights, but Lamb hadn't turned his on yet, and I wouldn't be the first to break. I asked him questions, just to cut the silence, but his answers were all one word or less. I could barely see anything but the back of his head. He never turned, not even to glance at the woods around him. I thought we'd come to search, to hunt. But Lamb was marching in a straight line, like he was being pulled along a track.

"Why do you think it always starts this time of year?" I asked. Maybe my twentieth question.

For a minute he didn't say anything, and I thought he'd given up even on monosyllables. But then he answered.

"Maybe it hibernates the rest of the year."

I couldn't tell if he was joking; his voice was stuffy, like he had a cold. I thought he'd turn and bare his teeth at me, try to scare me. But he kept his face forward.

"Like a bear?" I said, playing along. He shrugged silently. "Then why the rainy season?"

He said something, too soft to hear.

"What?"

"Maybe it lives in the water."

I didn't ask anything else after that. I wanted to turn my flashlight on, at least to try and keep from slipping. It hadn't yet rained much this year, but what water there was all settled into the bottom of the basin. As we moved deeper, the dirt softened into slick mud. My shoes made spongey sounds in the moss, and the water had already soaked through my socks. Maybe it lives in the water. It reminded me of something, some other story we'd been told. In our town—in any town with woods, any town with a place you weren't meant to go—there were loads of scary stories that got swapped at school, at sleepovers.

There's this thing. I remembered. A girl's voice, one of my classmates, but the memory was too old—stratified under layers of others—to remember who it had been. Her voice changed every time I got close to recognizing it. There's this thing. Called a Qallupillik.

Another voice, Lamb's, one I never forgot. I remembered the word whistling as he tried to repeat it back. One of his teeth had been half chipped off, the one on the left side of his mouth between front and canine. Not a fight. He'd been sliding in his socks through his kitchen, he told us proudly, and fallen, smashing his mouth on the corner of the dishwasher. Qallupillik, he said. Sounds like a laundry detergent.

It's an Inuit story. They—

I had interrupted to ask what an Inuit was.

Like an eskimo. People that live in Alaska. We learned about them in social studies, remember?

I'd nodded, even though I didn't.

Anyway, they live in water, under the ice.

The eskimos? Lamb, grinning, blowing air through the hole in his teeth.

Shut up, let me tell it! The Qallupillik. They live underwater and steal little kids. You hear them knocking on the bottom of the ice... knock, knock...

She'd rapped her fist slowly on the top of her desk. Lamb had shot me a look, rolling his eyes. We both knew where this was headed. I barely flinched when she jumped up and grabbed my leg.

Right before they surface!

It wasn't an especially scary story. Even in the winter, we barely got snow, let alone ice. It was just another name for the same bogeyman, the same monster translated to another place, another language. None of them relevant. They all stole kids, not lamps and books and TV sets. Still, anything can be creepy when you're thinking about in the pitch dark, with home a mile behind you, a mile over your head.

I didn't realize Lamb had stopped until I bumped into him, hitting my nose on the back of his head. I stumbled back, almost tripping over an exposed root.

"We're here," he said. No excitement. Just certainty.

I fumbled with my flashlight as Lamb moved forward, into an opening between two trees. "Wait," I said, my voice a little higher than intended. I couldn't find the switch on my light. I could no longer see the back of Lamb's head. "Lamb! Wait up!"

# The Basin

My fingers finally found the groove near the bottom of the flashlight handle. I switched it on and shined the light between the trees; the beam shook in my trembling hands, bouncing off the trunks, their bark peeling away from years of water damage. I finally managed to center the flashlight. The first thing I saw almost made me drop it.

A huge, black eye, reflective and shiny like the eye of a fish. I seized up in place.

No. Not an eye. A screen.

The TV set was half sunk into the slimy mud, it's cord coiled beside it like a garter snake. I let out a shaky breath, heartbeat thumping in my ears. I cautiously moved the beam around, stepping into the doorway made by the two pines. A wicker rocking chair piled with magazines, half of them soaked into one another like paper mache, colored ink bleeding down through the stack. Yellowing porcelain plates, scattered. Glass that had turned green and foggy with grime. A warped wooden dresser. I could see that the piles of things went back, disappearing past the throw of my flashlight. It was like a huge storage room, a basement that had flooded.

The beam slid across a face, and I let out a little shriek, moving the light around erratically until I found it again. Just Lamb. He was sitting atop an ottoman, half of it ripped open, stuffing bleeding from between silk cross-stitch like gray matter from a cracked-in skull. His eyes were half open, like he was drowsy. For a moment I couldn't say a word. All the bruises I'd ever seen on him, yellow and black, rings around his eyes and red burn-welts on his inner arm, seemed to be there all at once. It was like someone had laid them all down, double and triple exposures of the same picture.

He looked right at home, there among the stolen things.

I realized I was shaking. I wanted to say something to him. I wanted to say that this, all of this, was never what was meant to be stolen. I don't know what made me realize—the dates on the stone cross, how short the time was between birth and death, or how the basin had been formed, or why we learned about the things we did in school. I don't know what made me realize. I just knew.

"Lamb," I said, voice weak.

"Thanks for coming with me."

I blinked back tears, not knowing why I was crying. I wouldn't know until much later. "Lamb. It's bait. It's—"

"Thanks," He said again. He sounded so tired. "You should run."

My flashlight shuddered, blinking off. When the light was gone, there was another shape, another silhouette. Not yet close, but big. The light came on and it was gone.

"Lamb," I said, one more time. "You can't stay down here."

He'd closed his eyes completely. He lifted his hand, the one with his broken fingers, and pointed up. "Better than up there."

The light flickered. The shape—just barely humanoid, but too tall, head too long, shoulders too low. Closer. The size of a tree.

I ran.

## The *Anna Doria*

### Ellen Denton

"Cap'n, Is something wrong? You look like you've seen a ghost."

It was something far more unworldly than a ghost that Captain Jay Michael Roberts thought he saw, but he would not for all the world have told the bosun that. He glanced at him - his name was Thomas - then looked back at the gently rolling sea. For the third time, he raised his binoculars, was about to look through them once more, but let them drop back onto his chest.

"Nothing Thomas. I was just lost in thought." He turned to the Bosun again, who was eyeing him up with a vaguely puzzled expression. "Well, go on. What are you standing there for? Get back to work."

"Aye Sir!"

Thomas turned and sprinted off to check on some repairs being done amidships. Roberts placed his hands on the rail and squinted at the horizon. It was as flat and featureless as the bright, periwinkle sky.

He thought that what he had seen there five minutes before must have been due to being too short on sleep and too cooked on the rum he'd imbibed at lunch. After going down to his cabin, he dropped onto the bed without even bothering to pull off his soiled deck boots.

He was snoring within minutes.

If that had been all that occurred, the entire incident would have been forgotten - chalked up to an exhaustion-spawned illusion, or even to some freak, passing cloud formation with the sun glowing red in the double rifts at its center. He would have been content to think that the grinning devil's face, tall as a lighthouse, and seemingly hewn out of gray smoke and fire on the horizon, was nothing more than that. There was no real harm in his not mentioning it to anyone, nor at first, was there any consequence to his not reporting some of the other things he'd seen. He continued to execute his command in a way that was beyond reproach. A fatal error and pivotal moment occurred when he thought he saw, but did not tell anyone, about the Kraken. Had he done so, it probably would have prevented the subsequent death of his crew. Those not burned when fire engulfed the ship, drowned in the freezing winter seas.

By the time he saw the mythical sea monster rising up port side, reaching its monstrous tentacles toward him, it was one of many hallucinations he'd had over the previous weeks. Not long after the initial visions and voices started, he realized he was losing his mind and hid this, even from his own brother, the first mate.

Wondering why an insane person had and kept secrets upon which spun a coin of life and death, is about as useful as asking a serial killer to provide a good reason for murdering ten children. This report does not question or delve into why Roberts, fully aware of his deteriorating mental state, did not turn over his command, and ultimately led his crew into disaster; it only gives a summation of the events leading up to it.

As we now know, he kept a secret journal in which he recorded those things of which he would not speak. This he kept in a padlocked, waterproof box, and when not writing in it, kept the box hidden between his mattress and the wooden slats of his bed. He felt it vital to maintain the protective safeguards around the book at all times. He had a premonition of what was to come and wanted to ensure a record remained that would stand up to tides and time.

Indeed, it was through the disjointed and feverish writings in that secret diary, recently recovered from the wreck by salvage divers, that I was able to piece together the story of what happened to the *Anna Doria*.

The complete journal, appendices, index, salvage inventory list, corroborative reports, and final summary are attached to this preface, which I here provide as a broad overview that touches on some of the key points.

> **Entry of May 2nd:**
> *I've given the order that no one is to go off duty or sleep until every square inch of this ship is inspected and brought into peak operating condition, down to the last cotter pin, trunnel, sheave, and bitt. Every deck is to be swabbed and swabbed again, and if needed, swabbed yet again. I'm having every signal flag unfurled and mended of any tears, any loose threads snipped off, and their individual wooden cubbies painted clearly with their respective letters. I'm even having the treads on the rubber soles of everyone's shoes examined.*
>
> *The* Anna Doria *has always been a seakindly vessel, and*
>
> *I intend to save her at all costs. I know the crew is secretly grumbling over the extra work and even my senior officers are starting to privately question my actions. Yesterday, I came upon the second mate and chief engineer standing by the binnacle, whispering and gesturing to each other. I saw the guilty looks on their faces when they saw me. I know they were talking about me.*

By the time Robert's made the above entry, the

unraveling of his mental faculties was starting to escalate; he failed to any longer be cognizant of his own declining condition and had also become obsessive about small and relatively insignificant things.

Compare, for instance, an earlier journal entry from April 18$^{th}$ with the above, later one, from May 2$^{nd}$ and then one from May 6$^{th}$. It can be seen from these that Roberts was in a dangerously unwell state, and that this was getting rapidly and progressively worse.

> ***Entry of April 18$^{th}$***
> *I saw a mermaid today. She rose up out of the ocean and stood alee, balanced on her tail. She sparkled like an emerald in the offing at the far end of a path of burnished gold, made on the water by the setting sun, and seemed the most beautiful thing I have ever laid eyes on. She sang to me in a haunting voice, which plainly, no one else could hear.*
> *There is no question for me anymore. I am slowly going mad. I no doubt suffer from a brain fever and fear I will soon be like a distempered dog, slobbering and running in circles. Perhaps a period of prolonged bed rest may cure the matter, along with some of my other maladies, but no. There is no time in a captain's life for such idleness. I will soldier on through it.*

It's evident from this entry that he was fully aware the mermaid was an hallucination and was doing his best to carry on with his duties and responsibilities.

The aforementioned entry of May 2nd shows him beginning to display questionable behavior that others were apparently starting to notice.

Then, some days after the mermaid sighting, there is this:

***Entry of May 6th***
*These fools! Are they blind? I was at mess when I saw the unthinkable. One of the saltcellars had white specks encrusted onto its lid. I ordered every last shaker emptied and cleaned at once in boiling water, along with the surfaces of every can, container, box, and bottle in galley stores to be scrubbed with lye and steel brushes.*

The entry continues on with a rambling account in which Roberts speaks of later racing down a passageway, stopping every few yards to stomp on rat-sized, black spiders he thought were skittering around on the floor. He then relays clubbing a deckhand on the head, because after he ordered him to swab up the bloody remains of what he thought were now dead, crushed arachnids, the puzzled sailor said he didn't see anything dead or alive on the floor "'cept you and I standing here captain.'

His writings for that day conclude with an account of looking in his shaving glass and seeing a quartet of devils swirling around behind him wagging foot-long, black tongues. He cracked the mirror into shards by smashing it with his water basin.

In this later entry of the 6th, he no longer shows any apparent recognition or suspicion that these apparitions existed solely in the hinterlands of his imagination.

As covered elsewhere in this report, the make-break point for Roberts on this appears to be when he saw the Kraken.

Prior to that, the unearthly visions he saw looming on the horizon were really no more or less than what has gone before. Sea-faring history abounds with sailor's tales of mermaid and sea monster sightings. Little harm has ever come from such, and if nothing else, they made for good banter in the dockside taverns, or in a seaman's later years, were colorful stories told from rocking chairs to wide-eyed grandchildren on their knees. Even the face of a devil in the distance was no more than an unsettling, but passing illusion for one with a superstitious mind.

Roberts was well aware of this, but after he could no longer explain away, what had become for him, almost daily, recurring visions as merely an effect of exhaustion, weather anomalies, or the generous quantities of rum he consumed with almost every meal, he began to write extensively about his concern over his mental state. He was clearly keeping this a secret, while attempting to carry on with his command, but there was nothing even hinting that he considered the things he saw were real.

What changed when he saw the Kraken, which he records on April 28th, is that it was not viewed as a self-generated apparition, and recognized as such, by a sad and secretive soul who had become resigned to the fact that he was slowly going mad. Roberts thought the beast was actually attacking the ship.

He describes, in quite explicit detail, a horrific thunder and lightening storm, and a creature, wider and taller than the ship itself, encircling it with tentacles until the vessel was half seas over and starting to break deep. Then, in a trice, the creature was gone, the sun was shining brightly, and the crew members working on deck were going about their business as though nothing had happened. Some sailors, now off watch, were shooting dice, while others laughed and whooped from the rigging as they skylarked in the light of an unseasonably warm, bright winter day at sea.

Every entry from that point on showed abundant evidence that Roberts truly believed that both he and the ship were under a concerted assault by evil, unworldly creatures and in deadly peril. It was also the point when he began to entertain the idea that his own crew was in league with the devil, and preparing to steer the ship into hell.

Compare, for instance, his first sighting of the mermaid, which he chronicled in the April 18th entry, with this one:

> **Entry of May 8th**
> *I saw the mermaid again today. As always, she was quite beautiful as she rose up in the distance, emblazoned against the backdrop of a setting sun. I gazed at her with loneliness and longing, until she blew apart and scattered like a thousand sea birds into the wind. I turned my gaze away with quite a feeling of sadness, then heard a sing-song voice that carried and called to me in the breeze. When I looked again at the water, she was this time only mere yards from the ship, gliding in pace with it, her green and gold hair flowing the length of her body in the rippling water behind her.*
>
> *She sang and called to me, so I hoisted myself up on the railing. She reached out her arms, and I would have leapt off the ship then and there, and in fact tilted my whole body forward to do so, but at the last moment, I saw that she was not a sea nymph, but a gorgon, with live snakes growing out of her head and writhing repulsively around her face. She stretched her mouth open so widely, I could no longer see her face, only a grill of needle sharp fangs long as a Bengal Tiger's. She then snapped her horrible jaws shut, her red eyes glowed with a chilling malevolence, and she reached out her arms to me once again. I pushed myself backwards as hard as I could and dropped once again to the safety of the deck.*

From here, things decline at a frightening rate.

On May 10th, he writes a long, jumbled entry about seeing thousands of beslimed leeches and beetles slithering up and down the bulkhead walls in the stokehold, seeing a pack of rabid dogs, with bloody saliva foaming out of their mouths, spinning in circles on the quarterdeck, and finally, approaching the helmsman, Rolly, (who is described in earlier entries as a cheerful, carrot-topped eighteen year old), who, while still facing front and holding the wheel, spun his head round and round 360 degrees, revealing a grimacing devils face on one side and a grinning hyena's on the other. He concludes by describing how his brother Jake approached. Roberts was greatly relieved to see his own kin, but states that as Jake came abreast, his entire head morphed into that of a snarling jackal's.

There is then another, later entry on the 10th wherein Roberts again states his belief that his crew and officers were in a secret conspiracy against him, and that there was a plan afoot to turn the ship over to the devil.

As you will see from the journal itself, the several entries following this were so muddled and deranged that it's hard to determine just what did happen on those days beyond that Roberts had obviously descended into a heavily disoriented state. Some of the writing is illegible, just a scribble of tangled lines and half formed letters. All of it conveys a sense of great confusion and turmoil.

From bits and pieces of somewhat cohesive sentences, really mere fragments at this point, it's clear Roberts was no longer able to conceal his maddened condition. There are mentions of him screaming, while being chased around the ship by creatures of every stripe and hue, and of his own officers "speaking with forked tongues" and turning into animals, raptors, and bugs, as they try to comfort him, reason with him, and eventually restrain him. These entries are as dark and chaotic as the events themselves must have been.

While we'll never know the full details of what did actually occur on the night the *Anna Doria* sank, Roberts' final journal entry, rather than sounding like the heated rambling of an unhinged madman, was ironically as clear, cold, and concise as the zing of a Samurai's sword. He had managed to barricade himself in his cabin, and penned a calm, chilling epilogue about what he intended to do to save his ship from sailing into what he thought was eternal damnation. From his last recorded words, we can envision what may have happened in those final hours.

"Cap'n?" Thomas held his distance as he peered at

Captain Jay Michael Roberts, who had just ascended onto the deck, and now stood spectral and silent in the dark against the backdrop of a moonless night.

"Stay right there Cap'n." The bosun turned and started to run off. He needed to alert the watch-crew that Roberts was there. He had only a fleeting thought about where the two sailors were who were supposed to be on watch outside Roberts' cabin door, because before he'd taken even five steps, he pitched forward and slammed down onto the deck, felled by a bullet to the back of the head.

Within moments, Roberts came up behind an unsuspecting Rolly in the wheelhouse and fired into his heart when the helmsman, wide-eyed and open-mouthed, turned to face him. There was a pounding of footsteps as both crew and officers converged on the area the gunshots had come from, but by the time they got there, Roberts was gone.

Moving with machine-like grim resolve, emptying one gun and pulling out another from the waistband of his trousers, Roberts summarily shot any crew members in his path, leaving blood and brains splashed across bulkhead walls, as he made his way to the lowest deck. Once there, he pulled out from his shirt, ignited, and dropped, one oil-soaked rag after another as he ran from stern to bow. He climbed up to the next deck and sped from compartment to compartment, doing the same there. The explosions of fire from the volatile oil blew upwards and spread so quickly, he himself never made it back topside to the surface of the ship.

With the powerful accelerant Roberts distributed at preplanned, strategic points on the vessel, it's doubtful it took even half an hour for fire to turn the ship into a blackened skeleton of wood. Had there been anyone nearby to hear it, the howling wails of the burning, and the whispered prayers of the freezing and drowning, would have indeed sounded like the damned descending into hell.

What I believe to be the real tragedy concerning the *Anna Doria* is that if seamen knew what we knew today, Roberts' so called "insanity", or at least the most drastic aspects of it, could likely have been handled in a matter of days, possibly even hours. Please see the attached, corroborative reports from the two medical experts I consulted as part of the compilation of this one.

From information Roberts himself provides in the earliest part of his journal concerning long-term, badly depleted galley stores of meat, poultry, and cheese, his refusal to eat fish due to an extreme dislike for the taste, the physical symptoms he experienced preceding the onset of his mental decline (bouts of fatigue, falls following a loss of balance, tingling and numbness in his arms and legs), and other related entries all indicate that his condition was no more or less than a severe vitamin B-12 deficiency. Even to this day, such a dearth often goes undiagnosed and masquerades as other ailments and mental derangements. It certainly wouldn't have been unusual in his time, especially on a long sea journey, where vital food stores could not be easily replenished.

As Doctor Ringler, one of the consulting medical experts observed, Roberts' mentions of worsening balance and muscle coordination issues, were in themselves, quite symptomatic of truncal ataxia (more colloquially known as "drunken sailor" gait), and sensory ataxia, a condition now well known to be induced by a severe B-12 deficiency.

It was also clear, from various journal entries, that Roberts drank copious amounts of rum on a daily basis. Excessive alcohol use can bring on a B-12 deficiency, and in his case, with the extreme lack of proper dietary safeguards in place, the rum, if nothing else, would have greatly exacerbated the condition. It's not surprising, in light of this medical data, that he eventually descended to the psychosis often present at the nethermost reaches of such a nutritional deficit.

"Dr. Ringler, more wine?"

"Yes, please. Thank you."

"I appreciate your accepting my dinner invitation. I wanted to personally thank you for collaborating in my research about the *Anna Doria*."

"It was my pleasure. Being a sailing enthusiast myself, I've always had a strong interest in historical, seafaring events. I enjoyed the opportunity to bring my medical expertise into play in regards to this one."

"It was quite satisfying for me too, with the help of specialists such as yourself, to unravel what occurred that resulted in the demise of the ship. I can't help but feel a bit sad though, when I think about the loss of that noble vessel, and all the souls aboard, to such a horrible death. Really, like something out of a nightmare, wouldn't you say?

Dr. Ringler took another sip of his wine and looked at the glass appreciatively for a moment.

"Yes, especially when there was, basically, nothing much

wrong with Roberts that a few good good T-bone steaks wouldn't have cured.

By the way, was there ever anything Roberts mentioned in his journal about that strange green and gold hair-like substance that was found between two of the pages?

"No, but I have both a biologist and an oceanographer working on it. For the life of me, I can't imagine what's taking them so long to figure out what that is."

## The Ghost Tree

Sharon Diane King

Emmaline said I should never tell about this because nobody would believe it and people might make fun of her. But I haven't paid her much heed since she went and blabbed to MaryEllen Fulksville about the strawberry mark in the small of my back. Now the kids at school call me Strawberry Jammie, and it puts me out.

It was a year ago, the first of May. It was already getting steamy in the afternoons, and the dogwood blossoms were starting to droop. Mom had finally given in and was letting me go on my first ever outdoor sleepover, for Emmaline's twelfth birthday. Her folks had a big place in the mountains almost a mile off the main road. It was an old farmhouse set back a ways in the trees, old oaks and hickory and sweet-smelling red cedar. I liked the cedars best because I could always see faces in the trunks, some ugly, some funny. Emmaline said there was a story about the cedars, that they held the spirits of dead people and would protect you. I don't know. They sure smelled better than most dead things I've ever come across.

Emmaline's party started out pretty lame. She was already dressed in a sparkly purple Mean Queen dress when mom dropped me off, so we couldn't go outside to swing on the swings or explore the yard. She and I and her two sisters ended up having cereal and milk and playing silly video games like *Worrywarts: Academy for Girls* for a couple of hours. It was hard to talk, though, because her dad kept yelling at the TV while he watched the game in the next room. Then her aunts and uncles and cousins arrived and Emmaline dived right into her pile of gifts. She about swooned over the Apple Pandowdy doll somebody got her—not me—and was all in a tizzy at the tiara and bracelet set her parents gave her. At least she seemed to like the Hootie Owl hoodie I had picked out, with Mom's help. She probably would have preferred it covered in rhinestones, but oh well.

Things perked up a little while they were setting out lunch. One of Emmaline's cousins, a tall skinny older kid named Petey, kept getting into into one dust-up after another. Most folks I know tend to settle down if you slide enough buffalo wings and potato salad their way. Not Petey. He had a funny laugh that grew lower and fainter as it went on, like it was skittering away from you, and he laughed a lot. I noticed he found a way or two to tap into the keg they had out back, and I think he also helped himself to the whiskey bottle Emmaline's dad kept in their cherrywood cabinet. At one point I heard a lot of doors slamming, yelling and cussing going on upstairs, and later a fat bearded guy was chasing Petey around the yard, hollering about some missing DVD's. It was all a lot more interesting—and real--than the *I Didn't Know I Was Stupid* show Emmaline's aunts were crowded around the TV to watch, that's for sure.

After lunch we all filed into the dining room. Emmaline's older sister and cousins had put together a funny video with Emmaline's face stuck onto a whole bunch of famous pictures, and we watched it on their big flatscreen. I especially liked that swirly weird one, *The Scream,* with Emmaline making one of her trademark fish faces. The harder we laughed, though, the more Emmaline got quiet and her face all scrunched up. Her mom hurried through the last slides. While the lights were still dim they brought out a huge pink sheet cake from Lie-Low (that's what Emmaline's dad kept calling the big box) and we sang and Emmaline blew out the candles. All the family crowded ahead of me and came away with big hunks of cake. I was handed a dinky piece without roses or writing, and barely a spoonful of ice cream. I set my plate down and snuck into the kitchen, where I slid a couple of chocolate bars in my vest pockets before heading to the restroom. When I got back I somehow ended up seated right next to Petey. He'd simmered down a little, as if the starch had been walloped out of him, and his pale blue eyes hardly looked up from his plate while he ate his slice of cake. For all that, he laughed his skitter-laugh a couple times at something I said, and he kept kicking my shins with his steel-toed boots under the table until I had three big black-and-blue marks.

That night things got even better. After Emmaline's relatives left, the four of us girls got to take our sleeping bags way out past the old barn to a little clearing in the trees. We made a fire in the stone pit, and her dad filled our plates with smoky ribs and chicken drumsticks dripping with barbecue sauce, and told us scary story after scary story. We loved the one about the Hook Man who left his metal hand swinging on the lovers' car door, and the drivers who kept hitting the Phantom Lady running across the road at night, only never to find her body when they went back. As we crunched through melty s'mores we whispered "Bloody Bones" over and over, relishing the tale of the skinless man who lived under the stairs, shivering as if Jack Frost himself had run his chill finger down our spines.

But my favorite was the one about the Ghost Tree. I'd never heard it before. Emmaline's dad told us that there was a bogey that would come after people sleeping outside in the woods just at dead of night. It especially liked children who didn't obey their parents and teachers. He said it could pull you right out of your shoes or out from your blankets, and we hugged our sleeping bags around us a little tighter. The ghost tree's branches would sweep this way and that in the wind, and if it found someone especially bad, it would catch hold of that person and carry them away. No one would ever hear from them again.

"What makes it take people?" I heard myself asking. Emmaline's dad nodded at me. "Nobody really knows. Some say it's revenge. An Indian father whose children were slaughtered by white men died of grief, and his spirit went into the trees seeking shelter. No one tree would hold such an angry spirit, so his ghost moves from tree to tree. It can never find rest, and it can never get enough of others' children to take away the agony over losing its own."

"What does the Ghost Tree do with the bad children?" Emmaline's littlest sister Sarah asked, her eyes wide in the flickering light of the fire. Her dad shook his head.

"Don't know. Eats 'em, maybe, swallows 'em whole. No one's ever found anything but teeth, maybe a bone or two, but we couldn't be sure they weren't from an animal."

He looked around the fire at all of us and grinned. "Well, it's late. Time to go to sleep!"

"Aw, Daddy—" Emmaline began, but he turned to her and pointed a finger. "You going to disobey me?"

We all lay down flat.

We giggled a little as we tossed and turned on the tarp-covered ground, swatting at mosquitoes and trying to get comfortable. We didn't chatter much, though. We didn't any of us want to tempt the Ghost Tree. It was cold and clear, and the stars and half a moon were out. Emmaline's dad threw some dirt on the fire, but left a lantern lit near us and wished us sweet dreams before he went back inside.

I don't know exactly when I drifted off. The last thing I remember was hearing an owl hooting, maybe two, high up in the trees.

I must have been dreaming for a while before the images took shape in my mind. I was running away from something big and faceless that screeched out my name. I ran fast and left it far behind me. I found myself deep in the woods, in a little clearing, and I stopped to catch my breath. All around me were tall craggy oaks, slender white aspens, flouncy-leaved maples, big sycamores with their jigsaw-puzzle bark. As I looked up, I saw they had faces--twisted, contorted, chilling faces. They were staring at me, their glares cutting through my skin. Their branches waved wildly, as if in a high wind, and the features in the trunks shifted and altered to form their clotted words. I couldn't understand a one. Finally the biggest of their number, a stately cedar tree, its green fronds studded with ice-blue berries, intoned something at a depthless pitch, like the lowest pedal of a church organ. I could barely hear it, though I could feel the vibrations in my bones. But it was plain the rest heard. They went silent, all of them, their faces shriveling back deep into the bark. Some decision had been made, for good or ill.

 I awoke to hear a shriek, almost in my ear. My eyes fluttered open. In the moonlight the branches reached over my head like eager claws. I sat up with a jerk and saw Emmaline, lying just to the right of me, screaming and thrashing as her sleeping bag was slowly dragged backwards towards the woods. Her sisters were yelling that it was the Ghost Tree. I lunged for Emmaline's hand but missed and watched in horror as a huge black shapeless thing that was pulling the bag...

... started laughing hysterically and let it go. The thing rose up, took off something big—it looked like a dark sheet-- and shone a flashlight briefly upward, showing us a grimacing face. Then it dropped the flashlight and rolled on the ground, laughing as if it could not stop.

It was Emmaline's dad.

Despite the cold, we all jumped out of our sleeping bags to beat on him in turn. Emmaline's mom, who had been filming the whole thing from a distance on a night-vision camera, finally stepped in and got him out of there, bribing us with the promise of homemade pecan pancakes in the morning. With extra butter and syrup.

We lay in the darkness whispering for a long time after that. We passed around leftover graham crackers while Emmaline and her older sister, Carol, went back and forth about which practical joke had been the best her dad had ever played. We decided it was a tossup between this trick and the one where he'd made up a product called No-Nest, something you sprinkled around to keep birds from nesting where you didn't want them to. He'd convinced Emmaline's mom that Wal-Mart sold it. She was pretty ticked off when she went there and nobody knew anything about it. Accused them of lying, hoarding, really read them the riot act. Carol and Emmaline had been in on the joke and couldn't keep a straight face. The story was so funny it kinda made me wish my dad were at home, too, but he had never been anything like Emmaline's.

It took a long while before we could fall back asleep. If I dreamed again, I don't remember it.

Screams once again jerked me awake. Lots of screams. Low and long enough to curdle the blood, seeming to come from deep in the woods.

*Here we go again,* I thought, and sat up feeling grumpy. A joke was a joke, but this wasn't funny any more. It was cold and misty, and I couldn't really see much; the lantern had gone out somehow, and a cloud had drifted in front of the moon. The horrible cries went on, mingled with pleas for help, with some swear words mixed in. *Something's wrong*, I thought, and swallowed hard. *Emmaline's dad never swore like that, even at the TV.* In the darkness I heard Sarah whimper. Emmaline tried to stand up but must have tripped over her sleeping bag; there was a thud, and then sobbing. Carol, next to her, began shrieking. I took a quick breath.

*The screams weren't ours.*

We started scrambling all over, throwing off our sleeping bags, trying to find our shoes. I guess we were screaming ourselves by then. A light went on in the big house, and Emmaline's dad and mom came racing out towards us.

"What's wrong? Are you OK?"

"Emmaline fell down," I answered, grabbing Sarah, who was trembling and silent next to me. My voice sounded weak and sick. Carol had finally found her flashlight and with shaking hands shone it all around us.

No one was there. Nothing but the trees.

We stumbled inside the house with Emmaline's folks, babbling our tale. It turned out they hadn't heard anything but our yells, which had woken them up. They wiped away our tears and sat us down. Emmaline's mom made toast and hot cocoa, while her dad put ice on Emmaline's forehead, where she had a nasty bump, and stopped her nosebleed. They called the police, too, but no one came. Her mom said they weren't likely to come out for a bunch of kids making up campfire stories to scare each other.

For a long time we lay with our teeth chattering on the warm beds they made for us on sofa cushions in the living room. Nobody wanted to be put in separate rooms. I must have drifted off, though, because Emmaline and Carol said I talked gibberish in my sleep, words they couldn't understand. And I cried out really loud at one point, waking myself and everybody else up in the process. Emmaline's parents weren't too happy about that.

    I don't remember talking, but I do remember yelling. I didn't tell anyone why. In my dream I was back in the woods, and the moonlight was bright; I could see almost as well as in the day. This time it wasn't me being chased. Instead I stood watching as somebody tall and skinny ran past me, screaming for all he was worth. I never caught sight of his face. As I watched, the high branches of a tall tree, an old oak maybe, reached down, grabbed him, and hoisted him in the air, still shrieking. He struggled hard; I heard twigs snap as the tree held him fast. Then the biggest of the branches caught his legs and ripped them off, one by one. I heard two separate thuds as they hit the ground. The second one fell at my feet. It had jeans on it with dark streaking stains, and a ratty white sock; I remember seeing a hole in the toe. Then the screams stopped. Something dripped down from the tiny leaves on the tree, hitting my face. It sounded like rain, but it wasn't cold like raindrops. I knew what it was--

    --and then Emmaline's mother was shaking my shoulder.

    We didn't say a word about what had happened near the

fire pit the next morning. We pushed the pancakes around on our plates—nobody had much appetite—while the sisters trash-talked our principal Ms. Appleton, who had her convertible repo'd right out of the school parking lot, and poor deaf old Mrs. Pyle, who had taught our sixth grade class and was retiring about a thousand years too late. I tried to smile at their words but my insides were churning. Then Emmaline started talking about the camp her parents were sending her to that summer, somewhere up north. From the way she bragged, it sounded like the log cabins had everything from hot tubs to maid service. I tried not to listen. The last thing I wanted to think about was staying in the woods overnight again, even if the bunk bed had thousand-count sheets and a mint on the pillow. I was glad when Mom showed up early to take me home.

And if she wondered why both my vest pockets were lined with melted chocolate bars, she never said anything.

On Monday, at school, word got around the playground that one of the boys at the high school, Petey Waite, had disappeared. Those who hated him said he'd been blown up in a meth lab explosion, those who liked him said he'd finally up and run away from home. He was always in trouble for one thing or another, I guess, stealing money or smoking weed or mouthing off to any grownup he didn't take a shine to. His mom, Emmaline's Aunt Britney, had kicked him out that night, right after the birthday party. For the gazillionth time. Petey'd put up a little tent underneath the trees behind their house to stay in, maybe a couple of miles from where we'd been sleeping that night. His mom had pulled late shift at the Quincee's and hadn't missed him until the next day.

When they went to look for him, they say, the tent was still there. So were his pillows and sleeping bag. And his steel-toed boots.

The bruises on my shin took a long time to fade away.

The leaden weight in the pit of my stomach is with me yet.

## The Orphan and the Whale

KA Masters

When entering the Charleston Museum, the first thing that you will encounter is the skeleton of a giant whale. It dangles from the ceiling menacingly. As you ascend the main staircase to visit the exhibits upstairs, you pass through the shadow of its mouth, through the menacing phalanges of its flippers, and through the shattered remains of its caudal vertebrae

The sign on the stairwell provides a description and a black-and-white photograph. Its garish details are softened by the grainy quality of the image, but one can clearly see onlookers posing over the dead thing in triumphant exultation.

The text states that in 1880, this thirty-five foot whale became lost in the Charleston Harbor, and after disrupting the shipping lanes with its presence, it was finally hunted down by dozens of citizens in rowboats. The corpse was put on display until interest dwindled, and it was promptly processed for oil. Its skeleton was donated to the local museum to remind townsfolk of the miraculous event.

But few know the full tale. For this is not a story of natural history, but unnatural terror. The banal paragraph describing the demise of the wayward whale veils over the casualties that it left in its wake. This is the true story of the Charleston Whale, who came not as a redemptive Jonah but as a menacing kraken…

"A whale cannot be rabid," Tristan Flaubert declared, slamming his fist on the table in emphasis. The impact rattled the teacups, and made the waif watching them jump in fear.

"Clearly, it can," his friend Albert declared calmly. "Did you see the way it charged that fishing boat? It rammed the poor sloop, then slammed it underwater? And then—what it did to those poor fishermen?"

"But it's a baleen whale. They feed on shrimp. This is no toothed monster, Al. This isn't like Moby Dick. Baleen whales are docile. Like a cow, or a sheep."

"Cows can go rabid," Albert contradicted him. "Remember your Aunt Jenny's farm? They shot six bullets into it before they took it down. And it trampled half a dozen calves and two dogs in the meantime."

"Yeah, but it had been attacked by a rabid raccoon," Tristan replied, taking a sip of his coffee to counteract the January cold, "How is a whale going to be infected?"

Albert shrugged, working out his hypothesis aloud. "Maybe a rat—jumped ship? There was that ghost ship they found off coast six weeks ago, with the crew murdered and chopped up. Maybe they went rabid, and killed each other? And the rats jumped ship, and spread the infection?"

Tristan dismissed the suggestion. "Firstly, the 'ghost ship' wasn't off our coast. It was off of Nova Scotia—half a continent's length away. And that supposes the whale went south. Everyone knows that they migrate north this time of year. Besides—how is the rat going to make contact with our whale? Will the damned thing crawl into its blowhole?"

"It probably ate the darned thing, thinking it was a school of fish…"

"Baleen whales eat krill, not fish. You're thinking of a sperm whale, not a bowhead."

"Well, what do you think has happened?"

"Damned if I know," Tristan grimaced. "But if we're the ones to capture it tonight, we'll be several hundred dollars richer."

"Tonight! Who says anything about capturing it tonight? The newspapers say…"

"The newspapers be damned," Tristan spat hotly. "Everyone's going to hunt the thing tomorrow. If we go hunting tonight, we can bypass the competition."

"Yes, but we need a plan. And we don't have one yet."

The waif returned, refreshing their coffee and removing their breakfast plates.

"What do you think it is? This whale business?" Albert asked her.

The child timidly looked down, shaking her head nervously.

"Hessie, don't be shy around Mister Flaubert. His mouth is detestable, but he's got a sweet heart under all of that sailor talk. Go on," he encouraged her, "tell us."

She looked up at him with eyes full of adoration. "Pastor Robbins says that it's the tale of Jonah come to pass. That Charleston has become Ninevah, and we must repent our sinful ways."

Tristan snickered.

"Jonah was trying to escape the Lord's plan for him, and got on a boat, but there was a big storm. The sailors cast lots to see who was responsible…"

"Casting lots?" Tristan laughed. "Oh, they cast lots. Let's see what casting lots can do." He rose from their breakfast table to enter the Norris' home, heading for the study.

"Don't mind him, Hessie. He's an atheist," Albert whispered in mock fear.

Hessie's eyes widened in surprise. "Why are you friends with such a man?"

"He was my roommate at university, and my dearest friend. Don't worry, he'll grow on you."

Tristan returned a moment later with a dusty old book. Placing it in the girl's hands, he said, "Here. Let's cast lots. Pick a passage, and God will direct our path."

She fingered through the book, noting, "This book doesn't have columns like the Bible I see at church."

"It doesn't matter. Pick," he commanded her.

Hessie opened the book and nervously spoke, "nam memini Hesionae visentem regna sororis. What Bible verse is this?"

"It's from the Aeneid, sweetie. Just nonsense that means nothing," Tristan laughed.

" 'The kingdom of Hesione'?" Albert noticed, alert. "Hessie, can you return this to my bookshelf?"

"Yes, sir," she spoke, and timidly withdrew from the table.

When she was out of sight, Tristan accused, "Of course the dumb tart would pick a line that has her name in it."

"She doesn't know Latin, Tris," Albert countered.

"She loves you, you know."

"I know," he grimaced.

"She has to figure it out soon—she looks just like you, but dipped in cocoa. Why don't you just tell her?"

"Tell her that she's one of my father's bastards? Are you mad? Then she'll ask for a portion of my inheritance. And then, the others will come."

"What others?"

"I found six already. Six alone in Charleston. Who knows how many more are out there, on his route…I can't! I'm not giving up my house and my income because my father bedded every woman in sight."

"Do you see the way she looks at you?" Tristan offered. "She thinks you rescued her from the orphanage because you love her."

"I do love her," he asserted. "She's my half sister."

"But to her, you're her knight in shining armor. Her Achilles. Her Hercules."

"And I will be her Hercules," he declared. "I have a plan."

Hessie stood on the dock of the Charleston Harbor and gulped in fear. Her eyes glowed in the lantern light, revealing a dewy expression of bafflement and terror.

"It'll be alright, Hessie. You can do this," Albert encouraged.

"Come on, then. Are you helping us, or not?" Tristan thundered.

"I've never been on a boat before. And it'll be night, and there's a whale out there…"

"…and Jonah isn't here to get swallowed up for us. Girl, come aboard or go home crying. We don't have time to dally," Tristan snapped.

Albert stepped off of the yacht to join Hessie on the dock.

"Mister Norris, I'm scared," she whispered.

"I know," he replied, tenderly placing a heavy life vest onto her shoulders. "And you know you can call me by name. I am your Al, remember?"

She snuffled a sob and nodded.

"Look, I'm tying this life vest around you—arms up! Let me tie this right," he said, securing the vest around her middle, "Everything is perfectly safe. I know it's scary, but it's also thrilling! Think of it—with the money we make tonight, you can buy a dress for the Spring cotillion. You'll be the prettiest twelve-year old there! All the gentlemen will flock around you, and your dance card will be full in half a minute."

She tugged on the life vest anxiously. Albert could not tell if she were trying to test its security or remove it, so he continued, "And think of what a hero you will be! You will help keep the town safe. All of the fishermen will go fishing again, and all of the boats out at sea will be able to use our harbor again. And you can use your third of the whale oil money to donate to the church, to feed the sick and hungry—or you can donate it to the orphanage I found you in. Think of how smug you'll be, being a benefactress of an orphanage, instead of a ward! How fitting!"

Still the child was silent, her trembling hands clasping

the neck opening of the safety vest as she searched his face for answers.

"What'll it be, Hessie? Will you let me be your Hercules?"

"Will you dance with me at the cotillion?" she asked hopefully.

"Of course I will! We'll be the best couple on the dance floor. We'll have to beat away your suitors with a stick." Albert promised desperately.

"You'll rescue me, right? You'll keep me safe?"

"Of course, Hessie. I'll never let anything happen to you!"

She threw her arms around his waist, not being tall enough to reach his shoulders. "My Hercules!" she cried, swept up in excitement.

"Ha-ha!" he countered, swinging her up in his arms and carrying her aboard.

While Tristan tied the rope around Hessie's life vest,

Albert distracted her with a story.

"Did you know that Hercules visited the fabled city of Troy?"

"Did he fight in the war to get back Helen?" she asked in wonder.

"I'm surprised they teach the Trojan War in your school. Isn't it blasphemy to learn Greek myths? Or do they tie it in with religion somehow, make Jesus walk on water across the Dardanelles to hide the Ark of the Covenant inside the Trojan Horse?" Tristan snickered, reveling in his sarcasm.

Albert addressed his snide remark with an exasperated look, then continued, "This was before the War. Laomedon, the first king of Troy, asked the gods to build a wall around his city. And he promised to reward them with gold, but then once they built it, he drove them out of the city without payment."

"You should always give thanks and tithes to God—er, the gods," Hessie parroted.

"Yes. So the gods sent a giant whale into the Trojan harbor—just like us!—and they made the king Laomedon sacrifice his only daughter Hesione into the whale's belly. But," he added quickly to allay her panic, "as they chained her to the rock on shore, waiting for her to be devoured by the beast, Hercules wandered by. He broke the chains, freed the girl, and slew the monster."

"I'm fairly certain that you're thinking of the story of Perseus and Andromeda," Tristan said. "You know, The Gorgon's Head, in Hawthorne's Wonder Book."

"We're reading that in school!" Hessie noted.

"It happened in Troy, too," Albert corrected them.

"Once he freed her, did Hercules marry Hesione?" she asked in innocent wonder.

"No," Albert replied carefully. "Hercules saw that she loved his best friend, Teucer. So he let them get married instead, and from that marriage, she became the mother of the mighty warrior Ajax."

"The strongest of the Greek warriors?"

"Yes. And he was strong because he had the blood of Greeks and Trojans within him." He took her caramel colored hands in his and squeezed them in encouragement. Even in the moonlight, their contrast was striking. She looked up at him in silent awe.

Tristan tugged on the rope attached to her waist playfully to end her reverie. "Are you ready, damsel-in-distress?"

"Are you sure it's safe?" Hessie asked again.

"Of course. You'll splash about in the water to attract the whale's attention. Once he gets within range, we'll pull you up, and in an instant you'll be right back on board."

"But…" she gulped. "Who will pull me up if you're both busy harpooning him?"

"I'll do the harpooning," Tristan boasted. "Your darling Hercules has terrible aim. He'll work the pulleys—see?" he gave a quick tug to the end of the rope and Hessie swooped airborne with a timid squeak.

Watching her feet dangling inches from the yacht's deck, she giggled and danced about like a child. Tristan released the ropes, and she returned to stand beside them.

"Are you ready?" Albert asked, giving her a quick kiss of

encouragement on the forehead.

"Yes, my Hercules," she smiled starrily up at him. "But Al?" she prompted him.

"Yes?"

"Hesione was a fool to marry Hercules' friend. Why marry a warrior, when you can marry a god?" She declared; she kissed his cheek and jumped overboard.

"I don't think we realized how cold the water would be," Tristan commented anxiously, as they scanned the horizon for the whale's spouts. "Yikes! I can hear her teeth chattering from here."

"She is determined, poor mite. She isn't even complaining. Doing her duty like a good little lass," Albert replied.

"Lovely story, by the way," Tristan groused. "Thanks for pawning her off to me, Hercules."

"I don't know what you're talking about," Albert chuckled.

"Was this part of the plan? While I play the mighty hero, her devotion slips from your shoulders to mine? You'll be free of a parasite, and I get to marry one of your father's mistakes?"

"Well, if you don't like her, I can introduce you to Rosalie, Robin, Annabeth, Cynthia, Charles, or Montgomery," Albert grinned. "Besides, that's not the plan."

"Good," he sighed in relief. "I had to wake up to your miserable face every day for four years at university; I cannot imagine a lifetime of waking up to your face dipped in cocoa."

"No, that's not the plan," Albert said glibly. "Her life vest is packed in wax-coated potassium. Within an hour, her body heat will melt the wax and liberate the potassium. And you remember from chemistry class what happens when potassium and water mix."

Tristan laughed, until he realized that Albert was serious. "You can't be, you're pulling my chain, old friend! Surely you must be joking."

"You saw me go to the druggist this afternoon," he replied casually, then pointed. "He's here! Look!"

A spout puffed in the distance. Hessie shrieked in alarm.

"It's coming! Pull me up!" she cried feebly, weakened by the chill of the water.

"Get your harpoon ready, mate!" Albert shouted, readying his aim.

"But Hessie--" Tristan called, but too late. There was a stifled scream, a sickening crunch, and blood straining from the monster's maw.

"Hessie!" Tristan cried, overwhelmed by the casual cruelty of his friend.

And then he fell backwards, as the impact of the whale's bite activated the chemical reaction in Hessie's life vest, sending forth a violent explosion that ripped apart the jaws of the whale.

"Quickly—harpoon it!" Albert cried; having braced himself for the explosion, he was now ready and poised to strike.

Tristan stared, aghast, at his friend's actions.

"Come on! For Hessie! Help me spear this fellow, or she died for nothing!" Albert gave a war-whoop, and lodged both harpoons into the whale's flesh.

The struggle quickly ended. The dark waters, stained by the blood of an innocent life, were saturated by the gore of the whale.

"We did it!" Albert sighed with utter satisfaction, helping Tristan rise to his feet.

Tristan looked overboard, saw the mangled remains of the orphan and the whale, and vomited violently.

"You're a monster," he moaned between heaves.

"Did you think I was going to just let her live in my house for the rest of her life? Give her a dowry, pay to put her children through school? Of course not, old fellow. Now, will you help me with the rest? I have five more to track down."

"But..."

"If if makes you feel better, you can donate her portion to the orphanage I found her in. That'll ease your guilt a bit, I bet. But I have to thank you—your plan was brilliant!"

"My plan?"

"Yes, with the 'casting lots' nonsense. I was just going to throw her overboard—but instead, I fed her to a whale! Because of you! Thanks, ol' pal!"

Tristan merely looked up at him in speechless horror.

## Acknowledgements

Dragon's Roost Press would like to extend its sincerest gratitude to a number of people.

First and foremost, we would like to thank the authors whose works fill these pages. Thank you for taking us to strange places and introducing us to a wild menagerie of cryptids. Your new take on familiar – and some not so familiar – beasts is truly inspiring.

The editing staff would also like to thank all of the authors who submitted during our open call, but whose stories were not selected. Even after extending the project to two volumes, we still had stories which we loved but simply did not have room for. We wish the best to you all.

Enormous thanks to all of our Kickstarter supporters: fill in the names here. This was our first time running an "all or nothing" campaign and we were more than a little worried. Without your support, these books simply would not exist.

Thank you to Luke Spooner whose art graces our covers. You captured the look we were aiming for exactly. We are sure that everyone is tired of us whipping out our phones to show them the beautiful covers.

We tip our glasses to the members of the Great Lakes Association of Horror Writers, the attendees of AthanorCon, and all of our friends in the writing and horror communities. You inspire us.

Acknowledgements

Thank you to all of the friends and supporter of Dragon's Roost Press who follow us on the blog, on social media, and who visit us at our convention appearances, as well as all of our readers (including you, yes you, holding the book right now!). You are the reason that we do what we do.

Thank you to our Kickstarter Backers: Asher, Rose M Anderson, Josh Bowen, Lat Brown, Andy Busch, Nicole Castle-Kelly, Anton Cancre, Dan Chisholm, Aleta Clegg, Crispymayhem, the DeVito family, Sarah Doebereiner, R Fletcher, Peter Guenther, Ivan, Jen Haeger, Josh Hendren, Stephen Hunt, jrho, jmrozanski, Jonna, Justin, Connie Lagge, James Lucas, Alexander Lyle, Kurtis Primm, William Robertson, Tori Smith, Edward Stasheff, Liz T, Alana Thibert, Rebecca Try, Cindy Williams, Andrew Wright, and those who wished to remain annonymous.

Long walks and warm snuggle to assistant editors Tesla and Titus. Thank you for putting up with long hours and the computer and for making us take breaks when we needed them.

Finally, all of my love and appreciation to Ruth Pinto-Cieslak who puts up with a ridiculous amount of nonsense with a smile and a nod. There is no one I would rather go hunting mysterious creatures with.

## About the Contributors

Mark David Adam ("The Costs and Benefits of Lake Monsters") lives on an island off the coast of British Columbia. When he is not foraging for edible and medicinal wild plants, playing funk guitar, or working at his day jobs, he writes short stories and works at finishing his first novel.

It is believed that Jennie Brass ("Wake") descended from a line of changelings, this would explain her fascination with the creatures beyond the veil. Her work has been in various publications including Gold Fever Press, Bards and Sages Quarterly, and winner of the Rochester Public Library 2018 novella contest. Follow her writing on www.facebook.com/BrassQuill/

Jeff Brigham ("Sky Dinosaur") lives in Southeastern Wisconsin. He has been writing short horror fiction for over twenty-five years. When he is not writing, he is reading, working, or spending time with his one-year-old son.

Lauren Childs ("The Basin") studied Children's and Young Adult Literature at Eastern Michigan University, but her lean in terms of writing has always been speculative fiction and horror. "The Basin" is her first published work.

Maggie Denton ("The Anna Doria") is a freelance writer living in the Rocky Mountains with her husband and three demonic cats who wreak havoc and hell (the cats, not the husband). Her writing has been published in over a hundred magazines and anthologies. She as well has had an exciting life working as a circus acrobat, a Navy seal, an exotic dancer on the starship Enterprise, and was the first person to reach the summit

About the Contributors

of Mount Everest. (Writer's note: The publication credits are true, but some of the other stuff may be fictional.)

Eric J. Guignard ("Something in the Strawberry Fields") is a writer and editor of dark and speculative fiction, operating from the shadowy outskirts of Los Angeles. He's won the Bram Stoker Award, been a finalist for the International Thriller Writers Award, and a multi-nominee of the Pushcart Prize. Outside the glamorous and jet-setting world of indie fiction, he's a technical writer and college professor. Visit Eric at: www.ericjguignard.com, his blog: ericjguignard.blogspot.com, or Twitter: @ericjguignard.

Lawrence Harding ("Hounded") is the literary alter-ego of a PhD medievalist from Cambridge, England. After filling his life with medieval literature and folklore on the one hand and fantasy fiction on the other, it was inevitable that he would combine the two. This is one of the results of that (un)holy union.

In between penning stories and marking essays, Lawrence also reviews at exploringotherwheres.wordpress.com and can be found lurking on Twitter at @lhardingwrites.

Haley Holden ("Nancy's Rumble") is a lifetime author, who participated in her first writing contest at the age of eight. Since then she has been published in Palaver, Linden Avenue Literary Journal, Pretty Owl Poetry, and The Gateway Review. She is currently a senior at Bowling Green State University, studying to become a starving artist.

B.D. Keefe ("Night Quarry") "B.D. Keefe lives with his wife and two small children in Providence, RI. His work has appeared in HelloHorror, Massacre Magazine, The Flash Fiction Offensive, as well as several anthologies. He is currently at work on a novel of psychological suspense."

About the Contributors

Sharon Diane King (Ph.D., Comparative Literature, UCLA) ("The Ghost Tree") is an Associate at UCLA's Center for Medieval and Renaissance Studies and moonlights as a character actor for film/TV (Zombie Strippers, Gene Simmons Family Jewels, Lady Gaga's Telephone, My Haunted House). Scholarly publications include books (City Tragedy on the Renaissance Stage in France, Spain, and England), translations (J. Prevost's 1584 Clever and Pleasant Inventions, the first book on sleight-of-hand magic in French), and essays in the anthologies Of Bread, Blood and The Hunger Games (McFarland 2012), Supernatural, Humanity, and the Soul (Palgrave 2014), and The Last Midnight: Critical Essays on Apocalyptic Narratives in Millennial Media (McFarland 2016). For nearly 30 years, King's theatrical troupe Les Enfans Sans Abri (www.lesenfanssansabri.com) has presented short medieval and Renaissance comedies in translation in the United States and Europe. King's published fiction includes stories in Kaleidotrope (Autumn 2014), in the anthologies Keystone Chronicles and Monstrosities by Third Flatiron Press, and in the anthologies Desolation: 21 Tales for Tails and Eldritch Embraces by Dragon's Roost Press. She and her husband do volunteer work for reptile and amphibian rescue (www.RARN.org).

 KA Masters ("The Orphan and the Whale") is a fantasy writer who specializes in twisted fairy tales and zombie-infested historic fiction. She attributes her passion for Greco-Roman mythology and Germanic folklore to her alma mater, Dickinson College. Her debut novel, The Morning Tree, was published by Indie Gypsy in Summer 2016.

Kyle Miller ("Dendrophillia") is the author of short stories, poems, and essays appearing in such places as Betwixt Magazine, Lackington's, and Thoreau on Mackinac. He currently resides in Michigan, his lifelong home and the birthplace of his imagination. He is probably wandering around the wilderness trying to talk to oaks and aspens. One day, he'd like to become a

About the Contributors

hermit.

Gregory L. Norris ("O Christmas Tree") is a full-time professional writer, with work appearing in numerous short story anthologies, national magazines, novels, the occasional TV episode, and, so far, one produced feature film (Brutal Colors, which debuted on Amazon Prime January 2016). He's a former feature writer and columnist at Sci Fi, the official magazine of the Sci Fi Channel (before all those ridiculous Ys invaded). Gregory worked as a screenwriter on two episodes of Paramount's modern classic, Star Trek: Voyager. Two of his paranormal novels (written under his rom-de-plume, Jo Atkinson) were published by Home Shopping Network as part of their "Escape With Romance" line—the first time HSN offered novels to their global customer base. Gregory judged the 2012 Lambda Awards in the SF/F/H category. His stories have notched Honorable Mentions in Ellen Datlow's Best-of books three times. In 2016, Gregory traveled to Hollywood to accept HM in the Roswell Awards in Short SF Writing. Follow his literary adventures at: http://gregorylnorris.blogspot.com.

Soumya Sundar Mukherjee ("Moonlight Forest") is an admirer of engaging Sci Fi, Horror and Fantasy tales. He is a bi-lingual writer who lives in West Bengal, India, and writes about stuff strange dreams are made of. He teaches English in a school and spends his leisure time in writing, studying the myths and legends of different cultures around the globe and drawing monsters both horrifying and cute. His works of fiction have appeared/ are scheduled to appear in Mother of Invention Anthology, Occult Detective Quarterly, Mother's Revenge Anthology and a few others. When he is not writing or making any interplanetary journeys in his pet-spaceship, he plays with his cats who are, in a different reality, gods and goddesses from ancient civilizations.

Aimee Ogden ("A Cruelty That Cut Both Ways") lives in

Wisconsin with her husband, three-year-old twins, and very old dog. A former software tester and science teacher, she now writes stories about sad astronauts and angry princesses. Her work has also appeared in Shimmer, Apex, and Escape Pod.

Danielle Warnick ("Lifeboat") spends most of her time, when she's not writing, with her insane French bulldog/ beagle Raz. She loves fiction with teeth, and aims to jam fangs and sharp edges into everything she writes. Other than writing, she extremely interested in communing with the dead, UFOS, and other odd, bizarre hobbies

Kevin Wetmore ("You Will Be Laid Low Even at the Sight of Him") is an award-winning short story and non-fiction author whose short fiction has appeared in such anthologies as "Midian Unmade," "Enter at Your Own Risk: The End is the Beginning" and "Strangely Funny III," as well as magazines such as "Devolution Z," "Mothership Zeta," "Weirdbook" and "Cemetery Dance." He is also the author of such books as "Post-9/11 Horror in American Cinema" and "The Theology of Battlestar Galactica." Lastly, he is an actor, director, professor and fight choreographer/stuntman who lives and works in Los Angeles.

## About Last Day Dog Rescue

Last Day is more than just a name, it's the situation all the dogs were faced with. Because of LDDR these wonderful dogs get another chance at life. All dogs coming into their rescue were saved from high-kill animal shelters or being sold for research.

A Little About LDDR:

Last Day Dog Rescue is an ALL volunteer based organization. They do not have a physical location; all of their dogs are placed in the care of foster homes until they are adopted.

The group focuses on rescuing dogs from the "Urgent" list in shelters and pounds across lower Michigan and parts of Ohio with an emphasis on those shelters who euthanize by gas or those shelters who sell the dogs in their care to research labs where they are used for barbaric and most times painful testing and experiments. They hold a special place in their hearts for the big and black dogs, even 'ugly' dogs (whom they don't find ugly at all!) and the special senior dogs. These dogs most often get overlooked and passed up in shelters and pounds everywhere for puppies, small breeds, and the "prettier," lighter colored dogs.

Dogs found in shelters are there for many reasons; some are owner surrenders, strays, cruelty or abuse cases, and some dogs are found abandoned, left to fend for themselves in vacant homes, fields, ditches, and some have even been tied out in the woods and left to starve. Last Day Dog Rescue does not discriminate and feels that each of these dogs, no matter their size, age, color, or the reason they are there, deserve a second chance at life…they help all those they can.

Donations via check and money orders:
Last Day Dog Rescue
P.O. Box 51935
Livonia, MI 48151-5935

Donations also accepted via PayPal:
http://www.lastdaydogrescue.org/info/

**Dragon's Roost Press** is the fever dream brainchild of dark speculative fiction author Michael Cieslak. Since 2014, their goal has been to find the best speculative fiction authors and share their work with the public. For more information about Dragon's Roost Press and their publications, please visit:
http://thedragonsroost.net/styled-3/index.html.

A portion of the proceeds from all sales of *Hidden Menagerie Vol 1* will be donated to the Last Day Dog Rescue Organization.

Be sure to check out the companion volume *Hidden Menagerie Vol 2*.

# Also Available from Dragon's Roost Press

Robotic Animals
Televisions Which Reveal Alternate Universes
Inanimate Objects Brought to Life
People Struggling to Survive in Apocalyptic Wastelands
Sentient Cutlery

and much, much more

*Desolation: 21 Tales for Tails* is a collection of dark speculative fiction whose stories all focus on themes of loneliness, isolation, and abandonment.

Enter into strange worlds envisioned by some of the most inventive writing today.

Combine the mind splintering horror of the Cthulhu Mythos and the heart shattering portion of that most terrible of emotions -- love -- and what do you have? You have *Eldritch Embraces: Putting the Love Back in Lovecraft*.

This collection of short stories from some of the best authors working in the fields of horror and dark speculative fiction blends romance and Lovecraft in a way which will make you sigh, smile, weep, or leave you the hollow shell of your former self.

A portion of the proceeds of each sale of *Desolation: 21 Tales for Tails* and *Eldritch Embraces: Putting the Love Back in Lovecraft* benefit the Last Day Dog Rescue Organization.

# Also Available from Dragon's Roost Press

## The Maiden's Courage

by Mary Lynne Gibbs

The best man on the pirate ship is a girl named Alex.

Alexandra "Alex" Gardner is the reluctant cabin boy on *The Bloody Maiden*, a ruthless pirate ship run by the charmingly evil Captain Montgomery. The crew is convinced she's a boy, and she hopes it stays that way until she has the chance to avenge the deaths of her mother and brother at the hands of the crew. All goes well until the ship takes a handsome captive. Could her feelings for him ruin her charade?

Sebastian Whitley is a young man in love. He sails on his father's ship, trying to find the beautiful girl he's lost. When he's captured by *The Bloody Maiden*, the annoying cabin boy saves his life – and makes it more difficult at the same time. His savior is actually a girl, and if Sebastian doesn't keep quiet, it could mean both their deaths. Together, they have to thwart a mutiny, get revenge, and get off the ship before Alex's secret is revealed. If not, it's the plank for both of them.

# Also Available from Dragon's Roost Press

## Jericho Rising

by Mary Lynne Gibbs

In post-World War III, small town Michigan, a self-proclaimed, violent, and insane High Priestess has taken control, reducing the remaining men to nothing more than slaves and playthings. Jericho, the reluctant leader of the Resistance, must fight her own family to preserve the freedom and equality of all in her care – male and female alike. She's torn between love and duty, and with traitors around every corner, she has no idea who to trust anymore.

## Jericho's Redemption

by Mary Lynne Gibbs

The battle is over, but the war has just begun. Jericho returns to the Obsidian camp, only to learn that her sister Candace destroyed it as part of a plot to dismantle the resistance movement that brought down their mother, the High Priestess. The rest of the resistance blames Jericho for the deaths of their friends, but that's the least of her worries. Not only does Jericho now have to right the wrongs her sister has done, she must contend with a few guests to the camp who bring secrets that will change her life forever. Either she'll redeem herself in the eyes of her comrades, or she'll die trying.

# Also Available from Dragon's Roost Press

## Hell Hath No Fury

by Peggy Christie

Ever wonder how you might handle a sabbatical from work? Think the bible told you everything there is to know about the Devil? What if the noises coming from under your child's bed weren't just in his imagination? Crack open *Hell Hath No Fury*, a collection of 21 tales of horror and dark fiction, to learn the answers to these questions. Discover stories of psychotic delusions, ghosts, a murder victim's revenge, and a family brought closer together through torture.

## Sex, Gore, and Millipedes

by Ken MacGregor

Ken MacGregor, known for pushing boundaries in horror, for shoving the reader outside of their comfort zone, has finally gone too far. *Sex, Gore, and Millipedes* is a collection of the sickest stuff you've ever read. This book will hit your triggers. Hopefully, all of them. You've been warned.

**Coming Soon From Dragon's Roost Press**

From Award Winning Author

Sarah Hans

**Dead Girls Don't Love**

and

**An Ideal Vessel**

Made in the USA
Middletown, DE
24 December 2023